S0-BKV-866

Dear Reader,

We are extremely excited and proud that many of our favorite Arabesque romances have come to life on BET. In fact, giving these wonderful stories a new way to affect and delight audiences is the reason why Arabesque and BET merged in the first place. However, books and movies are very different, and at times, we have had to adjust parts of the stories in order to make them more visual and "TV friendly." While we recognize that these few changes may come as a bit of a surprise to fans of the written word, we are confident that the movies are wonderful in their own right.

Thank you for being part of the Arabesque community. And don't forget to look for made-for-TV movies on BET! You won't be disappointed. . . .

Kelli Richardson
Vice President and Publisher
BET Books

RHAPSODY

Felicia Mason

BET Publications, LLC
www.msbet.com
www.arabesquebooks.com

ARABESQUE BOOKS are published by

BET Publications, LLC
c/o BET BOOKS
One BET Plaza
1900 W Place NE
Washington, D.C. 20018-1211

First Printing: June, 1997
10 9 8 7 6 5 4 3 2

Printed in the United States of America

This one is for all the friends who helped me through a difficult 1996, and in particular, for Belva, Pam, Marion and Roz, who each in his or her own way helped tremendously. Thanks, guys, for being there, for the encouraging words, the phone calls and those late-night conversations. I couldn't have gotten through without you.

ACKNOWLEDGMENTS

Sincere thanks to Dr. Paula Barnes, English professor extra-ordinaire, who found a new genre to study and was willing to share her expertise on commas and English literature.

Shout-outs also to Derek and Angela McLendon; Beverly Williams; Michelle; Ed Bacon who is already a hero; Liz Primas who keeps the 'do together and got a kick out of discovering how characters are named; and to MaryAnne who solved the eleventh-hour problem.

Special thanks to all the songwriters and musicians, in all musical arts forms, who have followed the muse and given the world joy through song, composition and melody.

Prologue

Diamonds twinkled and sequined gowns sparkled in the auditorium. The best and the brightest, the up-and-coming, as well as the wannabes, the used-to-bes and the just plain curious filled the hall for this—the most important night in the music industry. Murmuring intensified throughout the audience as the tuxedoed presenter on stage began the next category.

"The nominations for songwriter of the year are Craig Sentinel and Jenny Lawman for 'Maybe Yes, Maybe No'; William Buster Dixon for 'Soul Fire'; and Wright Samms for 'Jukebox Gigolo.' "

A hush whispered through the crowd as the presenter ran a hand through his overly moussed hair, raised his eyebrows, then tore open the envelope.

He read the winner's name to himself, whistled in appreciation, then broke into a broad grin.

"Get on with it!" a heckler yelled from the far reaches of the balcony.

The audience twittered and then fell silent.

"And the winner is . . . Buster D! . . ."

The name of the nominated song was lost in the pandemonium that ensued. As the refrains of the soulful ballad
filled the air, a chant started somewhere in the balcony's
cheap seats. "Bus-ter! Bus-ter! Bus-ter!"

The diamonds and sequins seemed to shine brighter as
spotlights scanned the crowd, then locked in on the man
named Buster. The women in borrowed diamonds and
designer-original sequins smiled broader and clapped
harder in the precious few moments when the cameras
flashed on the faces their plastic surgeons created.

Buster knew the exact moment when the panning cameras found him and focused in on his reaction. He kept
a smile, or what could be interpreted as a smile, plastered
on his face, even while he endured the kisses a young
actress planted all over his cheek.

Buster took a deep breath and bowed his head. To the
music fans watching the live awards program at home on
television, and even to the hundreds of people in the
audience, it looked as though the songwriter offered up
a short prayer of thanksgiving before accepting his award.

It was a prayer all right. But not the one that would have
been expected of a man—who in being named songwriter
of the year—had just swept the awards ceremony with nods
in six different categories.

"Dammit, why me? Why this damn song?" he mumbled
to himself as he raised his head and made his way past the
well-turned-out knees of men and women sitting between
him and the aisle.

His back got slapped, and he shook hands with folks
who thrust their own hands at his. Buster knew some of
the congratulatory wishes were sincere; others were solely
for the benefit of the cameras.

By the time he made his way to the end of the row and
bounded up the four steps to the stage, Buster was grinning
from ear to ear. It was expected.

No one, not a single person in the audience or viewing at home, would suspect that this, which by all appearances should have been the shining highlight of his career, was actually the most miserable night of Buster's life.

Chapter 1

The woman beside him in bed was obviously naked. A tanned shoulder the color of rich sandalwood gave way to firm breasts with large nipples and dark areolae. Her chestnut brown hair with streaks of blond dyed in it fell in soft waves around his pillows and spilled over his arm. She was pretty.

Buster Dixon wished like hell he knew her name.

He frowned, trying to remember where he'd met her, when he'd met her, and just how she wound up in his bed. Since he was just as naked as she was, he could assume they'd done the nasty.

Buster couldn't remember.

He wasn't even sure he wanted to. Right now he just wanted to be left alone to wallow in his misery.

What was this woman's name? Linda? Leticia? Lenore?

His eyes widened with that thought, and then he remembered—not her name but why he had been attracted to her sometime late last night or maybe this morning. The excessive amount of celebratory alcohol had something to do with the attraction.

Buster extracted himself from the bed and tried not to wake the sleeping woman. She mumbled and turned— the cotton sheet had covered the lower half of her body. Buster sucked in his breath and felt himself stir. Mercy. He still couldn't recall her name, but his body had total recollection of the wonders her mouth had brought through the night.

Lenore. He'd been thinking of her a lot lately. Thoughts of her had a way of sneaking up on him. And then there was the song.

Buster felt the partial hard-on soften. He cursed himself and stomped into his bathroom. By the time he showered, shaved, dressed and finished a cup of coffee, he knew he'd met the woman at an after-party. Across the smoke-filled room, she'd reminded him of someone and of the days when picking up a girl or two at a party was standard operating procedure.

But when the woman who was in his bed this morning walked barefoot into his kitchen dressed in nothing but one of his shirts, Buster wondered how he'd *ever* mistaken her for that woman from his long-ago past. The woman before him now just served to remind him that he was old—too old to be waking up with a stranger in his bed.

She smiled. "Uh, I couldn't find my dress," she said, gesturing to his shirt.

Over the rim of his coffee cup, Buster looked at her. Be polite or throw her out? The latter had a great deal of appeal, but his manners and his uncertainty about the situation won out. What if she were the daughter or wife of some record company exec?

"No problem," he answered her. "I made some coffee. Want a cup?"

Buster turned around to refill his cup from the Krups coffeemaker. He knew how to do two things well: make music and make a cup of coffee. As for getting rid of unwanted females, he obviously needed some more training in that department.

"No, thank you. I'd better go."

Thank God.

"My dress?"

"On the back of the door in the bath," he answered.

He'd seen the dress as he'd showered. It was what had reminded him so much of Lenore. Lenore had worn a similar dress to a party years before. She'd made Alpha Kappa Mu, the national honor society, and to celebrate, he had taken her to a party given by a group of musicians previewing their demo tape. Lenore's red dress was too short, too tight and too revealing, she complained. He agreed wholeheartedly. Seeing her in it made him too hot. She looked stunning. All night he had to fight off the hounds who sniffed around her.

"Excuse me, Buster?"

He turned around, looked at the woman who was a stranger to him, surprised to see her still in his house. The red dress this woman was wearing, like the one so long ago in his memory, was designed to entice a man. The only good thing Buster could say about the previous night was that he'd seen used condoms in the trash. At least he'd had sense enough to use some protection.

"I'm sorry I spilled that drink on you last night. No hard feelings, okay?"

"Okay," he answered easily. What drink? he wondered.

He turned and fiddled with the coffeemaker, wracking his brain for a clue to her identity. At a loss as to how to get rid of the woman without being overly rude, Buster put his cup on the counter and walked toward the living room. Maybe she'd take the hint.

She followed him. That was good.

"You don't remember my name, do you?" she asked.

Busted! "Uh . . . Last night was . . ." Last night was mostly a big blur.

She smiled sadly. "That's what I thought. You called me Lenore all night long. By the way, it's Donna."

Dumbly he echoed her. "Donna?"

Shaking her head, she went to a glass-topped table and picked up a tiny beaded evening bag that matched her red dress. "Congratulations on winning the awards, Buster."

"Thanks," he mumbled.

Great. She had to go and remind him. He'd managed, albeit briefly, to put that whole fiasco out of his mind. He knew he was going to have to do something about that awards business. And soon. But what? He also recognized that there was more to life than making money. Since his best friend's death, Buster had been giving a lot of thought to things like his own mortality, like leaving his mark on the world by finding a wife and having some kids.

To the millions of fans who bought his records, and to the people whose careers he'd launched, Buster Dixon had it going on. He owned a multi-million dollar recording studio and a couple of nightclubs. He'd produced enough Grammy–award winning groups and singers to have him set for life. He had the cars, the clothes, the bodyguards and the penthouse suite. In the industry he had a solid reputation for being smooth as silk, a perfectionist but easy to work with.

But Dixon knew it all to be a facade. Sure, he had money, he managed it well and he could croon a silky love ballad just as easily as he could direct the production of a music video. But what did those things count for when it was all said and done? If he dropped dead tomorrow, would he be able to say he'd lived life to the fullest?

No.

In his younger days, he'd partied with the best of them. More than half the time, the party didn't even begin until he, Buster Dixon the Music Man, arrived. But now, all he had to show for his life were regrets—things he coulda, shoulda and woulda done if he'd known then just half the things he knew now.

Regrets. Maybe he'd write a song about regrets. Alicia Rae, the new artist he'd signed to his label last month, had a break-your-heart voice that could pull off a bluesy Billie Holiday type song about regrets. He'd give it some thought.

"Buster?"

He blinked and looked at the woman in the red dress. She was standing there, looking at him like he'd forgotten something important.

Then Buster got a clue.

From his back pants pocket he pulled his wallet. Taking out four crisp one hundred dollar bills, he thrust the money at the woman and smiled.

Several moments after the front door slammed, he could still feel the stinging crack of her palm against his cheek.

Buster sighed. He looked at his hands and shook his head in the empty penthouse suite.

"If she was so insulted, why'd she take my money?"

Making his way back to the kitchen, Buster didn't hold out any hope that he'd ever understand women.

A few minutes later, Buster knew what he needed to do. He needed to be away from the pollutants in this city, the chemical pollutants and the human ones.

He looked around the immaculate penthouse. The expensive apartment had been the first thing he'd bought when he'd made it big. A white grand piano occupied the place of honor, overlooking a panoramic view of the ocean. Buster walked to the music room. All around him was evidence of his success: gold records, platinum records, double-platinum hits, framed pictures of him with movie stars, recording artists, and even two U.S. presidents. Every music industry award imaginable was in this room, on shelves, on pedestals, being used as bookends and paperweights. His six awards from last night would also wind up in here.

Buster hated the room.

And he hated the penthouse with all its fancy trappings. Buster needed to escape, and he knew just where to go.

A phone started ringing. He ignored it.

Taking nothing with him, Buster left the apartment and didn't look back.

When he wanted some peace and quiet, a place to think, to get in touch with his roots, Buster went home. He now owned the house his old man had lived in. The small house was just like he'd left it the last time he'd come. The housekeeper still did her duty because everything was clean and neat. When he came home to this house, all he had to do was bring food.

With both his parents gone now, this house as well as his mother's house in Florida belonged to him. He didn't make it to either place very often but of the two residences, he felt more at home here. His father had loved music just as much as Buster did.

Music and dreams of glory had done in his parents' marriage. For a long time, Buster Dixon maintained that the best way to stay out of divorce court was to not ever get married. Funny how these days, that line of thinking seemed immature.

Buster dropped the bag of groceries on the kitchen counter and looked out the small window over the sink. The tire swing still hung from a tree limb in the backyard. He smiled. He came here for inspiration and rejuvenation. He needed both in megadoses. Buster ran his hands over his face, shook his head, then put the food away.

Hooking his rental car keys on a small ceramic keyholder next to the door, Buster smiled remembering the day Lenore had nailed the craft project to the spot. He could never find his keys, and she'd had the solution for him. Anal as she was, Buster loved her.

Still did.

As he opened the back door and stepped out on the patio, he wondered where she was, what she'd done with her life, whom she'd married, how many kids she had. He grinned. Lenore had always had childbearing hips.

But he was spending too much time thinking about Lenore, and it was all Marvin's fault. In the weeks since Marvin had died, Buster had been doing a lot of thinking about the past . . . and the future.

Buster spent a week at the house, seven whole days of solitude as he came to grips with what he needed to do . . . what he *had* to do. Coming clean was his only recourse.

A week at his father's house served to remind him how far he'd come and how far he had yet to fall. In the last week, he lived the life of a regular person. He cut the grass, read the Sunday newspaper, bought milk at a grocery store and consulted with his neighbor over a backyard fence on the best barbecuing techniques.

Buster missed being a regular person.

At the end of his stay, he'd come to a decision. It was gonna piss off a lot of people, and he was gonna hurt a whole lot of folks.

"But sometimes," he said as he locked the front door and made his way down the steps and to his car, "sometimes, a man has to take a stand for what's right."

Chapter 2

Lenore's summons to this California law office brought back memories, memories that belonged buried in the past.

Lenore had been in only one other law office. That other one, with its dollar-store prints and thrift-shop style sofa, paled in comparison to this opulence. Rich teak, original oils and museum-quality antiques graced the room. A tapestry that should have been hanging in a museum covered one complete wall. If old money had a smell, it smelled like this place.

Lenore didn't particularly care for lawyers. But Marvin Woodbridge had died, and Lenore was here for the reading of his will. Lenore could only wonder what the man had bequeathed her. Sure, they had been close in college, but that was years ago . . . a long, *long* time ago, when she had been young and in love for the first time. She'd been in love with Marvin's roommate, Billy Dixon.

But Billy hadn't loved her. Not the way she loved him. She would have died for William Dixon . . . then. But he'd walked away from her love, from their relationship. Part of Lenore withered and died when Billy turned his back on her. But she couldn't afford to give in to despair, not then and definitely not now. Lenore fought down the quick anger that bubbled up in her. She wondered why the painful memories of the past had to be dredged up now, now that she'd finally gotten herself and her life together.

Lenore Foxwood sighed. Thoughts of Billy Dixon were best left in dusty scrapbooks and faded memories. The problem was Billy Dixon refused to be relegated to the past. Without knowing it, he'd even had a hand in breaking up her marriage. Billy had been her first love, and he'd both hurt her . . . and touched her like no other man had been able to before or after. Billy Dixon was a fire in her soul that refused to be extinguished.

Even her marriage, where Lenore had learned the difference between breathing and suffocating, hadn't robbed her of the things Billy stole: hope, innocence, self-worth, and most importantly, the capacity and ability to love freely.

It had taken a long time to recapture those things, to become strong and independent. But she'd done it one step at a time, one day at a time. She'd walked through the valley, survived the wilderness, and clawed her way out of an emotional pit. She'd done it twice: the first time when Billy left; the second time after her marriage crumbled. She'd rebuilt herself after Billy and after her divorce. Lenore wasn't sure she had it in her to survive a third emotional makeover. A third round was likely to take her out and down for the count.

"Dr. Foxwood?"

Lenore looked up at the cooly efficient secretary.

"Mr. Hobbs will see you now."

Lenore stood. Smoothing the material of her suit skirt with one hand, she slipped the strap of her Coach bag over her shoulder with the other.

As she followed the secretary, the heels of her black pumps made no noise in the deep carpeting.

* * *

The last thing Buster wanted to be bothered with was this appointment with a lawyer. It was bad enough that the man's office was clear across town. Stepping out of the high-rise where he kept his own offices, Buster winced in the bright sunshine. After returning from his father's house, he'd spent the last two days holed up in his office, figuring out how to mitigate the damage he was about to cause. He'd surprised his staff and given everyone bonuses—in cash. He hoped they all remembered his generosity a week from now. It was major league doings he contemplated. After carefully reviewing all his options, Dixon knew he really had only one option.

But before he could get to that, he had to deal with Gil Hobbs. He wished he could put off this lawyer thing, but Hobbs had been insistent. If he hadn't gotten out of the squirrelly lawyer the fact that the meeting was about Marvin, Dixon would just have blown both the meeting and Gil Hobbs off.

Shielding his eyes from the harsh glare of the sun, Buster dashed to the curb and ducked into the waiting limousine. Charles slammed the door shut behind him. Buster winced again, this time in pain.

"Jeez, show a little mercy, will you," he grumbled.

In the last two days, he'd had little sleep and lots of alcohol. Unfortunately the liquor hadn't dulled his senses, but it sure left a headache.

In moments the car smoothly pulled into the street traffic. Buster leaned his head back on the soft leather and closed his eyes. He stretched his legs out in front of him and crossed his feet at the ankles.

Buster didn't have to look at himself to know he was what the ladies called fine. Usually he cultivated the image. Today, like most days in the last week, he didn't care about his public persona any more than he cared about his manager's four hundred phone calls or fretting. Buster knew he needed a haircut. If his hair got any longer or nappier, the style might be mistaken for dreads.

Buster figured he needed to unwind, to get himself together. A week at his father's old house hadn't been enough. Sarge Watson, his agent and manager, was talking about a national tour, the talk-show circuit, lots of public appearances to play up his virtual sweep of last week's record industry awards. Buster was still saying no to that notion. In a few days, he'd be persona non grata anyway. The talk shows would want him all right, but not for grip-and-grin appearances. Possibly, after a little time, he'd grant Barbara Walters an interview. Or maybe Oprah would do a special. If he was gonna talk, it had to be to a journalist he could respect.

Maybe he could hide after first figuring out what Gil Hobbs wanted and then taking care of the business he had to do. He could go on another personal retreat; maybe this time he'd go someplace where he *would* be recognized, a place where he could get some TLC, drink some carrot juice and find someone named Inga to give him back massages. Buster figured what he needed most was some R&R, rest and relaxation. The last thing he needed was more emotional upheaval in his life.

If Lenore had been expecting an ancient, shriveled-up man to be Mr. Hobbs, she got a pleasant surprise. Gilbert Hobbs proved far from old or shriveled. As a matter of fact, he looked more like a linebacker than a lawyer.

Lenore gave him a subtle but appreciative once-over as the man walked toward her. Then she noticed the gold band on his ring finger. She sighed inwardly but gave him a bright smile.

"Hello. I'm Lenore Foxwood. I have a two thirty appointment."

"Come right on in, Dr. Foxwood. I've been expecting you."

Lenore let the man usher her into a sumptuously decorated office. The outer office paled in comparison to this. Rich burgundy hues and deep blues constituted the color scheme. Lenore guessed the large desk to be cherry. A Ming-looking vase stood on a cherry pedestal a few feet from the desk. A hint of decadence in the office made her look around, trying to pinpoint why furnishings would make her think that way. But professionally decadent was the only way she could describe the room. More oils decorated the walls. From a museum exhibit she'd taken her students to view, she recognized an original Renaissance piece on one wall. But not even the tasteful nude painting seemed to be the source of the just off-kilter, slightly uncomfortable feel of the room.

Then Lenore turned. Gilbert Hobbs watched her. Goose bumps broke out on her arms. It wasn't the room that exuded avarice so much as the man standing before her. But quick as a flash, the look of debauchery vanished and the handsome lawyer stood before her with a slightly amused expression on his face.

Hobbs nodded. "Please, have a seat," he said, indicating what was obviously an antique settee.

Lenore looked around for something a bit more contemporary to sit on. The last thing she needed to do was break something in this office. It might take the next ten years of her college professor's salary to pay for one of the pieces so casually scattered about at this firm, like that pretty porcelain vase. It probably *was* an original Ming.

Finally guesstimating the settee to be her best bet, Lenore perched on the edge of the seat.

"May I get you something?" Hobbs asked. "Tea, a glass of wine?"

"No, thank you. I'm really curious about why I've been called here though. Marvin Woodbridge and I were just casual friends in college. I was sorry to learn of his passing, but I haven't seen Marvin, let alone heard from or about him for about fourteen or fifteen years."

Lenore slipped her handbag strap off her shoulder and placed the bag on her lap. She noticed, but ignored, Gil Hobbs's gaze linger on her legs. She cleared her throat and continued, compelling him to meet her direct gaze.

"We had, at that time, a . . . a mutual friend."

Well, that was one way to describe Billy, she thought.

Hobbs smiled, and Lenore felt like Little Red Riding Hood facing the big, bad wolf. This man wanted to gobble her up. But Lenore wasn't about to be baited or bait.

"Another party will be joining us shortly. I thought I'd wait until his arrival, so I don't have to repeat everything. Are you sure I can't get something for you?"

Lenore shook her head. "Can you tell me how Marvin died."

Hobbs moved from in front of her, where he'd been crowding her space, and positioned himself behind his desk. Lenore hadn't realized she was holding her breath until he'd moved out of her personal space.

"Mr. Woodbridge died of complications as a result of pneumonia."

"Oh, that's terrible. Poor Marv. When we were in college, he was always the picture of health, even if he rarely went to class."

Hobbs smiled. "No. Classrooms weren't very high on my client's list of life priorities. He preferred to get his education in other ways."

Lenore wondered at the tone the lawyer used when he referred to "other ways," but before she had time to dwell on it, the office door opened and a dark breeze blew in. The blur was followed by the perfectly coiffed and attired secretary.

"I'm sorry, Mr. Hobbs. He just barrelled right in."

Hobbs waved his secretary away. "That's all right. Please hold all my calls for the next hour."

"Yes, sir," the woman said.

"Gil, this better be important. I have better stuff to do than hang around and play your little games today."

Lenore's heart stopped. Then it beat triple time. She blinked. It couldn't be.

Almost afraid to turn around, she took a deep breath. That voice was Billy Dixon's. It had been years, but the timbre and slightly southern drawl was unmistakable.

For so long she'd dreamed about seeing Billy again. She'd often wondered what had happened to him, how he'd turned out, whether he ever thought of her. She'd spent months and lonely years wondering if he even knew how much he'd hurt her, how much she had needed him.

Lenore stood up.

With a slow, even motion, she turned. And there she stood, face-to-face with the man who'd haunted both her nightmares and her erotic dreams for the last fifteen years. He looked the same, and he looked different. The careful speech—honed over the years to oratorical contest perfection—that she'd prepared for just this moment fled her mind. The words caught in her throat, gobbled up by the pounding of her heart.

"Billy"—the sound a quiet rush of certainty.

"Lenore?"

They both spoke at the same time.

He squinted at her as if trying to determine if she was really the person he thought she was.

"Wh-what are you doing here?" she managed.

"Well, as I'd assumed, introductions won't be necessary," the lawyer said.

Lenore blinked and glanced back at Gil Hobbs. When her gaze connected with Dixon's again, she opened her mouth to speak but no words came.

The past slammed against the present. He was really there, standing in front of her as if nothing had ever passed between them. Lenore's breath caught in her throat. She stood startled and tongue-tied. First, in surprise and a joy she hadn't thought possible. Billy! Then anger seeped in with fury riding shotgun. Part of her wanted to leap into his arms, the other part wanted to rip off one of his arms.

He had no right to just show up in her life like this. He had no right to be so drop-dead gorgeous.

The gamut of perplexing and contradictory emotions whipping through her left Lenore breathless, unsure.

She swayed on her feet.

"Dr. Foxwood?" Gilbert Hobbs dashed to her side, his arm sliding around her waist to support her. She leaned against him and closed her eyes.

Dixon's eyes narrowed at the cozy way they snuggled together.

When Hobbs started fanning her with a yellow legal pad, Dixon raised an eyebrow.

"Are you all right, Dr. Foxwood?" the lawyer asked. "Here, have a seat. Let me get you some water."

He tried to seat her, but Lenore stood rooted to the spot, afraid to fully open her eyes, afraid to face the one person she most wanted to see in the world and the one person she hated most in the world.

Then she felt *his* hand on her arm. Even after all the time that had passed between them, she knew his touch. Her skin suddenly felt inflamed, so hot, so electric that she idly wondered if the imprint of his hand would remain on her arm—like a brand, like a mark of ownership.

Her eyes snapped open the same moment she jerked her arm free of his light, supporting touch. Hobbs stroked her arm in a soothing motion.

"Maybe I'll just stand over here and give you two some room," he said.

Lenore's gaze followed Billy's as he took slow steps backward. Unconsciously she pushed at Gil Hobbs. "I'm all right," she murmured. "Just taken by surprise."

She moved to the settee but didn't sit. She watched Billy's eyes track her, then his scowl at Gilbert Hobbs. Just like old times, she thought. Any man who dared even look at her got the same frost treatment the lawyer was now receiving.

But Hobbs took it in stride. He even grinned at Billy.

Lenore watched Billy's eyes narrow. Jealous? He couldn't be. What was there to be jealous of? When she would have strolled over burning coals to be with him, Billy didn't want her. Why would fifteen years, eight months, three weeks and a day make any difference?

Reluctantly yet greedily she drank in the sight of him. The years had been kind. He'd grown into the face that fifteen years ago had had the smooth lines and angles of youth. Thick, slightly arched eyebrows highlighted the upper portion of his face. And his eyes! On more than one occasion she'd drowned in the brown pools of Billy Dixon's eyes. His skin, a rich chestnut brown, glistened with a fine sheen of sweat, or maybe oil.

She let her gaze move away from that too compelling face. The bottom of the fraternity brand she so vividly remembered was visible from the short-sleeved shirt he wore. Muscles, more than she remembered, flexed there.

He had been a boy the last time she saw him. He was a man now. Lenore fought back a soul deep longing that welled up inside her. She couldn't still want him, wouldn't still want him. Not after what he'd done. But she did, and that fact galled her.

She hid the embarrassment she felt by looking down. Muscular thighs were encased in jeans that could have been on a male model's body. Memories of hot nights and cool sheets cascaded over her. Lenore took a deep breath. It suddenly seemed unbearably warm in Mr. Hobbs's office. Deciding it was safer to look somewhere else, she cast her gaze upward. Up, up, up to his broad nose and laughing brown eyes. He was laughing at her!

Lenore whirled around to Mr. Hobbs.

She almost upset the glass of water he held before her.

"Here you are, Dr. Foxwood. Why don't you have a seat? You, too, Mr. Dixon," he said to Billy.

"Oh, so it's Mr. Dixon today, Gil?"

The attorney ignored him, and Lenore wondered at the byplay. Accepting the glass, and hoping the cool liquid would lower her temperature, Lenore took a sip as she covertly studied him.

The jeans fit the way jeans were supposed to fit a man. The rumpled shirt and scuffed-up Nikes made her wonder just what he did for a living. Now that the first wave of shock over seeing him had subsided, she saw the tiredness in his eyes, the hair that needed a trim and the five-o'clock shadow on his face, even though it was early in the day.

Notwithstanding her body's initial reaction, she felt safe. The man standing a few feet from her was just that, a man, a stranger, not the boyish Billy Dixon she'd fallen in love with so many years ago. They were both different people now. They'd led separate lives. Lenore's mouth turned down briefly. As she sipped from the water again, she wondered how differently things might have turned out had he stayed around.

Except for twenty nagging pounds and a strand or two of gray hair, Lenore knew she looked the same on the outside as she did fifteen years ago. But she was a new person on the inside, where it counted. The naive innocence that had been her unconscious shield in college had long since been shattered—by Billy, by her ex-husband and by the adult responsibilities she now had. In the place of that innocence, she'd built a concrete wall with NO TRESPASSING signs posted at handy intervals.

"Dr. Foxwood . . ." Hobbs began.

"Congratulations," Billy interrupted, giving her a small salute with a nod of his head. "I always knew you'd follow and find your dreams."

Keeping an uninterested, nonchalant expression on her face, she sipped from her glass of cool water and silently thanked Mr. Hobbs for the small physical shield the tumbler offered.

"If the reunion is over, shall we begin?" Hobbs said.

Lenore kept her attention on the attorney, but from the corner of her eye she saw Billy cross one foot at the ankle, the heel of one sneaker propped on the toe of the other. She smiled at the memory of that familiar pose.

"You always had a beautiful smile."

Lenore's mouth dropped open, then snapped shut.

Her gaze lifted to his. A tremor shivered through her when she realized he studied her just as intently as she had been trying to covertly study him.

Fifteen years was a long time, the kind of time that filled out a boy and made him a man.

"As you both know . . ." Hobbs continued.

Lenore reluctantly brought her attention back to the lawyer.

". . . Mr. Marvin Woodbridge passed on a month ago. He left a considerable estate to be administered. His family, employees and, all of his, uh, significant others met here last week for the reading of the will. At Mr. Woodbridge's specific request, the two of you, his closest friends from his college days, were to meet here a week after the general reading for his bequests to you."

"Mr. Hobbs, it's been many years since I've seen or even thought of Marvin. I find it difficult to believe he'd leave something for me in his will. If you don't mind, I'd like to just waive—"

Hobbs smiled and held up a hand.

"Before you start waiving claims, Dr. Foxwood, I think you ought to hear just what it is Mr. Woodbridge wanted you to have. You'll probably change your mind."

Lenore glanced at Billy. His eyes were closed and his head back on the rim of his chair. The pose didn't fool Lenore for even half a second. Billy Dixon was more alert now than ever. The I'm-so-bored-with-this-conversation-that-I'll-just-take-a-quick-snooze look was one Lenore remembered he'd perfected in college.

"Are you awake, Mr. Dixon?" Hobbs asked.

"You know I don't want to be here, Gil. Get on with it."

Unaccountably hurt, Lenore took the insult at face value. So he thought so little of her that he didn't even want to be in the same room she was in. Mr. Hobbs clearly said Marvin wanted them both there. Billy's desire not to see her had apparently been expressed to the lawyer at some earlier point. Fine, if that's the way he wanted to play it.

Lenore wondered what she'd ever done to earn Billy Dixon's contempt. In her eyes, the only crime she'd ever committed was falling in love with him. His crimes, on the other hand, were numerous and contemptible.

With a sardonic smile and shake of her head, she turned her attention back to Mr. Hobbs. She'd paid for her crime, while he'd gotten off scot-free. Falling in love with Billy Dixon constituted a punishment in and of itself.

As the lawyer droned on, Lenore realized with surprise and with a growing sense of pleasure that the one thing she wanted from Billy Dixon was vengeance.

Chapter 3

Later that day, Buster lounged across the back of a big leather chair in a friend's office.

"For someone who's supposed to be on the top of the world, you sure look like hell."

Buster looked at the man in the slick Italian suit. Sergeant Watson constituted the best in the business. Lucky for Buster, they'd been business associates long before either of them tasted the first fruit of fame. Sarge had never been in the military, but he ran his business like a drill sergeant. Unlike Buster, Sarge had managed to keep his affairs and flings discreet, behind the scenes. Every move Buster made got duly recorded, dissected and displayed on TV, in the tabloids and the trades. He lived in a fishbowl. If Buster Dixon sneezed, that fact somehow managed to be construed as front-page news.

Sarge wasn't gonna like what Buster had to say today.

"Didn't your mama teach you that you're supposed to say 'Good morning,' which, by the way, it isn't."

Sarge got up from behind his desk and came around to take in the full effect of Buster's presence. He watched his longtime friend and business partner and wondered what he was up to now.

Sarge Watson was meticulous. He kept his nails trimmed and manicured, his suits were tailor-made and he didn't keep clutter on his desk. Just two things he deemed important enough to be on his desk, and all he really needed to operate his artist management company: an instrument and a reminder.

The instrument was a telephone, and his biggest client, Buster Dixon, had picked up and was playing with the reminder: a marble paperweight with an engraved brass plate on it that read SHIT HAPPENS. DEAL WITH IT.

Sarge got the feeling that Buster was about to lay something heavy on him. "Do I need to clear out the office? Bring in the shovels?"

Buster didn't look at him, and he ignored the attempt at humor. "Lenore's in town," he said.

"Lenore? Is this supposed to ring a bell with me?"

Sarge crossed his arms and leaned back on the desk. His feet securely planted on the floor; he inspected the shine on his Stacy Adams shoes.

Buster sighed.

Sarge's eyebrows rose. He'd never seen Buster in this kind of mood: edgy, practically dejected. And in all the years he and Buster had run together, Sarge had never seen his boy look so unkempt. It's a wonder the guards recognized him and let him in the building.

When Buster failed to answer his question, Sarge asked again. "Do I know a Lenore? Should I?"

Buster fiddled with the paperweight, then placed it on the edge of the desk. Automatically Sarge reached out and lined it up near the telephone in its proper spot.

"I was in love with Lenore."

Sarge snorted. "Call the eyewitness news crews for the special report. So what else is new, Buster? You're in love with a different woman every month."

That got Buster's attention.

"No, not in love with them, in lust with them. There's a difference."

Sarge glanced at his Rolex. "Is there a point to all of this, Buster? I have an important meeting in about a half hour."

Buster got up and walked around the large room. Gold and platinum records and oversized pictures of Sarge and famous people decorated the walls. In a lot of ways, Sarge's office reminded him of the music room he abhorred at his penthouse apartment. But Buster liked this room; he liked the feel of it . . . and the security of it.

"Buster?"

The musician turned and looked at his agent/manager. Sergeant Watson was a big man, as tall as Buster's own six foot two. But Sarge outweighed Buster by a good sixty pounds. Sarge was known for two things: looking good and making megadeals. Unlike the rest of the men in the business, Sarge didn't drink, smoke, do drugs or publicly cheat on his wife. His only vice, it seemed, was not knowing when to leave the dining room table.

Buster sat down again and stared at the words on the paperweight.

"This is all your fault, you know."

"I'm going to be late to my meeting."

"Who are you meeting with?"

"Buster, what is the problem? Is somebody pregnant? Did you punch out a photographer?"

It was Buster's turn to snort. He sat back in his chair and kicked his Nike–clad feet up on the edge of Sarge's desk. "I left that life-style a long time ago. You know that."

Sarge looked at the feet but didn't say anything about that. He had another bone to pick with his biggest client.

"My phone has been ringing off the hook about you. And you up and pulled a disappearing act on me. Don't even think that little flimsy message you left about being out of pocket for a few days counts for anything. Where the hell have you been?"

"At home. I've been at home."

"Negative!" Sarge snapped back. "I've been calling there nonstop for a week. A whole week? Do you know how much time that is, how much momentum you've lost? How could you do this to me?"

Buster got up and walked to the windows that even through the smog gave a panoramic view overlooking the city.

"I was at my real house."

Sarge pushed back from the edge of the desk, went around and sat at the huge chair he'd had custom made. "You mean that hideout with no phone, no computer or modem, no fax machine, no links to the modern world. We've known each other for years, Buster, and I've never seen that place. I don't think it really even exists. Were you at Betty Ford?"

Buster shook his head. "I really expected more faith from you, Sarge. You know I don't mess with that stuff."

"Well, being on drugs is the only answer I can conjure for somebody who sweeps the biggest awards night in music and then disappears off the face of the planet for a week."

"I told you I was at home. I had some thinking to do."

Sarge glanced at his watch again. "Well, what did you come up with by way of conclusions after this pilgrimage?"

Buster whirled around. "Look, Sarge, you can cut the crap, okay. I didn't feel like being bothered with the press. I had a headache. Still do. I woke up with some strange woman in my bed, and I knew it was time for me to get away for a while. If it caused you some problems, I'm sorry. I'm sure you managed to milk every moment for what it was worth."

Sarge grinned. "As a matter of fact, I did. I just signed two new acts. Met them at one of your celebration parties."

Sarge eyed Buster. "What's the deal, Buster? I really don't have all day."

"Like I don't have enough problems already, Lenore is in the city."

"I'll ask again—who is Lenore?"

Buster smiled. Sarge blinked. It was, he realized with a start, the first real smile he'd seen from Buster Dixon in many years. It transformed his friend's face, made him look like the young idealistic songwriter he'd met more than a decade ago.

"Lenore is . . . Lenore is the woman I should have married. Sit down, Sarge, this is going to take a while."

Sarge stared Buster in the eye. It was a test. They both knew it. Sarge lost. Buster had the power and called the shots. Sarge sighed and punched a button on the telephone console.

"Reschedule my appointment and hold all other calls. No exceptions," he told his secretary.

Sarge folded his arms and leaned back in the chair. "This better be good, Buster. You probably just cost me five hundred grand."

But Buster wasn't listening to hollow threats. He was thinking about the past . . .

When his dorm room door slammed behind his math tutor, Billy rolled his eyes and glanced at the open textbook on his desk. The tutor had gotten in a huff because he wasn't paying attention.

Math held no appeal for Billy.

"When I'm rich and famous, I'll have accountants deal with the numbers. I'll just sign my name on the back of the checks." With that, Billy shut the book, leaned back on the hind legs of his dorm room desk chair and punched a button on a black boom box. Moments later, the high-pitched intro to Tom Browne's "Jamaica Funk" reverberated off the walls.

Over and over again, Billy listened to the riffs, the chords, the lyrics, the syncopated beat, dissecting what made the song work, what made it such a danceable hit.

Almost an hour later, he went to the closet that would

have been his roommate's, had his assigned roommate actually lived in the dormitory. Billy had turned the closet into a storage facility for the records that constituted his thriving business. Billy organized parties and DJ'd on the side. He favored off-the-yard house parties where booze could flow freely and the babes were less inclined to worry about missing their curfew.

Satisfied that he had everything under control, Billy snatched the concert ticket from his desktop. Yeah, after the stupid classical concert he had to go to tonight for music appreciation, he'd come up with a slow jam play list for the Saturday night Block Party. He set the alarm and locked his dorm room door. Only his phantom roommate and his best boy, Raheem, knew about the alarm system. Billy had too much money and too much equipment invested in his DJ business to rely on just the campus security force to safeguard his valuables.

Outside, Billy made his way to Campus Hall, where he'd have to suffer through this tired old music for two hours. It beat listening to a lecture though. When his music professor broke out of the boring textbook and started talking real life experience, that's when Billy usually woke up.

Listening to Haydn and Bach, two dead white guys from Europe, didn't do much for him. But the extra-credit points he'd get for hanging out at the concert would. All he had to do was stay awake long enough to hear a few of the pieces. Then he'd slip out a side door, write up his one-page impression of the symphony performance and he'd have instant brownie points.

Billy ignored the scowl from an usher who looked pointedly at his ripped jeans and baseball cap. Billy's insolent look challenged the older woman. She backed down and walked away, shaking her head. Billy grinned, took the baseball cap off his head as he entered the hall, then made his way down to his seat, Row H, Seat 1.

"Damn, I would be right up in the front."

With undisguised longing, he took in all the occupied seats around him and especially the ones near the doors.

Billy sighed, plopped down and hoped for the best.

"Excuse me, you're in my seat."

Billy looked up and fell in love.

Big brown eyes stared at him; a mouth made for kissing was almost within his reach. He could write a song about that mouth. He let his gaze drift over the rest of her. That black dress she was wearing, with its white lacy collar, looked like something the pilgrims wore way back in the day. But the girl sure filled out that proper little dress in a lot of wicked ways. Gloves, she even had on little black gloves. How cute!

But there was something else about her—something calling to him beyond the physical. Billy's eyebrows rose at that thought, then he smiled.

They'd have a traditional wedding. The church would be filled with flowers and candles. She'd walk down the aisle in a long, white dress made just for her by an Italian . . . no, by a French fashion designer. He'd be waiting for her at the altar in black tails. And Stevie Wonder would be playing "Isn't She Lovely" on a white baby grand.

"The performance is about to begin, and you're in my seat."

Billy grinned. Then he patted his lap.

The girl gasped, looked embarrassed and then shot her gaze about looking for an usher.

"You have to leave," she hissed. "This is my seat. I'm a season ticket holder."

"Is there a problem here?" an adult voice asked.

"Yes, ma'am. This gentleman is in my seat," the girl said as she handed her ticket stub over to the usher.

Billy nodded when she called him a gentleman. He liked that.

"Let me see your ticket," the usher told Billy.

Billy patted his shirt—that had no pockets—then looked up at the usher and shrugged.

"Your ticket stub, please." The tone wasn't exactly accommodating. Some people just had no sense of humor.

Billy searched his jeans pockets. When he came up empty, he remembered. He leaned over, looked around on the floor and then triumphantly held up a crumpled ticket stub.

The usher shook her head, then took the ticket and studied it.

"You're here on the wrong night. Your performance is tomorrow," she told Billy. "This seat belongs to the young lady. You'll have to leave, sir."

"Thank you," the girl murmured. She slipped a shiny black purse under her arm and waited for him to move.

Billy could just imagine that in her mind she was busy tapping her little foot. He glanced down her body, pausing briefly at hips that had potential. Then he grinned. She *was* impatiently tapping her foot. Her shiny black shoes matched the shiny black purse. She looked like she was going to a funeral.

If her choice of clothing was any indication of what the music was going to be like, it was gonna be a long two hours. Good thing he didn't wear a watch—he'd be looking at it every minute.

Billy rose from his seat, tipped his cap to the girl, who slid into it with a soft "Thank you," then he turned to the usher.

"Ma'am, I was really, really hoping to hear this evening's performance. I've anxiously awaited this for some time." Billy glanced at the girl out the corner of an eye while keeping an earnest expression on his face for the usher.

The usher raised an eyebrow and pointedly looked at Billy's casual attire. The house lights began to dim.

"Please, may I take that seat there?" Billy said, pointing across the aisle and one row behind the girl. "If anyone comes for it, I promise I'll leave."

Violins and other strings concluded their preperformance tune-up.

"Jeans are not the proper attire for the symphony, young man," the usher scolded.

Billy managed a chagrined look, then chanced a quick glance at the girl. "I know. I was studying and lost track of time. If I changed, I would have been late. Please, may I stay?"

The usher nodded as the house lights completely dimmed and the conductor walked out on stage. The audience's polite applause drowned out whatever else the censoring usher had to say.

Billy grabbed a program from the woman's hands, said "Thanks" and plopped into the aisle seat.

The girl looked back at him and smiled shyly.

She *had* been listening! Yes!

He nodded and smiled back. When she turned her attention to the musicians gathered on stage, Billy grinned.

This wouldn't be too bad after all.

The conductor said a few words of introduction, declared some unpronounceable name as the title of the first song and then the violins started squeaking in earnest. Billy winced. He could be back in the room, listening to some real music. But no.

He looked around at the people in the hall. Of the faces he could see, they all seemed to be enjoying this. He sat up as he took in the number of babes in the house. Quite a few, and some of them were sitting alone, like his future wife was.

Billy's attention moved back to the girl in the funeral dress. He leaned forward in an effort to see her a little better. In profile, her face held a serene beauty. She was pretty, yes. But she also seemed so, so . . . for lack of a better word, Billy came up with calm. She just looked calm, peaceful. Sort of like the music playing; it reminded him of pictures he'd seen of a mountain stream.

"Hmm." Billy glanced down at the program in his hands but couldn't see much in the dark.

With another look at the girl, who now had her eyes

closed and a soft smile about that gorgeous mouth, Billy
settled back in his seat to see why someone would want to
have season tickets to listen to this music. If you couldn't
dance to it, what was the point?

Thunderous applause filled the hall. Billy sat in his seat
dazed. Absolutely incredible, this music was incredible. As
the lights came up he looked at his program. The program
notes had a lot of information. This Haydn dude had
actually been influenced by Bach's style.

A concertgoer accidentally brushed Billy's arm.

"I'm sorry."

Billy looked up, "That's okay, man."

Then he remembered—the girl!

His wife was headed up the aisle and out the door. Billy
hopped up, then elbowed his way through the throng. He
caught up with her in the lobby.

He folded his program in half and tucked it in the back
pocket of his jeans. "Hi."

She turned. Wide eyes and soft mouth beckoned him.
But playing the hound dog probably wouldn't earn him
any points.

"Hello. Wasn't it a lovely performance?"

Before Billy could respond to that, she continued. "I
heard what you told the usher. That's how I've been about
this series. When one is over, I can hardly wait until the next
one. Which composer is your favorite, Bach or Haydn?"

Oh, is that how they're pronounced. Billy had figured
the names to be pronounced like they were spelled: *batch*
and *hay-den*. But she'd said *bok* and *high-den*.

"Uh, Bach," he said.

Her bright smile lit up the lobby. "Mine, too!" she
exclaimed.

Billy took his opening. "Are you a student here? May I
walk you to your car or your dormitory?"

"Why, yes. That's so nice of you. And yes, I'm a sopho-more."

"Me, too," he said. Well, almost, sort of a sophomore. A GPA of one point three didn't exactly put him on sound academic ground. If he flunked this semester, he'd be booted out.

He guided her out the door and down the steps. When she moved to turn left, he steered her to the right.

"We can walk around the building and take in a little of the waterfront."

She smiled up at him. "Okay."

Billy breathed a sigh of relief. If his boys on the block saw him with this babe in the funeral dress, he'd never hear the end of it.

"My name's Billy Dixon," he said.

"Oh, that's right. We didn't get introduced. I'm Lenore. Lenore Foxwood."

She glanced up at him. "You tried to embarrass me back there. I wouldn't even consider sitting on your lap."

"I know," he admitted. "I'm sorry." Sometimes it was better to play 'em straight. "You were looking so prim and proper, I just wanted to see you smile."

She glanced at him and then away, clearly not sure how to respond. Then after a moment: "How long have you liked classical music?" she asked.

"You could call me a new convert," he said. "There was just something about it. I don't really know how to put it, something soothing and gentle even when there was a lot of cymbal crashing. Dynamite horn section, too."

If Billy was surprised to hear the truth come out of his mouth, he didn't show it. They left the sidewalk and walked in the street, headed to the lake that rimmed a portion of the campus.

"I'm not that familiar with all of Haydn's work," she said. "Now, Bach, that I love. What's your favorite?"

Uh-oh.

"Well," he said. "There are so many songs, I just can't say which is my favorite."

She turned to him, a quizzical expression on her face. "Why do you call the compositions songs?"

Oops. Tactical error. Billy thought fast.

"Well, I do a little composing myself. I think of all music in terms of songs because I always use lyrics."

Her smile turned him on.

"Really? What have you written?"

"Oh, just a few things here and there. Nothing you'd have heard unless . . ."

She paused. "Unless what?"

Billy reached for her hand to tug her along as they strolled through the grass. She followed. "Unless you go to dance parties."

Lenore shook her head. "I went to one my freshman year. It was horrible. There was beer all over the floor. It was hot and dark and sweaty."

"Different parties have different atmospheres. That sounds like it was a union sweatbox dance."

"Do you mean at the campus Student Union?"

When he nodded, Lenore continued. "That's not my thing. I like classical music."

"What about jazz?" he asked. She had to like jazz.

"Some of it is okay, I guess."

Billy frowned. So far they had zilch in common. Time to change the subject.

"Where are you from?" he asked.

"Philadelphia. And you?"

"A Philly girl, well, all right." There was hope.

"I'm originally from Chicago, but my mom just moved to Florida. My old man is in California. L.A."

"Oh, your parents are divorced. I'm sorry."

Billy looked at her. "Why be sorry? I'm not. It's best that they're on separate coasts. No state is big enough for them both to live in at the same time."

"What do they do?"

"Moms is an insurance administrator. My pops is in the business."

"What business?" she asked.

"Show business. He books acts for shows at nightclubs."

He looked at her and caught the tail-end of a frown when he said "nightclubs." If she was one of those ones who went to vespers every Tuesday and never missed Sunday school or chapel service, he could hang it up right now.

"What's wrong with nightclubs?" he asked her.

"They're just so loud. I like quiet things."

He took her hand in his and slowly ran his thumb over the back of her palm. When she didn't resist, he moved in a little closer as they strolled along the trim grassy banks. A mallard crossed in front of them, then waddled to the jagged lakefront, over the rocks and to the water.

"It must be nice being a duck," she said.

Billy grinned. "Why do you say that?"

"Well, the only thing ducks have to worry about is where to get a little food and where to get in the water. Most of the ones around here get fed by students all the time so they don't have to search for food, and the university maintains the lake. I figure a duck has it pretty easy."

Billy paused. Lenore still walking, stopped and looked at their joined hands.

"What?" she asked.

"I was just thinking that maybe it's too early to try to kiss you. We only just met."

Chapter 4

Sarge sighed, then yawned. At the rate Buster was going, the telling of this little tale would take two weeks. He glanced at his watch. So much for that deal. Not only was he going to miss his appointment, he was gonna miss lunch. And that cheapskate Murphy had planned to pick up the tab.

Sarge had things to do. Listening to Buster wax poetic about kissing a girl wasn't one of those things.

"That's all very romantic, Buster. Your first love and whatnot. What does your little story have to do with today? With music? With my lost five hundred grand?"

Buster jumped up. "Don't you understand? She is my music." He faltered. "Or rather, she was my music. Lenore was the inspiration for my first hit."

"And?"

"And she's in town. I just saw her over at Gil Hobbs's office."

"Hobbs? What were you doing with that snake?"

"Gil's not a snake, maybe a shark, very sharp, very cagey. And I was over there because he was Marvin's lawyer."

"Oh, yes. The dearly departed Mr. Woodbridge. So what'd you reap from the ashes and the spoils of the International Playboy?"

Buster frowned at the sarcastic tone in his friend's voice. "Have a little respect for the dead, Sergeant."

Sarge assessed Buster and then nodded. He'd gone too far and he knew it. Buster didn't take to people talking about his friends. And Buster rarely pulled rank on Sarge by calling him by his first name. That was twice today Buster had put him in his place. Sarge didn't like it, but he also knew the primary source of most of his own personal wealth.

Buster looked at his longtime friend.

"Marvin left me the one thing I can't have."

"What's that?" Sarge asked.

"He left me Lenore."

Across town, Lenore talked with her old college roommate. Kim had been living in California for about ten years. The small upscale fashion boutique she owned thrived. With the store, the fashion design she did for some of Hollywood's most affluent and the costume work she did for feature films, Kim lived and breathed clothes, color and style.

In college Lenore had been the quiet, studious, anal one. Kim had been a hard-core party girl. Their dorm room had been a study in the odd couple: Lenore, proud of the soothing setting she created with her cool whites and pale pinks, was constantly affronted by Kim's constant experiments with one wild color and design theme after another. How they ever managed to get along still confounded them.

Lenore looked around the big room. With screens and contemporary, uncomfortable-looking furniture, Kim had created an effect of separate rooms in the space. Kim's house was actually a gutted-out warehouse. With swatches and bolts of material and glitzy accessories here, there and everywhere, the place looked more like a costume factory than personal living quarters. A life-sized stuffed giraffe graced one corner of the room, wispy trails of cream chiffon draped from his papier-mâché neck.

"Are you going to tell me about the giraffe or am I supposed to guess?" Lenore asked.

Kim glanced at the animal and chuckled. "That was from a low-budget shoot. We were looking for a jungle, Wild Kingdom—type effect. I did the clothes, some art students made the giraffe, a rhino and a couple of monkeys. It turned out okay. The clothes were fabulous, of course."

Lenore laughed. "Of course."

"Now tell me, what do you mean Marv left you Billy? That's the craziest thing I've ever heard. Turn around."

Lenore obeyed Kim and slowly turned in the high heels she wore as Kim pinned the hem on a long indigo-colored, strategically transparent evening gown. Blue sparkles, shades lighter than the material, twinkled like stars while just barely covering certain significant body parts.

"This dress is gorgeous, but why aren't you hemming it to a client's specifications?"

Kim, humming along with a contemporary R&B song on the radio, tucked a pin in the bottom, then put three in her mouth while she reached for a small marker. One by one she pulled the pins from her mouth and tucked them here and there.

"Stick your leg out like you're doing a Mae West pose," she ordered.

Lenore did as she was told.

"This isn't for sale or for a client. It's for show, tell and entice. It's a 'tease me, baby' dress."

Lenore smiled at her best friend's description of the dress. "That's for sure." She glanced down, then straightened when Kim tsk-tsked. "Are you really going to have that much leg showing? You're going to need someone bold to wear this get-up outside.''

"I don't create 'get-ups.' My designs are all created to make statements." Kim sat back and studied her work. She cocked her head to get a different perspective.

"This one's statement is peekaboo, come and get me," Lenore said.

Kim chuckled. Then, with a critical eye, she assessed the hem. "Actually I was thinking it's a bit too low. I may inch it up. And stop trying to avoid the issue. You haven't answered my question. How did that fine brother Marvin Woodbridge leave you a person in the form of Mr. Dixon?"

"I was hoping you'd forgotten about that," Lenore said dryly.

"Not a chance, sweet babycakes. Spill it. And turn to your left."

Lenore did as she was directed. Then sighed.

"Kim, I swear, seeing Billy was like being thrown into a time machine. All the past, all the history came rushing back to me."

"Like what?"

"Like the jazzy pencils he gave me to replace my dull yellow number-two pencils, and like what he wanted to do on that fake bearskin bedspread you had. Remember, the one with the head? And I remembered the first time he kissed me, the first night we met. I was excited about a classical concert at Campus Hall.

"When I got there, he was in my seat. I had to get an usher to make him move. Then I felt him staring at me through the whole performance. I could barely concentrate on the movements. After it was over, he caught up with me and started asking me all kinds of questions." Lenore smiled at the memory. "He walked me back to the dorm. Bach has held a special place in my heart since then."

Kim rolled her eyes. "You always did like that boring music. And only you would remember something as mundane as pencils." She chuckled. "I wonder what ever happened to that old bear spread."

"Maybe someone shot it and put it out of its plastic and fake fur misery," Lenore said.

Still in the fond mist of reminiscence, Lenore smiled dreamily. "I still have three glitter pencils he gave me. He said the boring yellow number-two pencils were for the masses. That I could show my style and verve with some pencils with attitude. The two of you taught me about attitude."

"Billy Dixon used the word *verve?* From my recollection of your complaints, he was about one failing grade from being booted out of school. Turn. Small step."

Lenore simply shrugged and made the move so Kim could see better.

When another song came on the radio, Kim straightened up, grooved to it a little, then grinned at her friend. "You should give rap, hip-hop and some of the new artists a chance, Lenore. Loosen up. Live a little."

"You sound like Billy used to," Lenore said. She caught the wistfulness in her own voice and sighed. "I thought I'd gotten over Billy. And as for rap and hip-hop, I'll leave that to those of you who *think* you're still twenty-five."

Kim chuckled. "Hey, in my line of work, you gotta keep current."

"Why does seeing him hurt so bad?" Lenore asked. "I thought I'd gotten over him once and for all."

"Len, I thought you knew by now. Take another small step to your left."

Lenore complied. "Knew what?"

"You never get over your first love. Besides," Kim added with a pointed look at her friend, "the two of you have some major league unfinished business."

"I don't want to talk about it."

"You never do," Kim replied.

"I didn't come over here to get hassled."

"Don't jump all testy on me, sisterfriend. Take that mess out on Dixon."

"Sorry," Lenore mumbled, chagrined. "If you never get over your first love, why don't I see you pining after anyone."

"Ah ha! So you admit it finally."

Lenore huffed. "Admit what?"

"That after all these years, you're still pining after Billy Dixon."

"Puh-leeese. Spare me. Don't even go there."

"Me thinks she doth protest too much."

"Granted, I'll admit that he still looks good, even if he looked kind of scruffy and tired today. The whole will business was odd. I'm sure that was the last time I'll see him."

"Um-hmm."

Lenore leveled a slit-eyed look at Kim.

"Don't try to throw one of those Evilena looks at me. Won't work. I'm used to you. I knew you before you were a big-shot Ph.D. That evil eye might scare your students but not me."

"Yeah, well, I knew you when Polly and Esther were close personal friends of yours. Where's your Rolodex so I can call *W* magazine and give them a scoop."

The two women laughed together at the good-natured threats.

Kim stood up and offered her hand. "Here, step down. Be careful. Go take a look, but watch out for the pins."

Lenore stepped off the pedestal and walked to the three-way mirrors Kim pointed to across the room.

"From everything I've seen, heard and read lately, Buster D should be tired. He produces and writes music nonstop, for himself and a bunch of other artists. I did some costume work for one of the music videos he produced about a year ago. Girl, don't you read *Ebony*? They featured his penthouse and his recording studio a while back. He owns a couple of clubs, too. I've been to one of them. Nice place. It's well managed. No riffraff. That's where he show-cases some of the new talent before he takes them nation-wide. He calls all the shots. The brother has come a long way since those dance parties he put together when we were in school.''

Lenore, eyeing the dress and the way it hugged her form, at first missed her former roommate's words. "This dress is awesome. I couldn't imagine wearing it outside where people would . . . what did you say?''

"Huh?''

"What were you saying about Billy and somebody named Buster?''

The intro to a sexy slow song came on the radio. Kim grinned. "I tell you, Lenore, every time I hear this song I just want to crawl all over a man.''

Lenore turned to look at Kim, who had her eyes closed and was swaying to the tune. She, too, had heard the song on her car radio once or twice and had always liked it. "That's your problem, Kim. You've always been over-sexed.''

"Don't hate me because I'm beautiful,'' Kim said.

Lenore chuckled at the old joke between the two. In college, whenever Kim headed out on another date with yet another guy, Lenore would just shake her head in wonder. Kim, decked out in one of the outfits she'd designed, would blow a kiss over her shoulder and say, 'Don't hate me because I'm beautiful, babycakes. Get out there and get yourself some.' Until Billy, Lenore had always declined. Through the ensuing years, men and relation-ships had come and gone, but the saying between the two women endured.

"This was one of his biggest hits.''

Lenore, never one for keeping up with the names of all the fly-by-night, one-hit wonders, asked the obvious. "Who?''

"Buster. He produced this song.''

"That song, Miss Know-it-All, is called 'Indigo Dreams,'

and it's by a recording artist named Alejandro.'' She stuck her tongue out at Kim in a so-there gesture. "Who is this Buster you keep talking about?"

"Alejandro recorded it. Buster Dixon wrote it and produced it.''

"Who is Buster Dixon?"

Kim opened her eyes and stopped swaying. "You're joking, right?''

At Lenore's blank look, Kim shook her head. "Jeez, oh man. What have you been doing in that ivory tower of yours?''

"I've been scrambling my way to tenure and taking care of my responsibilities. What are you talking about?''

"Have you ever heard of Buster D?" Kim asked.

Lenore huffed. "Yes, I'm not *that* backward and behind. J.D., as well as some of my students, are always talking about his music. 'Shake 'N Bake' is one of his songs.''

Kim's burst of laughter competed with the radio. "Shake 'N Bake is for your chicken,'' she said chuckling. "The song was 'Shake it Babe.' "

Lenore rolled her eyes. "Same difference for all the sense it makes.''

"So tell me, how *is* that too fine J.D. doing these days?''

"Just fine, thank you very much. And don't even think about it.''

"What?" Kim innocently asked. "Make sure to tell him I said hi.''

"I'm sure I'll forget by the time I get home.''

Chuckling, Kim walked to Lenore, who stood in front of the mirrors with hands on hips.

"We'll talk some more about him later,'' Kim said. "Right now, Lenore, there's obviously something you need to know about Buster. It's important.''

From her reflection in the mirror, Lenore looked at her friend, concerned about her serious tone. "What?''

"Lenore, Buster Dixon the record and video producer, Buster Dixon the man who every now and then records a slow jam himself, Buster Dixon, the hottest ticket in the music industry is Billy Dixon, *your* Billy Dixon. He just won about five or six music awards last week."

Lenore's disbelief was apparent. "Get out of here."

"It's true," Kim said. Kim started helping Lenore out of the shimmery gown.

"Buster D is a big-time record producer. He hangs out with movie stars and is responsible for some of today's rising stars, even I know that much. The Billy Dixon I knew in college didn't have enough ambition in him to do all that. He just liked to party."

"Um-hmm. People change, you know. And have you ever seen a picture of him?" Kim asked.

"Well, not exactly," Lenore admitted. "And I know all of that because a couple of my students gave me the four-one-one."

Kim laughed. "Whoo, chile. Trying to talk hip now. I don't think they said that back in the seventeenth century, where you like to hang out in your dusty books."

Lenore rolled her eyes, then smiled. "Forget you, Kim."

Lenore stepped out of the sexy evening gown and handed it to Kim.

"I'm serious though, Lenore," Kim said as she carefully arranged the gown on a padded hanger. "The man we knew in school as Billy Dixon is Buster D."

Lenore went to the chair where she'd left her clothes. "That's the stupidest name I ever heard of. Who would run around calling himself Buster D?"

"That's the street name he goes by. I saw an interview with him on one of those entertainment shows. It was a while ago, and he was saying how he's had the nickname all his life, that it started with the Buster Brown shoes his mother bought for him. Adding the D gave him a contemporary moniker. You know, so he'd fit in with the hip-hop crowd."

"If you knew who he was all this time, why didn't you say something?" Lenore accused.

"What was there to say? I thought you knew. Everybody in the world knows Buster D's real name is William DuBois Dixon."

Everybody in the world except me, Lenore thought.

"That's always been the problem," Lenore said as she tugged her blouse over her head. "Billy and I have always lived in two different worlds."

Kim handed Lenore her slacks.

"So what are you going to do?" Kim asked. "About Buster, I mean Billy. And about Marvin's will?"

"Nothing. I'm going to go back to my hotel. Take a nice long bath, go to bed, and then get on a plane tomorrow and head back to the real world. You can keep your sunny California."

"Are you going to spend your entire life running away?" Kim quietly asked.

Lenore slipped on her shoes and glared at Kim. "One, I don't know what you're talking about, and two, I'm not the one who did the running away."

Chapter 5

Lenore slid under the mountain of bubbles the Jacuzzi's jets kept frothed up. She'd done just what she told Kim she planned to do. She'd stripped off her clothes, checked her flight time and ordered room service. The wait for her meal would be about an hour, so she had time to relax in the tub. Problem was, she couldn't get her mind off of Billy, off Billy being Buster, Marvin being dead and two hundred fifty thousand dollars she suddenly had at her disposal.

Marvin Woodbridge had no business leaving her that kind of money. What in the world was she going to do with it?

"What was the man thinking?"

Lenore stretched one long shapely leg up out of the water. Watching the white bubbles slide down her leg reminded her of Billy. He liked sensual things and was always trying to embarrass her. She skimmed one hand along the surface of the bubbles and thought about how long it had been since intimacy and simple joys like cuddling or holding hands had been a part of her life.

Wrinkling her nose, she thought about the unpleasant sexual encounters she'd had with her ex. He blamed her unresponsiveness on a low sex drive plus the fact that by nature she was cold and frigid. "A man could get more warmth out of a bag of ice cubes," he'd accuse before finishing himself off with himself in one hand and a men's magazine in the other.

Every now and then, sex with Simon had been pleasant. Those occasions had been rare though. Then, after a while, with nothing else to base the lovemaking experience on, Lenore started believing what her husband said about her. Vague recollections of heat and warmth and a building pleasure she'd found in Billy's arms had long since faded. She simply attributed those distant thoughts to a memory that wanted to make things better than they actually were.

Maybe the reason she'd liked the song "Indigo Dreams" so much was because it reminded her of her past, of a time when she'd been young, in love and on the threshold of an awakening passion. Passion, obviously, was something she wasn't meant to experience.

She thought of the man she'd met in the lawyer's office this afternoon. He'd been Billy, but he had also been a stranger. He was cocky and arrogant, insolent and oh-so-fine.

"Some things don't change, Lenore. You should know that by now."

Her ex hadn't changed, even after the expensive marriage counseling they'd suffered through. Lenore wasn't even sure why she'd tried to save the marriage. Things went south two months after the honeymoon. She and Simon really had little in common. But they were considered the golden couple in academic circles, both of them on the fast track at their university. Lenore published papers and pulled in grant money, while Simon had been quickly promoted up the administrative ladder. But Simon had come home one too many nights with lipstick on his collar and the enticing perfume of some young undergraduate mingled with the sweat of his body.

Lenore filed for divorce and applied for a teaching position at another university. It meant a move and starting from scratch toward her goal of tenure. But it was worth it. She reclaimed her own name and found a home at a small, conservative liberal arts college where the emphasis was on teaching and community service instead of research. She still got her work published in all the right academic journals, but she wasn't in a neck-to-neck, do-or-die competition with her husband to see who could succeed the fastest. More counseling and countless workshops on self-esteem had healed her.

"Best thing you ever did was dump that loser," she said aloud. Sure a few doubts surfaced every now and then—that was only natural and to be expected. Sometimes her nights got lonely. She'd had dates and relationships since the divorce. But nothing she considered significant.

"Now if you could just get Billy Dixon off your mind, everything would be okay."

Reconciling the fact that the megaproducer Buster Dixon was in actuality the Billy Dixon she'd known as a girl, was going to take a while to get used to. She tried to think of any of his songs she might have heard. But she drew a blank. Lenore didn't listen to contemporary music. She taught her students about long-dead poets and writers, and tended to draw her musical tastes from the same periods as those long-gone masters of art and literature. Every now and then, she'd catch a new tune on the car radio before tuning in to the classical or public radio station she liked. Classical and operatic works remained her favorites.

J.D.'s tastes were more contemporary. They'd had more than one argument about music. He considered himself a great composer. But Lenore heard mostly noise when he played. Granted, he was gifted; piano came naturally to him, and he played several instruments. But the fact they could never agree on anything these days was unsettling.

Lenore liked all her relationships to be rock steady. In the last year, their fights had grown lengthier and louder: She didn't like his friends. He said she stifled his creativity. His hair was too long. She was too uptight. And so it went, back and forth, until every now and then they called a truce to enjoy for a while the simple novelty of peace.

Lenore sighed, not really sure how to handle that situation. She and J.D. had had another squabble before she'd come out here. Resolving *that* problem awaited her return. Dark clouds seemed to follow her everywhere she went.

It seemed like all the men in her life caused her nothing but grief. Billy, like her ex, was bad news for her mental psyche. But just the sight of him in that lawyer's office this morning made her think about what might have been. Simon's complaints about her technique and lack of zest for intercourse had their roots in Lenore's own doubts and insecurities about her sensuality.

She hadn't been woman enough to keep Billy interested beyond a few times. He'd grown bored and moved on—literally right out of her life. She had a pile of "Return to Sender" letters from the post office to prove it. Billy Dixon stole her virginity and left her to slowly and painfully fall out of love with him. She remembered her thought process at the time: If Billy didn't want her after the time and effort he put into wooing her, what did she have to offer a man?

"A lot, that's what." She could boldly claim that now, now that she'd come into her own being. And she'd done it without Billy, without Simon.

Slipping a little lower in the bubbles, she smiled. "*Dr.* Foxwood, you've come a long way, baby." Lenore let the frothing bubbles tickle her nose. She lifted a hand in the air and watched the slick trail of water and bubbles slide down her arm.

She imagined Billy's hands following that trail. She closed her eyes and moaned. Would his mouth still feel the same? Would his hands, with those long, nimble fingers, still hold and caress, shape and mold her pliant flesh? Lenore shifted in the Jacuzzi so the jets of water massaged her. She sighed then opened her eyes.

"Water jets just aren't the same."

A little while later, Lenore was just stepping out of the tub when room service knocked on her door. Wrapping one of the hotel's big, fluffy white robes about her, she shook her hair down and went to claim her dinner.

When she opened the door, Billy Dixon pushed in a cart.

Lenore's mouth dropped open the same moment she clutched the folds of the robe to her neck. "Wh-what are you doing here?"

"I tipped the waiter and sent him back to the kitchen."

Despite her shock at seeing him, she eagerly took in everything about him. He'd shaved, gotten a haircut and put on some decent clothing. White slacks and the white shirt with banded collar gave him a sophisticated but relaxed look. He looked like the Billy she remembered from so long ago. If she didn't already know him, he would have been a man she'd like to get to know better.

But then she remembered all he'd done and not done. She remembered her anger at being abandoned. All the hurt, the confusion and the despair he'd caused her. Billy Dixon had been her first real boyfriend, her first love. But to him, she was obviously just another conquest that he quickly tired of.

He stood there with an easy smile and watched her struggle with the decision to throw him out or not. He'd spent most of the day thinking about Lenore. Talking to Sarge had really opened the floodgates for him. Lenore had been sunshine and music in his life. For years after he'd moved to California, he thought of her.

For the last few weeks, he'd thought of little else but her. Marvin's death had been a wake-up call for him. He'd begun an agonizing personal assessment of what really mattered in his life. At the top of the list had been Lenore's name. Seeing her today, after so many years, after so many fantasies, was like a rainbow after a storm. Except Lenore was both the rainbow and the pot of gold.

Nothing in his wildest fantasies of late could have prepared him for the sight of Lenore wrapped in a soft white robe. The ends of her hair were damp, as if she'd just gotten out of the shower or tub. Dixon's body responded to the mental image of a naked Lenore covered with nothing but streams of water and him.

"We need to talk, Leni," he said, putting the accent, like he always did, on the second syllable. From his lips, the name was a caress.

Lenore jerked back as if he'd assaulted her. In actuality he had: He'd given her the nickname. "Don't call me that. You no longer have the right to call me that. As a matter of fact, you don't have a right to be here, so why don't you leave."

He didn't move. The room service cart sat between them.

That sexy half smile played about his mouth. It was his tolerant and amused look. And it ticked Lenore off.

"Are you leaving, or do I have to call security?"

He didn't say anything. He just stared into her eyes.

The silence between them grew. Her breathing slowed. It was almost as though no time had passed between them, as though he'd just walked in and picked up on a long-ago seduction scene. Heat slowly washed through her as he watched her. She stared into his brown eyes and saw everything she wanted to see: desire, love, hope, passion. Or was that merely a reflection of what shone in her own eyes?

She gripped the doorknob for balance when her knees grew weak. Then she remembered the robe, and with one hand on the doorknob and one hand holding the robe tight against her body, she fought all the sensations that roiled through her. She just knew he could see through the robe's thick fabric clear to her naked damp skin. Heat swirled in her lower abdomen, and she felt her breasts grow heavy.

"Don't look at me," she said.

Billy smiled. Then he walked behind her and shut the door. Lenore practically leaped away from his nearness.

Turning back to her: "You're still as beautiful as the last day I saw you."

Lenore inched around the cart, putting distance between them. "Why are you here? How did you find me?"

Billy shrugged. "Gil Hobbs got sick of me calling every five minutes. He finally gave me the name of your hotel. From there, it was pretty easy. A big tip and an autograph got me your dinner from the room service guy, who'd just rolled up to your door."

"And I suppose life has just been pretty easy for you."

"Not necessarily. We can talk about that though. We need to talk about Marvin's will. We need to talk about us. Let's catch up on old times. How've you been?"

Lenore shook her head. Could he really be standing there with that cocky attitude just chitchatting her up? For fifteen long years she'd wondered what had happened to him, why he'd dumped her without so much as a goodbye note. In counseling she'd learned that she held on to issues too long. Billy Dixon was raggedy old baggage she should have traded in long ago. But right or wrong, she was still emotionally attached to him. She couldn't help that fact. Right or wrong, he still had the power to make her run hot and cold. That he had any power over her at all, pissed Lenore off royally.

Her conflicted emotions, that in just this one day had run the gamut from desire to anger, from longing to bloodlust, had taken a toll on her. And now he stood there cavalierly asking how she'd been for the last fifteen years.

Something in Lenore snapped.

Before she even realized she'd thought of it, she slapped him with everything she had in her.

"How dare you barge in here. You have no right. Get out!"

Billy didn't flinch, he didn't even move.

"I used to wonder sometimes if you'd haul off and hit me when you saw me again. I guess I deserve it."

"You guess? Let me set you straight if you're not sure." Lenore's militant pose, somewhat deflated by the fact she was just wearing a robe rather than full body armor, let him know she wouldn't think twice about hitting him again.

"Do you want to know what I thought I'd do when I saw you again?"

"No," she fired back. "What I want you to do is leave."

He smiled. "I can't do that, Lenore. I've waited too long."

"Waited too long for what?"

Wrapping one arm about her waist, Billy pulled Lenore to him. When his mouth crushed over hers, she struggled.

She resisted. She didn't want this. She didn't want him. Then she stopped lying to herself. This was the only place she wanted to be.

Her hands crawled up his chest and draped around his neck. She curled her body into his and felt his arm slide around her waist.

The kiss was a whispered memory, an apology, a temptation and a promise of things to come. His lips parted hers in a soul-reaching message that Lenore both wanted to hear and received loud and clear: I love you; I want you. The divine ecstasy was just like it was the first time he'd kissed her. The earth moved when his tongue danced with hers. Fireworks exploded and their joining sent swirls of fire to her stomach. Lenore had come home to paradise, to the arms of the man she'd never stopped loving.

And she hated herself for carrying a torch that long.

She pulled away from him and wiped her mouth off with the sleeve of the thick terry robe.

"Don't ever do that again," she hissed.

Billy released her. "Man, was I ever a fool."

"What does that mean?"

He grinned. "Your steak's getting cold, Lenore. Come on and eat your dinner." He pushed the cart to the dining table in the lounge area of the hotel suite.

Lenore cinched the belt at her waist and folded her arms. "I want you to leave."

Billy turned to her. The understanding in his eyes infuriated her. "I know you hate me. I know you're angry. I also know you're hungry and that this has been an exhausting day. You ordered enough food for four people, so come on over here and eat it."

Pulling a pack of Kools from his pocket, he tapped one out and lit it with a gold-inlaid lighter.

Lenore watched him inhale and then exhale.

"That's a disgusting habit," she said.

"Gotta die of something."

"If you're hastening to an early grave, maybe I'll stick around for a while."

Billy grinned. "I see you got some spark in the last fifteen years."

Fifteen years, eight months, three weeks and then today, she thought.

With the cigarette dangling from his mouth, Billy held his hand to her in invitation while pulling out a chair for her.

Lenore didn't move.

"I'm not going to bite, Leni."

"I don't want my clothes, my room or my food smelling like cigarettes."

Billy grinned as he snuffed out the cigarette in an ashtray on the room service cart. Too late she realized her comment was the tacit invitation he'd been waiting for.

"I wish you'd leave," she said.

"No, you don't," he said.

And that, Lenore knew, was the truth.

That kiss had seared her to her toes. Lenore didn't like admitting that fact even to herself. She didn't want to want him. Yet she wondered if, when a man wanted a woman, he felt anything like what she was feeling this moment. If so, it was a wonder people didn't just spontaneously combust with desire.

Lenore had never wanted Simon like this, and they had been married six years. She couldn't even remember ever wanting Billy like this. She needed a strong defense. Clothes would help.

Dabbing her mouth, she excused herself from the table where he heartily ate and where she'd merely pushed food around her plate. A few minutes later, she came back wearing hose and penny loafers, slacks and a bow blouse and cardigan. Half-rim reading glasses perched on her nose.

She watched Billy's eyebrows rise. Then she frowned at his amused smile.

"Sorry, Leni, it won't work," he said.

"What're you talking about?"

"You can try to shield yourself in the armor of those drab clothes, but it won't work. I know what's under all that scholarly cloth. I know the shape of your breasts, the feel of your thighs, the heat of your passion."

"You threw my passion away."

"And I've regretted that for the last fifteen years."

Lenore caught her breath. She folded her arms across her chest. "Why are you here, Billy?"

He came to her and tugged on her arm until she followed him to the two love seats that faced each other in the lounge area. Lenore sat down. She watched him grab the bottle of wine they hadn't touched during dinner. Since Mr. Hobbs's firm was picking up the tab for her stay, Lenore didn't feel any qualms about the expensive addition she'd ordered with her meal. Now she had second thoughts.

Billy was going to try to get her drunk.

Well, it wasn't going to work.

Lenore breathed a sigh of relief when he took a seat on

the opposite sofa. He opened the bottle, filled two glasses and left one within easy reach for her on the small marble table that separated the green brocade love seats.

While she sat tense and perched on the edge of her seat, Billy, as usual, made himself comfortable. He held his glass in salute to her, then took a swallow.

"Mmm. Nice tastes, as always."

"Why are you here?" she asked for the third time.

"I want to apologize."

"For what?

This time his smile was rueful. "I think you know. I walked out on you fifteen years ago. I never said goodbye. I never got in touch with you. I didn't do right by you. I'm sorry."

She crossed her arms and legs. "Don't you think it's a little late for that?"

Billy leaned forward, the wineglass casually held in his hand. "It's never too late to make amends, to try to make amends," he added. "I've thought about you through the years."

"Have you now?"

Shaking his head at her caustic tone, he smiled and sat back. "I deserve your animosity."

Lenore, silent, watched him. Animosity. My, he must have looked that one up before coming over here. "If you're waiting for me to disagree, you have a long wait ahead of you," she said.

Billy drank from his glass, then put it on the table. "Look, let's just start over, okay? I've been a bastard, but that was then. I'm a different man now."

Lenore assessed him. He *was* different. He carried a man's sophistication about him. Maybe Kim was right, maybe he had changed. Not only did a level of maturity surround him, he couldn't have made it to where he was today without some business and professional acumen. Maybe she'd give him the benefit of the doubt . . . for now.

She loosened up, removed the glasses from her nose and reached for her wine goblet.

"Tell me about this Buster D business. Where did that come from?"

Billy grinned, and he was the fun-loving guy she knew as a college sophomore. Lenore had to smile back. That infectious sunny outlook on life was one of the things she first liked about him . . . that and the fact he loved classical music.

"Ah," he said, leaning back. "Buster is a facade, a public persona so to speak. Buster D hangs out in all the latest clubs, he's down with the homies. He's on a first-name basis, A-list for the parties, have-your-people-call-my-people kind of brother. He's from the 'hood and the 'burbs. He's from uptown, downtown, Brentwood and South Central. Buster Dixon is so many things to so many people that sometimes I forget and lose track."

"And who are you?" she asked.

"Me? I'm just a black man trying to make a living in America."

Lenore's look, decidedly skeptical, made him laugh.

"I didn't say I was scrimping to make a living," he said. "And my standards, admittedly, are kind of high."

Chuckling, Lenore slipped off her shoes and tucked her feet under her on the sofa. She sipped from the glass and asked another question. "Why didn't you ever try to contact me?"

Billy looked down, then away, and then straight in her eyes. "I did. Every time I wrote a love song."

Chapter 6

"I'm not familiar with your music."

Billy sighed. "I think I've been insulted."

Amusement flickered in Lenore's eyes. "Not necessarily. My kids all know you. I just listen to . . ."

"Classical. Haydn and Bach," he finished.

Lenore thought of the night two young kids walked on a college campus after a concert of classical works: her shyness, his assertive yet endearing entreaty. Tonight she looked at him and knew that he, too, remembered the night they met. The shared moment made her realize just how much she'd missed him.

"I've expanded my tastes through the years," she said.

One raised eyebrow was his question.

"I like Yanni, and I've even ventured into a little jazz." In spite of herself, Lenore chuckled at his pained expression. "What? You don't like Yanni?"

He wiped a hand over his face. "Uh . . ."

"Don't answer, Billy. I'd rather not have you incriminate yourself."

He looked up. "Billy. No one's called me that for years."

66 *Felicia Mason*

"What do people call you?"

"Buster, or if it's somebody kissing up for a favor, it's Mr. Dixon."

"You're right. Billy seems rather juvenile now. What should I call you?"

"So you're saying I was juvenile then," he asked with a grin.

She returned his smile. "Let's just say we were both young and impressionable at that time. But that was then. What shall I call you now?"

"What do you want to call me?" he countered.

Lover man might be nice. To him she simply shrugged.

"Why don't you try Dixon if you don't like Buster," he offered.

"It would be like we're getting to know each other anew." Then after a pause, "You can call me Dr. Foxwood."

His laughter, a full-hearted sound, made Lenore's insides weak. Small laugh lines at his eyes, lines she hadn't noticed before, enhanced his face in the way only a man could be enhanced. Billy was a man who should laugh often. She wondered if he did. He sat there looking good enough to nibble on. His back, she remembered from watching him play ball, was broad and well defined. She liked his mouth with those full lips. She remembered, vividly, the way they merged with her own. He was filled out now, not wiry like he used to be. Lenore licked her lips. This new Billy would know how to stoke a slow-burning fire. Simon had been a two-minute wonder. She'd just bet the Billy Dixon sitting before her now was more like a two-hour feature film at the movies.

Lenore cleared her throat and wondered when her thoughts began to take such an uncharacteristic carnal streak.

He got up and refilled her glass, a glass she didn't even realize she'd sipped down. He topped off his own and moved to join her on her love seat. She scrunched her long legs up closer to her body.

"No need to get all tense, Dr. Foxwood," he said. "I'm not going to jump your bones . . . yet," he added under his breath.

"I'm not afraid of you," she said even as she unfolded her legs and sat facing him. "You made it perfectly clear this afternoon that you weren't thrilled to see me."

"Huh? Leni, you read me all wrong if you mistook my surprise for anything except joy and delight at seeing you again. Had I known that fart Gil Hobbs was going to have you there, I wouldn't have come in looking like a rumpled college kid."

Lenore took in the cool whites he wore. "I noticed the haircut and the shave."

Dixon grinned. "Hobbs and I aren't exactly tight. We've had our differences. And you, Dr. Foxwood, are still a master at changing the subject."

Lenore took a final sip from her wineglass, then put it aside. It didn't take much to make her tipsy, and she needed to keep all her faculties about her when dealing with Billy Dixon. "What do you mean?"

"I mean the way you were checking me out a minute ago. Do you want to know what you do to me?"

Lenore jumped up. "No! I, uh, I think it's time you left."

"Lenore, sit down. You're acting like a scared rabbit. You know I'm just messing with you."

Lenore didn't know any such thing, and she wasn't taking any chances—not with him and definitely not with her errant, not to mention wanton, thoughts.

"Why would Marvin leave me so much money?" she asked.

"Chicken," he taunted. "But that's okay. Now that you're back, we have lots of time to get to know each other."

"I'm leaving in the morning, and I have no idea what

you're talking about," she said as she walked about the room. She fingered a vase here, trailed a hand over a chair there.

Dixon smiled, tolerant and amused. "Okay, Dr. Foxwood. We'll play it your way for now." He sat back on the love seat and propped one foot on top of the other. "As for Marv, who knows what was going on in the man's head at the time. Maybe he was just thinking of you and wanted you to know it."

"Two hundred fifty thousand dollars is a lot of thinking, Billy . . . I mean, Dixon."

"I like the way you say that."

"Say what?"

"My name. With the accent drawing out the *i*. I can hear that southern belle in you."

"I'm from Philadelphia."

"But you went to school in the South, so that counts," he said. "Tell me about school. I see you got that Ph.D. you wanted."

She nodded and turned to him, her hips leaning against the dining table. "I went straight through after . . ." She paused for a moment. "Undergrad."

"What's it in, English lit?"

She nodded again. "You remembered."

"I remember everything about you, Lenore. And most of all, I regret the way I treated you."

Folding her arms, she asked the important question. "Why did you leave?"

Dixon got up and walked to the sliding glass doors of the suite's balcony. Sliding them open, he lit a cigarette and inhaled. "I was busy chasing my dreams of becoming a big-time star. I wanted to change the world with my music, be somebody. But my future was uncertain. If I failed, I didn't want to drag you down with me. You deserved more than I had to offer. You deserved more than a life of trailing after me from city to city and club to club while I built up a name. I always knew you'd be somebody."

He blew smoke out toward the balcony, then faced her. "I didn't want you regretting that you'd hooked up with a failure." He paused and then turned his back to her. "I didn't want to be the nobody you got stuck with."

"You had too many smarts and too much hustle to be a nobody."

"And you were a naive little virgin who didn't deserve to be hustled."

"Did you try to hustle me?"

"No," he said quietly. He took one more drag on the cigarette, then tossed it over the railing. "I cared about you too much to ever do anything to hurt you."

But that's just what you did, a part of her raged. Yet humbled and oddly touched by his admission, she kept that thought to herself.

"Dixon, why are you here?"

He nodded his head for her to join him outside. Lenore went to him. The spring night in California was warm. Back home it remained cold, wintertime. Spring break from school didn't mean the weather cooperated with the name of the vacation. But here, roses growing in pots on the balcony added a fragrant essence to the air. Her room, overlooking a courtyard, could have been anywhere in the world—Paris, Madrid, Jamaica. The quiet night, the scent of flowers, the pensive expectancy that flowed between them, all these elements surrounded Lenore and made her wish life had been different.

Billy, the boy she knew then, never admitted to love or regrets. Dixon, the man she'd met this afternoon, was someone with the capacity to feel and love deeply. He also seemed to harbor more than a regret or two. Lenore wanted to know that man, the complete man he'd become.

Taking her hand, he raised it and pressed a gentle kiss there. Then letting her go, he stepped to the railing and looked out over the courtyard.

Resting both elbows on the railing, she, too, looked out at the night. "It's beautiful here."

He harrumped. "The outer shell of beauty masks the inner corruption of this place. But California is the golden state, the land of opportunity."

"Is that why you came out here? For your golden opportunity?"

He looked at her and nodded, then like Lenore, rested his elbows on the balcony railing. "I know a lot of people. I've done a lot of things. I made a lot of money, a whole lot of money."

"I hear a 'but' in there," she said.

"But something's missing. I've known that for a while. It wasn't until today that I realized what it was."

"What happened to you today?"

"My future walked back into my life."

She straightened and looked at him. "If you're talking about me, Dixon, I don't think that's going to work."

"I *am* talking about you. And why? Lenore, when I walked into that office and saw you there, it was like a sign from God. Since Marv died, even before he died, I'd been thinking how I haven't left a significant mark on the world. When I die, all that'll be left are records. The music I write for my artists, it's contemporary stuff. Sure, they'll make money, the songs will be hits. But twenty-five or fifty years from now, it won't matter."

Taking her hands in his, he willed her to see the things he saw. "When I first got out here, I was a wild man, I did it all. I'm not proud of some of the things I did. Then when the music really started happening, I got myself together. I recognized then, just as I recognize now, that I've got to change direction in my life. I want to truly settle down. I want to right the wrongs I've done so I don't die with regrets. I've acquired all these *things*. When I'm outta here, I can't take them with me. I want kids, boys who'll bear my name and girls who'll make their daddy proud."

Lenore shuddered involuntarily. "What makes you think having children will make a difference in your life?"

He grinned. "Hey, I know kids give you grief. When I think about the changes I put my folks through, that makes me pause."

"Dixon . . ."

"I know this is a lot to dump on you, but I want you to understand that what I'm saying isn't something that popped into my head yesterday. These thoughts—thoughts of you and what I left behind—have been with me for a while now."

"We can't just pick up where we left off, as if nothing's happened. We're different people now. You say you loved me, or rather that you cared for me. Do you know you never once told me that back when it counted—back when I would have walked through a hurricane to be with you. The person you supposedly cared for then has changed, just like you're not the same person you were fifteen years ago. I'm different in lots of ways, most of them ways you can't see because the change is on the inside."

He took her hands in his. "I don't want to make it like it was, Lenore." He gently squeezed her hands. She glanced down at that one small, decidedly insignificant place their bodies met. He was just holding her hands, yet her heart beat so rapidly and so loudly she was sure he could hear it.

"Look at me, Leni."

When she did, his lips covered hers. The kiss, brief but searing, left her wanting more.

"I don't want to go back to where we were or to pick up where we left off. We were both kids then. We're adults now. I need you. I want to start fresh. I'm not going to lose you a second time."

Lenore tugged her hands free and walked to the sliding doors. Silhouetted from the light inside the suite, she studied him. She memorized every detail of his face, his body.

She'd take that mental photograph of him and find comfort in it when she returned to the reality of her own world.

"What if I'm not available?" she quietly asked him. Then she slipped inside the suite.

She wasn't at all surprised to hear him follow, to hear the balcony doors slide shut and the click as he flipped the lock.

She went to the door of the suite, not seeing any of the fabulous furnishings that had soothed her when she first entered the room. Lenore couldn't think of anything that might soothe her right now. All she could focus on was getting him out the door and then surviving his leaving.

But Dixon didn't go. He sat on the sofa.

"You're not wearing his ring, Lenore. You're a traditional kind of woman. If you weren't available, you'd be wearing his ring."

Lenore, not facing him, gave a soft half chuckle. After all these years, he still thought he knew her so well. He was deluding himself if he thought she'd been sitting in her room wasting away with thoughts of him. She'd done that for a while, but he didn't need to know about it. He had no right to know, just as he had no right to come in here and try to sweet talk her off her feet.

"Dixon . . . Billy, I suggest you leave."

He must have heard—and finally believed—the finality in her voice. She felt more than heard him move. Lenore held her breath when she sensed his nearness. But he didn't touch her.

He opened the door and looked at her; she could feel his eyes all over her. She refused to meet his gaze.

Lenore started when his finger lifted her chin. She didn't want to look him in the eyes. If she did that, she knew she'd be lost, caught up in the sensual web he'd been spinning all evening. His pretty words were just that . . . words. By his own admission, he made a lot of money writing love songs, pretty words and hollow promises. It would take more than a smoldering look and a pretty

RHAPSODY   73

speech on the patio to make her forget what he'd put her through.

So she didn't look into his eyes, those brown pools of seductive promises. She looked to the right of him. From the corner of her eye, she saw the half smile about his mouth.

"This isn't over, Lenore."

And then he was gone. The door shut.

Lenore stood by herself in the suite's entryway.

She, too, knew it wasn't over. It had just begun.

Chapter 7

From the bottom of her soft-sided suitcase, Lenore pulled a slim volume. The pink and white cloth cover was faded and worn in some places. She snapped the suitcase shut and placed it on a folding rack in the spacious closet. Then with a reverence generally reserved for holy relics, she carried the volume to her bed.

The turndown service offered by the hotel included a beverage, chocolates and magazines. Lenore tossed the magazines aside, climbed into bed and placed the volume on her lap.

At the last minute, she'd decided to include the journal in the things she packed for this quick trip to the West Coast. Her rationale at the time had been if the reading of Marvin Woodbridge's will was going to dredge up old memories, she may as well go at it whole hog—no use in dragging out the pain. So she'd found the journal, the one from college that featured Billy Dixon. She hadn't read or really even thought about that journal for years.

But now it was time to either say goodbye to yesterday or to see if there was anything worth salvaging from the relationship that had been significant in molding her into the woman she was today.

Lenore took a deep breath, smoothed her hand along the well-worn cover and then opened the volume to the first page.

I met a boy today. His name is Billy Dixon . . .

She'd slapped him, hissed at him and pushed at him. But she'd also kissed him back with fire and with passion. That's the part Dixon focused on. Her justifiable anger gave way to other emotions, ones he hadn't dared hoped she still had for him.

But he'd held her and felt her body mold itself to his. He'd kissed her and confirmed his destiny.

She was even more beautiful than he remembered.

Dixon closed his eyes and took a drag from his cigarette.

The last thing he'd been prepared for today was to walk into Gil Hobbs's office and face his past, particularly when his future looked so bleak. He'd gone off on a tangent this afternoon with Sarge and hadn't gotten to the real reason he'd wanted to meet with the super agent.

Lenore Foxwood. Dr. Foxwood. The woman looked good!

The long, straight hair he'd remembered had been precision cut and relaxed. It fell beyond her shoulders in soft waves. He'd stood in her hotel room not touching her, not running his hands through the fragrant mass of her hair. Yet he ached for her. Part of him would have been satisfied with one of her radiant smiles.

But the rest of his body remembered the shape of her, the feel of her. By his best estimation, he'd been in some state of arousal from the moment he'd seen her sitting in that chair. Then tonight, on her hotel balcony, he'd wanted her so badly he itched and twitched with need. She'd stood amid the roses, silhouetted by moonlight and looking like an angel.

Dixon stared out the window of his penthouse apartment. "Marv, old pal, whatever game you're playing from the grave better have me as a winner. Her reentering my life right now could only be a sign from above."

Leaving the window, he walked to the grand piano. Dixon opened the instrument and sat on the bench. Snuffing out the cigarette, he began to hum. Then his fingers picked up the melody playing in his head. The pieces came as fragments and he built bridges, weaving the music into the magic of a song.

Several hours later he'd put notes and words on paper. Using the precision pencil he composed with, he wrote the title of the song at the top of the sheet: "Angel at Midnight."

When Buster Dixon finally fell across his bed in the wee hours of the morning, he drifted to sleep knowing he'd just written a hit . . . and that Lenore, his muse, was responsible.

Lenore awakened slowly. Stretching like a contented cat in the afternoon sunshine, she turned this way and that. The cool sheets with a faint scent of jasmine beckoned her to stay. Lenore smiled and more comfortably tucked the big fluffy pillow under her head. Then her eyes flew open. Her pillows weren't soft and fluffy. As a matter of fact, she'd had in the back of her head for some time now that it was time to buy new ones. And her bedsheets at home didn't smell of jasmine; they smelled like whatever fabric softener was on sale that month.

She sat up with a start, trying to get her bearings. A pink book on the big bed brought it all back in a rush. Billy. Dixon. Dinner. Her journal. Her flight home!

Lenore glanced around for an alarm. The clock radio on a stand next to the bed flashed eleven thirty.

"Oh, my God!" Throwing the covers aside, Lenore leapt from the bed.

Between the emotional rollercoaster she'd been on and

staying up late reading through portions of her old journal, she'd overslept.

Lenore glanced at the beside table and frowned at the clock. She couldn't have slept through the alarm. Jabbing the buttons on the top of the clock radio she discovered her error. She'd set the alarm for 6:30 P.M. instead of A.M.

Her flight was supposed to leave LAX at eleven forty-five. She wasn't dressed. She wasn't packed. She didn't even know where the airport was. A car had picked her up when she arrived two days ago. Was she supposed to get a cab back?

Snatching up the telephone, she called the front desk but was put through to the concierge on her floor.

"Not to worry, Dr. Foxwood," the man said in his clipped precise English. "Everything has already been taken care of. A car is here at your disposal whenever you are prepared to depart."

"But I missed, or rather, I'm about to miss my flight," she said, glancing at the clock radio. "I have to call the airline and see if there's something else. I need to get home." I need to get back to the real world, she added to herself.

"That is what I made reference to, ma'am. Your flight has already been rescheduled for a later time. You can leave whenever you are ready. Would you care to order breakfast or brunch, Dr. Foxwood?"

Lenore shook her head, then realized he couldn't see her. "No. No, thank you. I'll be down as quickly as I can."

"By your leave, ma'am."

Lenore replaced the receiver and stared at the telephone. In all her years, she thought she'd been to a couple of places that had great service. This hotel topped them all.

She made fast but careful work of packing her clothing for the trip home. She'd spent the first night in Los Angeles with Kim. Her former college roommate had pressed what had to be thousands of dollars of clothing at her. Despite

Lenore's protests that she not only couldn't afford the outfits and had no place to wear them, Kim was shipping the garments to Lenore's Ohio home.

All Lenore would have to do was find about a half dozen society cocktail parties and movie premiers to attend. Yeah, right, she thought. Like all the other get-ups Kim had sent through the years, this latest set was bound for the closet in the spare bedroom of her loft.

Lenore thought about home. After her divorce, she'd eagerly traded the big house in the suburbs for something totally uncharacteristic. She left Philadelphia and those bad memories of her marriage. She'd moved to Ohio, and into an old factory that had been converted into eight loft units. Lenore saw the place and signed a lease on the spot.

"Billy would be proud of me," she'd told the leasing agent.

"Billy?"

Then, like now, Lenore smiled wistfully. That day almost two years ago she'd just waved him off as an old friend. Today, standing in a Snoopy nightshirt in a luxurious Los Angeles hotel suite, she recognized that he was more than that.

"You can recognize it, but you don't have to accept it," she said. With that, Lenore finished packing and dressing.

When she was ready, she looked around the suite once again, then hefted her suitcase in one hand and her brief-case stuffed with papers to be graded in the other and walked out of the room carrying her bags.

It never crossed her mind to call a bellman.

A few minutes later, when the elevators whooshed open, she realized the oversight. Two anxious and fretting bell-boys dashed to her side and relieved her of her burdens.

"That's okay, I have—"

The concierge swooped in. "Dr. Foxwood, you should have called. Come right this way. Your car is waiting."

Gilbert Hobbs had obviously taken care of everything. Lenore shrugged and followed the man outside where a sleek late-model slate gray limousine purred at the curb. A doorman held the door open for her. Lenore slipped into the car.

"Man, the other half sure knows how to live," she said.

"Yes, ma'am."

Lenore blushed when she realized she'd spoken her thought aloud.

Less than a minute later, the car pulled from the hotel. A fat white envelope with her name on it rested on the top of the bar. Curious, Lenore opened the bar. It was well stocked . . . with all her favorites.

"Hmmm."

She poured a small glass of tomato juice, then reached for the envelope, opened it and read the letter on top.

Marvin Woodbridge, it seemed, had even more surprises for her.

He'd put this off as long as he could. The more he delayed, the worse it was gonna get. Dixon sighed. Today he was Buster D. Actually, today, by the time people stopped chewing his hide he was gonna wish he was John Doe.

He glanced at the Rolex on his wrist. It had been a gift from a record company. He'd busted all the sales figures and made himself, Sarge, and the record company a lot of money. Lenore, he'd noticed, still sported a reliable Timex. Envisioning her bright smile and uncomplicated ways, he stepped off the elevator.

The receptionists and secretaries waved him through with a "Howzit going, Buster" or "Good morning, Mr. Dixon."

At last he stood at Sergeant Watson's door. He had to do this. It was for the best. Buster brought Lenore's image to the forefront. That was what he would focus on to get him through this ordeal. Then with a deep breath, he walked into the office to face the music.

Sarge looked up. As usual, Buster hadn't knocked.

Sarge stood to halt Dixon's progress into the office. "Buster, if you're here to tell me another insipid story about the beginning of your torrid love life, I'm really jammed up to the wall today."

"Sit down, Sarge. This is important."

"That's what you said yesterday, and I listened to a long tale about you kissing a girl in college. I had to reschedule two appointments, and I missed lunch."

Buster rested his hands on the back of a chair in front of Sarge's clean desk.

"I'm quitting the business, Sarge."

That got the big man's attention. "What the hell did you say?"

"I'm getting out. I have to get out."

Sarge held up a hand as if to stop his biggest client's thoughts. "Hold on a minute."

With a speed Dixon didn't know he was capable of achieving, Sarge hit his door and yanked it open. "Claudia," he barked at his secretary. "No calls, no disturbances. No exceptions."

Startled, the secretary mumbled, "Yes, sir."

The agent slammed his door and faced Buster Dixon.

"What the hell are you talking about?"

Buster came around the chair and sat in it. His voice when he spoke was flat, emotionless.

"I've made a decision, and I want you to hear me out. This isn't a spur of the moment thing. It's been on my mind for a while. I'm sick of living like this. Do you know I can't remember the last time I had a real vacation—"

"You've been to three countries in the last six months," Sarge cut in.

"Work, all work, and you know it. We were in Japan for two weeks, and what did I see—the Tokyo airport and a hotel. It's not just vacation, Sarge. It's quality of life."

"Quality of life? What did you do—go to a New Age chant-fest or something? What are you talking about?"

Buster steepled his fingers and leaned forward in his chair. "I've decided to cut back. No more songs, no more producing. The clubs and the studio run themselves. I have good management teams in place. Sarge, I want to have kids—"

"So go buy one or something. Take one of mine."

"I want to grow old knowing I made an impact on the world. I've made my decision, Sarge. It's a moral one."

Sarge stomped around his desk and yanked open a drawer. He pulled out a folder and slapped it on his desk. The file folder slid on the smooth surface of the desk until it stopped at the edge, about to topple over. Just like Dixon's life.

"You see that?" Sarge said. "Screw your moral decision. Those are legal decisions, contracts, Buster. Those are contracts that will tie both our asses in knots if you're sitting there thinking about doing something stupid. Not to mention the contracts, I've got you booked on Leno, Letterman, MTV, BET and even public television."

Buster shook his head. "I told you I didn't want to do those things."

"You don't have a choice, Buster. Promotion is in the contracts."

"Forget the contracts, Sarge."

Sarge jumped up. "Forget the contracts? Have you lost your mind? Do you know how much money is tied up in the endorsement deal I'm finalizing for you?"

"I don't care about the money," Buster said.

"I don't care about the money," Sarge mimicked. "Well, I do. What's this all about, Buster? I told you yesterday, if you need to check into Betty Ford for a while we can do that. We can do it quietly, no press. We'll get you dried out, cleaned out and then you'll be thinking straight again."

"I don't have a substance abuse problem."

Sarge snatched the folder off the edge of the desk and waved it in Buster's face. "Then what is this all about? What is this moral decision crap?"

For a long time, Buster Dixon was quiet. Then he looked up and into the anxious and angry eyes of his agent, manager and friend.

"Part of this is your fault," he said.

"My fault?" Sarge asked, folding his arms.

"As a favor to you I wrote some words down and put some music to them," Dixon said. "Sure, I'd been writing songs and producing a couple of small-time acts. But you said we could go places, that we could make a lot of money."

"There's nothing wrong with making a lot of money," Sarge said.

Agreeing, Dixon nodded. "As long as you make it on the up and up."

"And as for being a favor to me, you were practically a panhandler when I offered you that job. You needed the work."

"I had a job."

"Oh, sure," Sarge said sarcastically. "If you call writing jingles to second-rate products a job. What did you make then, fifteen grand a year max?"

"Money isn't everything," Buster said.

"Damn straight. It's the only thing."

Buster sat back. He smiled at Sarge's conviction. Sarge grew up poor and had scrambled, scraped and hustled his way to where he was today. Money was important to Sarge. It was important to Buster, too. But there was something even more important to him. Buster liked all the things money could buy: power, respect and prestige from other people.

But money couldn't buy his own self-respect.

"You and April have been together almost twenty years now. How'd you know she was the one?" Buster asked.

"April? What does my wife have to do with the conversation?"

Buster thought of everything he could have had with

Lenore. "I'm talking about love, about honesty, about relationships."

"Well, I'm talking about the bottom line. What's the deal, Buster?"

"I'm gonna give all the music awards back. I can't accept them."

Breath whooshed out of Sarge Watson.

"This is a joke—right, Buster? Tell me this is a joke."

When Dixon shook his head, Sarge looked at him closely. "This has something to do with the girl. With this Lenore, right?"

Dixon steepled his fingers and nodded.

Chapter 8

"So, what's the deal?"

"I can't in good conscience keep the awards, Sarge, particularly Songwriter of the Year."

"Why the hell not? You earned it. You earned them all."

Buster looked at Sarge and wished what he had to say next didn't hurt so much.

"I *have* to give the awards back, Sarge. I plagiarized the music."

Sarge couldn't have been more shocked than if Buster had said he was a convicted ax murderer.

"Buster, this ain't funny." But one look at Buster Dixon, at the pain and the regret etched into his friend's face, told Sarge that this wasn't a joke.

"Holy shit. You're serious, aren't you?"

Dixon got up and walked to the windows in Sarge's office. He turned and faced his friend.

"I'm serious, Sarge. I'm sorry," he added in apology.

Sarge cussed a blue streak, then kicked his desk so hard Dixon heard the hardwood splinter.

"You are not standing there, calm as you please, telling me about some Milli Vanilli give-the-awards-back shit."

Dixon weathered the storm. "I'm serious, Sarge. I wish to God I could tell you it's all a joke, but it's not. I made the music but I stole the words, all of them, most of them. Verbatim."

"Most of them, all of them. Which is it? Oh, Jesus, just wait till the press gets a hold of this. The reporters are gonna have a field day." Then Sarge thought of something even more important. "Have you been served a lawsuit by some songwriter out there?"

Buster shook his head. "No. Not yet."

"Not yet," Sarge mumbled, totally disgusted. He looked Buster over, reassessing all that he thought he knew about the musical genius he'd known for so many years.

Sarge took a deep breath. He counted to ten, then twenty. He glanced at the marble paperweight on his desk and the message on it. For half a second he contemplated hitting Buster upside the head with the rock in the hope of knocking some sense into him. Then the big man sighed, stomped to his chair, plopped into it and closed his eyes while rubbing his temples.

"Start at the beginning, Buster. And make it good."

When Lenore got to the airport, she was too numb to realize she'd been whisked from the limousine to a private jet. By the time she'd significantly recovered from the letter Gilbert Hobbs included with a handwritten letter from Marvin, she was on board and seated in a cabin designed with comfort in mind. Rich teak and deep, wide seats made her want to settle in for a while. This was nothing like the commercial jet she'd flown in for her trip to California. She'd been in first class then and thought she was flying in luxury. This beat that hands down.

A cabin steward served her tomato juice with celery and carrots cut in thin curled strips. Lenore wasn't surprised that her favorite snacks were being served without question.

Marvin Woodbridge, or someone, had done his homework.

"Excuse me," she asked the attendant. "Where are we headed?"

The single flight attendant's pleasant smile put Lenore at ease. "To your home, Dr. Foxwood, outside Dayton," he said. "I'll serve your lunch just as soon as we reach cruising altitude."

Lenore nodded. "And might lunch be grilled shrimp, Caesar salad and peach cobbler?"

"Yes, ma'am. Unless you would prefer something else?"

Lenore leaned back in her seat. It was more of an oversized recliner than the small seats she was used to seeing on airplanes. "No, no thank you. That will be fine."

The steward walked away. Somehow, some way, Marvin had known all the right buttons to push with her, right down to her favorite foods. Pulling his letter from her purse, Lenore reread the dead man's missive. Then she stared unseeing out the window as she evaluated her choices. The college had generous break periods. She had a little more than a week before spring break was over and she had to be back in the classroom. There was time to deal with the foolishness Marvin proposed to her from the grave, time to bury the past and get it out of her system once and for all. More than anything else, she needed closure in her life. With Marvin's proposition, she could get closure as well as a significant material bonus.

Lenore made her decision.

She rang for the flight attendant. He appeared at her side instantly.

"Tell the pilot I've changed my mind," Lenore said. "Take me back to Los Angeles."

The steward smiled, almost as if he'd expected her to make that request sometime before they landed in Ohio.

"Actually we're still in L.A." Lenore turned toward the

new voice. "Let's just chart a different course. There's a house in Santa Monica. Raul, let the captain know."

"Yes, sir," the cabin steward said.

Lenore watched Gilbert Hobbs ease into the chair next to hers. After Hobbs secured his seat belt, the steward handed him a drink then discreetly glided away to inform the pilot of the change.

"I didn't know you were on board. What is this about, Mr. Hobbs?"

"Please, call me Gil. We'll be getting to know each other fairly well if the decision you just made is any indication."

Lenore swirled her chair around to face him. "I have responsibilities, not to mention a life, in Ohio. I must be back at the university soon, so I hope this little drama gets played out before then."

Hobbs sighed. "Let me assure you, Lenore—may I call you Lenore?—there's nothing, not a single thing, that's little about this proposal," he said indicating the papers in her hand. "Mr. Woodbridge was in sound mind when he included the provision in his will."

"I don't understand something," she said. "Why me? Marvin and I couldn't claim to be close friends in college. I knew him because he was my boyfr . . . he was Billy, er, Dixon's roommate. Sometimes. I mean, sometimes he was Billy Dixon's roommate."

Hobbs smiled. "The scam my client ran on his parents eventually backfired on him, but he made the most of it, as evidenced by the estate he left for his children and his significant others."

Lenore leaned forward. "Marvin has kids? He never struck me as a family man."

Hobbs discreetly cleared his throat.

Lenore got the picture. "Oh."

"His daughters live with their mothers. I will tell you this much, the meeting last week required the assistance of a mediator and a referee."

Hobbs shuddered, apparently at the memory of the

meeting. Lenore smiled. This Gilbert Hobbs didn't exude the same aura of debauchery as the man she'd met and talked to just yesterday. Lenore wondered at the difference and then chalked it up to the environment. A cabin on a private jet was a lot different than a well-appointed law office.

When he sat back, loosened his tie and took a sip from his drink, Lenore's curiosity was piqued. Could this obviously handsome man make her feel fluttery inside as well as virginal and wantonly wicked all at the same time?—the way Billy Dixon made her feel.

She reached a hand to his jacket sleeve, pretending to pick a piece of lint off the material. The slightest touch from Billy Dixon made her run hot with a fever that burned from the inside out.

A small smile from Hobbs, and the beginning of a gleam in his eyes that she wasn't sure she wanted to decipher, made her pull away. Lenore instinctively knew that with this man she was playing way out of her league.

"You're an intriguing piece of work, Dr. Foxwood. I'm beginning to understand Marvin Woodbridge's interest in you."

"Excuse me?"

"Surely you know or knew of Marvin's reputation and his fascination with all things exquisite."

Lenore didn't indicate she knew anything about Marvin. In this case, her poker face was sincere. She *didn't* know much about Billy's roommate. "What does that have to do with me?"

Hobbs studied her, then raised an eyebrow and chuckled, an ironic sound in the otherwise relative quiet of the airplane's cabin. "You really don't know, do you?"

She was losing patience with this conversation. "Look, Mr. Hobbs . . ."

He held up a hand. "Please, call me Gil. And no, I don't suppose you would have known, at least at that time. Marvin Woodbridge was very, *very* jealous of William Dixon's relationship with you. He wanted you for himself and couldn't believe you actually preferred Dixon's company and time to his. Marvin was rich, athletic and handsome, yet you wanted his ghetto-bred, street smart, jive-talking roommate.''

Mouth open and totally incapable of comprehending his words, Lenore stared at Hobbs. "I beg your pardon?"

Hobbs chuckled. "This is a revelation to you, isn't it? The bottom line is when you were an undergraduate, you had two men competing for you."

"You're mistaken, Mr. Hobbs," she finally got out. "There was no competition for me between Billy and Marvin. As a matter of fact, I can probably count on one hand the number of times I actually saw Marvin Woodbridge. When we spoke it was just polite conversation, nothing more. And on two occasions he did something nice for me."

"Do you recall what those nice things were?"

Lenore smiled. "I remember like yesterday. But maybe that's a sign of old age creeping in."

She watched his gaze lower to her breasts, then on down to her legs, covered in sheer hose and crossed at the knees. Lenore felt exposed. The message she got from Hobbs was that he didn't think any part of her was old.

"You may not remember a conflict but believe me, it existed," he said. "What did Marvin do for you?"

She smiled, thinking a moment, about the time gone by. "Once he paid for me to come out here when Billy came to find his dad. And then the other time he'd blown in over the weekend because his parents were in town. They took us, all three of us, to dinner. We did a little window shopping after dinner. From a little store—now that I think back, it was probably a consignment shop— he bought me a necklace. It had some strange writing engraved on it. I wore it only once, but I still have it"— her face wrinkled in thought—"somewhere at home."

"The writing is Swahili. It roughly translates to 'love have in my heart for you always.'"

"How do you know what the necklace said? That was years ago, and it was a spur of the moment purchase. I didn't think anything of it at the time. Later, all I could figure was he didn't know it was so expensive."

"How do you know it's expensive?" the lawyer asked.

Lenore sharply glanced at him. "How do you know the language and translation of a necklace bought for me more than a decade ago?"

Hobbs smiled and for a moment, just a moment, Lenore questioned her safety on a private plane headed to God only knew where. No one knew where she was, not even Kim. What was the big deal about the necklace?

"You don't have to worry, Dr. Foxwood," Hobbs said as if reading her thoughts. "We're headed to Mr. Woodbridge's estate on the coast. You were telling me about the necklace."

Lenore, a grandmaster at the art of changing the subject, was not fooled by the conversational ploy. But she decided to play along. Maybe she'd find out what this was all about. "It's beautiful. But it's an odd size and color. I wore it to a party once, and so many people commented on it, including a couple of folks who said it was a rare find, that I took it to an African gallery for an appraisal. I was shocked about the value and wondered why Marvin had given it to me."

"Maybe he considered you a rare find, like the necklace."

"I doubt it." She assessed the lawyer. "I'm losing my patience, Mr. Hobbs. What is this all about?"

"It's about making amends, Dr. Foxwood. My client passed on regretting something he did to you. He never had the chance to do right by you. And now, even though he's gone, he has the opportunity to make things right."

Chapter 9

"I fell in love with her the night I met her," Dixon began as Sarge scowled at him. "There was just something about her, something pure and gentle and wholesome that just cried out to me. I remember the first time I kissed her. It was under a crepe myrtle tree . . .

. . . on a pathway stretching across campus, Billy kissed Lenore. His first touch was light, almost a whispered prayer. Then slanting his mouth over hers, he added pressure. He felt her arms slide up his chest and circle his neck. The taste of her was sweet and light, like Aunt Jemima syrup on warm pancakes. Billy moaned his satisfaction. He kissed her and felt like a breeze scampering over a river. Billy kissed her and met his future.

When it was over, he gazed into her dazed eyes. She blinked twice, as if trying to focus herself and her vision.

"You're beautiful, Leni. Thank you for that."

She merely stared at him, wide-eyed and with wonder.

Billy smiled. "I hope that dazed look means you liked it."

Lenore blinked as if awakened from a trance. Billy grinned, took her hand and started walking again.

"If we don't hurry, you'll be late for class," he said.

A few minutes later, at the door of her classroom, Billy kissed Lenore on the cheek, then waved as she walked into class backward. When she bumped into a desk, Billy grinned and blew her a kiss.

He whistled all the way back to his room.

The first thing he saw when he opened his door was his roommate's large Louis Vuitton duffel bag on the bed Billy used as a sofa.

"Oh, man. I got work to do this weekend."

Billy dropped the bookbag over the back of a desk chair and kicked off the sneaks. At least he had a little time to deal with this right now.

He picked up a tape and put it in the boombox. The music of a Brandenburg concerto filled the room. Billy plopped onto his bed and closed his eyes. He let the music wash over him, haunting, soothing, fierce.

"I see you finally managed to get some culture."

Billy opened one eye and looked at his roommate. Marvin Woodbridge had a towel draped over his shoulder and one wrapped around his hips. His bare chest was still damp from the shower he'd obviously just taken.

"Man, why are you here?"

"Folks in town this weekend," Marvin answered. "Where's the blow dryer?"

"Hook on my closet door." Billy swung his feet over the edge of the bed and rested his arms on his knees.

Marvin got the hair dryer, plugged it in and started on his head. Billy watched him for a moment, shook his head, then got up and turned the music down a notch.

"That's more like it," Marvin said over the buzz of the dryer. "Bach shouldn't be blasted from a box like that ghetto music of yours."

Billy didn't even raise an eyebrow. The argument was an old one. He and Marvin had been pretending to live together for two years now.

A few minutes later, the whirr of the dryer stopped. Marvin pulled some Royal Crown from his Vuitton bag and smoothed it into his hair. Then he brushed it.

Billy rolled his eyes.

"How long do you think you can pull this off? Don't your folks ever get suspicious?"

Marvin dried the rest of his body, then pulled from a second Vuitton bag that Billy hadn't seen, underwear, socks, jeans and a lightweight turtleneck sweater.

When he was dressed, he turned to Billy.

Billy looked him over, the inspection almost a ritual between the two. "Yeah, you pass," he said. "Where the books?"

Marvin went to the duffel bag and pulled out some textbooks. Billy started rearranging things on the desk that would have been Marvin's.

"The closet's gonna be a problem. I've converted it."

Marvin opened the second closet door in the dorm room. "Hmm," he said, eyeing the speakers, the board, the mikes and all the milk crates filled with records. Everything was neatly stacked, and there wasn't an inch of spare room. "You're right. Can we share?"

"You know," Billy said, "it would be nice if I could get a little advance warning about these visits."

"Little Mama just called this morning. I barely got here ahead of them. Their flight lands at eight twenty."

Billy grabbed Marvin's arm and looked at the Rolex. He cussed. "We don't have a lot of time."

In silence the two made fast work of transforming the dorm room from a bachelor pad into a room that looked like two students lived in it.

"Where's that gizmo Little Mama gave you the last time?"

"What gizmo?" Billy asked.

"You know, that thing with the silver balls that balance and click."

"Oh, yeah."

Billy went to his closet. From the back he pulled out a small box. The gift from Marvin's mother went on top of the dresser. Marvin pulled out a navy and gold pennant with the school name on it.

The roommates laughed out loud. Marvin pulled two thumbtacks from the bulletin board Billy had on the outside closet door and tacked the pennant up on the wall.

"What about the gig schedule?" Marvin asked as he looked at the large schedule of events Billy kept on the back of the room door.

"Have no fear, Buster is here," Billy said. From his closet he pulled out a large poster and unrolled Michael Jackson's image. The poster was a perfect fit over the schedule on the door.

The roommates high-fived each other. Then they looked around the room in a final check.

"Drawers," Marvin said.

Billy nodded. From the bottom two dresser drawers, he pulled back copies of his music industry magazines. Looking around for a place to put them, he decided on the footlocker that usually served as coffee table.

"Get that for me, Marv."

Marvin picked up the candles and incense holder on the footlocker and lifted the top. Billy dumped in the magazines, then got another armful.

After closing the lid again, it took Marvin just a few minutes to fold up clothes from his bag and neatly place them in the drawers. He zipped up the duffel bag and slid it under his bed. Then from the smaller bag he pulled out something and tossed it to Billy.

Billy caught the baseball cap. "Cool, man. Where'd you lift this?"

"Was down in the Bahamas for a few weeks. Thought you'd like that one for your collection."

Billy nodded. "Thanks, man."

A knock sounded on the door a moment later.

Marvin and Billy looked at each other and grinned.

"Let the show begin," Marvin said.

"At least I get some decent meals out of this gig," Billy said.

Marvin opened the door to his parents: Big Daddy and Little Mama.

Later that night Billy and Marvin both lay awake in the dark room.

"Marv, why do you go through this? Why can't you just tell them you don't like college?"

"Can't do that, Buster. I need the checks Big Daddy sends. Are you telling me you don't want the cut I give you?"

Billy shook his head in the dark. "The money's not it. Don't get me wrong, it's sweet to have that cool hundred coming in every month. I just don't understand what the deal is. Tell 'em college ain't your thing and go on 'bout your business."

"If you stood the chance of inheriting more than a million dollars and a sizable trust fund, would you turn your back on it?" Marvin quietly asked.

For a long time, Billy was silent. "It just seems like a lot of work to maintain two lives."

"It's not really that hard. Just the surprise visits cause problems. Remember that time I was in Mexico and they called here saying they were on the way?"

Billy chuckled. "I thought it was over then. Couldn't even tell a good lie cause I didn't know how it would play with your deal."

"It's a good thing Raheem came through. Both our butts would have been fried on that one."

"What about the grades though, Marv? It's got to be tough to swing that."

Billy could hear Marvin turn over in his bed. "Not really," Marvin answered. "The dude who's going to classes for me is actually doing okay. I got a B in geometry."

"You wouldn't know a geometry if one hit you in the head."

Marvin laughed. "For sho' you right, my brother."

Billy grinned. "Can that dude go to my classes, too? I think I punched another math test yesterday. I don't know why anybody thinks this stuff is important."

"Are you still on academic probation?"

The grunt of disgust that issued forth was Billy's only answer.

"Buster, what are you going to do when you flunk out of here?"

Irritated about the very same thought that had crossed his mind, Billy turned onto his stomach. "What do you mean *when?*"

"Yo, Buster, it's me you're talking to."

Billy flipped over again. "Yeah, I know. Maybe I'll go to L.A. and look up my old man. I bought the new speakers with the last check he sent. He has connections in the business and can hook me up. When he sent that check, he also sent me a picture of him and Quincy Jones at a party. It was the joint! *Jet* magazine even ran a picture from that party."

"Los Angeles isn't a kind place. There's some really ugly stuff going down out there."

"I ain't trying to be an actor, Marv. So you can stop worrying that I'm gonna be bussing tables and calling myself a producer on the side."

"You know, it's not so very difficult to go to class, take some notes and get a passing grade."

Billy sat up on an elbow. "And what would *you* know about going to a class? You haven't been to one since freshman orientation."

Marvin was silent for a moment. "You have a point there." The fact he let hang, that both of them knew, was

Billy's mom scrimped and saved to get him to college, while Marvin's parents didn't think twice about stroking tuition checks and sending so much spending money that Marv could afford to pay Billy one hundred dollars a month to help maintain his facade.

"I got a party to do tomorrow night and a date Sunday," Billy said.

"What's the flavor?"

"Naw, man. This one's not like that."

"Ahh," Marvin said. "That would explain the Bach."

"You know classical music?"

"Of course. That's part of my role as an international playboy."

In the dark room, Billy could hear the smile in his roommate's voice.

"Bach had twenty children," Marvin continued. "Several of them were musically gifted but none as great as their father."

Billy leaned back on his pillow and folded his arms behind his head. "That's what that book said."

Marvin sat up. "You read a book?"

Billy grinned. "Hey, miracles do happen."

"So tell me about the girl."

"Not much to tell yet," Billy said. "I'm working the groove. What else you know about classical music?"

For the next two hours the roommates talked, Marvin explaining, and Billy asking questions and soaking up knowledge.

Chapter 10

"Whatever happened to Raheem, the other friend? Is he the one you stole the music from?" Sarge asked.

Dixon winced at the word *stole*, then shook his head. "No, it wasn't him. Raheem was really good at picking up nuances and layering a song until it was filled out just right. He didn't write music. But he was an awesome DJ. Real organized."

"So what broke up the love-fest?"

"Lenore. We had a falling out about her. Raheem thought she was distracting me from business, that after I met her I wasn't committed to our bottom line. Lenore wasn't a distraction though. I was at my most creative peaks when she was in my life. And for a while, she was just always there. Raheem didn't like her aura. He said she carried the spirits of strife and confusion with her."

"Huh?"

Dixon waved Sarge's question away. "I never did understand what he was talking about. Raheem was my boy, but he could be kind of deep and strange at times. How he was back in the day could best be described as a mix of New Age mysticism, native American shamanism and Malcolm X.''

Sarge's eyebrow's rose at the description. ''What's he doing today?''

''Muslim. Raheem owns a black culture bookstore and health food store back in Jersey.''

Sarge leaned back in his big chair. ''Okay, so you and Raheem ran a DJ business, your roommate never went to class, and you fell for a girl named Lenore. Get to the plagiarism part.''

Buster got up and walked to the windows in the office. For a few moments, he stared out the tinted panes. ''That didn't come until later.''

''We got all day. Keep talking.''

Billy Dixon kissed me today! I couldn't believe it. I was too shocked to tell him it was my first kiss. I wish Kim would hurry up and get back here so I can ask her about this. She went to the mall to look for some material for a dress she wants to make.

I felt all tingly inside when his lips touched mine. I don't know what I expected a kiss to feel like. I've dreamed of my first kiss for so long I was taken by surprise at the reality of it. It was . . . it was nice!

It all started this morning. When I left the dorm, he was standing outside. Gosh, he looked sooooo cute. He had on blue jeans and an Izod shirt. And I love his book bag. It's very sturdy with double stitching. And my favorite color, too, blue. It's the kind I asked Mom to get for me. But she said they were too expensive, so I have the five-and-dime store special. It holds all my books, notebooks and class supplies though, and that's what's really important.

Lenore grinned as she settled more comfortably on the white chaise. ''Talk about anal retentive. You were waxing poetic about stitching, for goodness sakes.''

She reached for the glass of iced tea and sipped from it. Then still chuckling, she picked up her reading.

But anyway, oh, my gosh! When I went outside, I still had on my glasses. I hate those glasses. I look like a frog in them.

Billy Dixon saw me in my glasses—before I yanked them off. And he still kissed me! I'll remember that moment for the rest of my life. It was under a magnolia tree. The big waxy leaves canopied us on the walkway to my economics class. I'll always love magnolia trees.

And I think I'm falling in love with Billy Dixon. I know we just met the other day. But I think I know how I feel. I wonder if he feels the same way. I think we're going to go on a date to hear the Reverend Jesse Jackson speak. I can't wait. Maybe he'll kiss me again.

Lenore shook her head, marveling yet again at the ways William Dixon had affected her life. Love—she'd thought she was falling in love with him just because he'd kissed her. Because of Billy, her master's thesis had been on the metaphorical use of the magnolia in southern literature.

"If the things grew in Ohio, I'd probably have them in my yard."

In addition to the one big way he influenced her life, Lenore thought about some of the other, smaller, ways she'd held on to Billy—the contact lenses she wore to this day, for example, all because she thought he didn't like her glasses.

As for the minister's speech, that was a memory lost in the past. She didn't remember a word of it. But Lenore did remember, and if she tried hard enough, could even feel, the warmth and strength of Billy's hand as he held hers during the rally at Campus Hall.

Billy Dixon had matured. So had she.

Lenore glanced around the elegant sitting room at Marvin Woodbridge's estate. It was decorated in crisp white on white with green plants accenting open spaces and outlining in picture-frame fashion the spectacular ocean view.

"I could get used to this," she said. She'd live in luxury for another few days, and then return to the reality of making her own bed and cooking her own meals. Since she'd checked in with J.D. and knew he wouldn't begrudge her the extra days in California, Lenore was prepared to kick back and enjoy the hospitality.

Marvin Woodbridge obviously lived well. She still had a hard time accepting the lawyer's assertion that Marvin had been in love with her or that Marvin and Billy had competed for her attention.

"Must have been a guy thing, because I don't remember any of that."

Maybe the journal would yield some clues. But right now, there was something more pressing to deal with. Lenore carefully marked her page in the journal and then went in search of Gilbert Hobbs.

"And that's how it happened," Dixon finished for Sarge.

"That's really low, Buster. How could you do something like that?"

Dixon's shoulders slumped. "I never thought it would go so far. I never thought I'd feel guilty about it. It felt right at the time, and I had to produce to meet the demand. You were screaming at me for more, the record company wanted more, the fans wanted even more than that. My back was up against the wall. Can't you see my point of view?"

"Frankly, no. And I don't know what kind of spin I'm going to put on this." Sarge sat up in his chair and reached for the paperweight on his desk. "You haven't done anything stupid like call a press conference or anything, have you?"

"No. Right now, just two people know about what I did. You and Marv."

"Well, at least he has that secret safe with him in his grave. As far as wrongs go, Buster, it would have been easier to deal with if you'd been busted on a DWI or had a couple of hookers over for a party that got raided."

Dixon briefly thought about the prostitute in the red dress who had been in his bed the morning after the awards. "Well, that might come up, too," he said dryly.

Sarge closed his eyes and sighly heavily. "Oh, God. What else haven't you told me?"

Dixon shrugged, then made his way back to the chair in front of Sarge's desk. "So what should we do?"

"If you kill yourself now, I can turn this into big bucks for your estate."

"I'm not joking, Sarge."

The agent opened one eye and stared at Dixon. "Who said I was."

Dixon slumped into his seat. "We, I, have to do something fast. I want to get this behind me and then spend the rest of my life loving Lenore. Marv has given me the opportunity to make things right. I can't blow it with her this time."

"Humph," Sarge grunted. "Your behind needs to be concentrating on how we're going to handle this mess. She's caused enough grief as it is."

"Don't judge Lenore by my actions, Sarge. That wouldn't be fair . . . or warranted. I accept all the blame here. I'm the one who did wrong."

"Damn straight. Then you drop a shitload of trouble on my desk for me to clean up."

Dixon grinned, but it was, admittedly, a halfhearted effort at his usual joviality. "That's why they pay you the big bucks. You can handle it."

Chapter 11

The terms of the will were actually quite simple. She could take the two hundred fifty thousand in cash and run, or she could take that and add another one million dollars set up in a special scholarship fund for as many needy students as she deemed worthy. For the extra million, all Lenore had to do was spend a week living with William Dixon.

Under normal circumstances, that wouldn't be such a tall order. But there was nothing normal about her feelings toward Billy Dixon. And Marvin—even from his grave—knew that.

After reading Marvin's letter, Lenore was first angry, then heartsick and then resolved. The dead man's actions made a lot of sense—after the fact. Not only had Marvin been jealous, he'd acted on that jealousy in a deliberately malicious manner. By withholding vital information from Billy, he'd effectively closed the lines of communication between Lenore and the man she had loved then, the man she needed to come to terms with now.

Gilbert Hobbs claimed no knowledge of the contents of

the letter his client had left for Lenore. If the man spoke the truth, Lenore was grateful he didn't know. For just a moment, she'd quickly embraced the idea of combing the white pages or the national CD ROM telephone directory for anyone named William Dixon. She'd just explain the terms of the will to the man, offer him something for his trouble and then live with the man for a week. But Gilbert Hobbs nixed that notion before she could even complete the thought process.

"Violating the spirit or the intent of the codicil will invalidate your claim," the attorney calmly informed her.

Lenore latched on to the sole remaining life raft. "What exactly does 'living with' mean?"

Hobbs smiled. "Sharing living quarters. It could be here, at your home, or at one of Mr. Dixon's homes."

Now back in her room at Marvin's estate with her journal in her lap and a glass of tomato juice at her side, Lenore shuddered. She could no more have Billy Dixon bumping around her house than she could bring Marvin Wood-bridge back from the dead to explain his intent of this farce.

One million dollars.

It was a lot of money. Even though it wouldn't be going straight to her, the very idea of turning her back on money that could help her students gave Lenore reason to pause. She could help students like Theresa, who worked three jobs to pay her tuition bill at the private college. She could make the way easier for Roberto, who was majoring in English because his parents wouldn't finance the music degree he craved so much.

Could she afford to put her wariness about her still lingering feelings for Billy Dixon in front of real opportunities for her students? How many times had she wished she were independently wealthy and able to help the undergrads who had so much potential and so little money? She had lots of smart kids who could benefit by not having a financial burden. With a million dollars, she could touch a lot of lives.

Could she live with Dixon for a week? A week wasn't so very long. Living with him for seven whole days would tell her exactly what type of man he'd become and whether she could trust a very valuable part of herself with him. A week would let her know if she could afford to invest mental, physical and emotional resources in him. Could he redeem himself in her eyes in one short week? Lenore wasn't sure about the answer to that question. But she was willing to make the gamble.

She hadn't told J.D. that she was with Billy "Buster" Dixon. He didn't even know she knew the man. J.D. was another reason she'd stay for the week. They needed some alone time, though God only knew what mischief he'd get into in her absence. Would he understand her need to do this? Would he be able to forgive her?

Lenore wondered if she could have both men, or would her week with Dixon irrevocably change—to the detriment—her relationship with both of them. In her heart of hearts, Lenore knew what the problem was: She wanted them both because right or wrong, she loved them both.

In the end, Lenore realized she *had* to give Billy Dixon this last chance. She'd deal with J.D. when she got home. After all, she rationalized, it was for a good cause: kids who deserved a financial break as they pursued their academic dreams. The least she could do was provide them the backing they needed.

A week wasn't so very long.

And he probably had one of those huge mansions like celebrities on television and in *Ebony* magazine. They'd probably never even see each other the whole time. A week would go by fast.

"He'll be out with models and movie stars, and I'll be able to get papers graded and get that reading done for the next article I'll write."

A week wasn't bad. She could be under the same roof with him that long. It would be a snap.

Her decision made, Lenore started thinking up names for the endowed scholarship fund.

When the limousine pulled up to the small stucco house with its faded pink outer walls, Lenore knew she was in trouble. She scrambled to the other side of the car and tapped on the window separating her from the limo driver.

"Yes, ma'am?"

"There's been a mistake. This is Billy Dixon's father's house. We're supposed to be going to a mansion. One of Mr. Dixon's mansions."

"I'm sorry, ma'am. My instructions were to bring you here. You should find everything you need in the house."

Lenore's shoulders slumped. "I should have known there was a catch."

She powered her side window down as the big car came to a halt in the small driveway. The house was just like she remembered it: cozy, comforting. It looked like home. It was the perfect little house for, say, a newlywed couple. Just enough room for two.

Lenore closed her eyes and held her breath. She counted to ten.

When she opened her eyes, the house was still there. It hadn't been magically transformed into a multi-million dollar home with servants and lots of big rooms. It was the kind of house most Americans lived in. It said comfort, settling in, chicken soup and chocolate chip cookies.

Lenore was doomed and she knew it. A week in that house with Billy Dixon would be a test of her patience, her resolve and most especially, her virtue.

Everything was exactly as she remembered it. She hadn't been to this house in years, not since she and Billy came out to see his father. That had been an ugly scene. Like so much of the time spent with Billy, Lenore remembered it like yesterday. Lenore spent most of the weekend wishing she'd never left her college dormitory room.

Billy hadn't seen his father in years and was expecting to meet a big shot in the music industry. On campus he'd been bragging about the connections his dad, the music producer, had and Billy even had the proof: lots of photos of DuBois Dixon and the stars.

But Billy's father didn't turn out to be a hotshot deal-maker. He was a mover and shaker all right, but not in the capacity he'd led his son to believe: DuBois Dixon spent his career as a doorman and bouncer in trendy clubs and as the occasional celebrity bodyguard.

Billy had been hurt, angry and embarrassed to discover his parent's true occupation. He called his father a liar and a nobody. The softspoken Mr. Dixon, obviously hurting from the pain he'd caused his son, apologized again and again.

"I'm sorry, son. I didn't mean to lie to you. I just wanted my boy to be proud of his old man."

Billy stormed out the front door and left Lenore with his father. Not sure what to say or do, Lenore had hugged the man and then sat with him on the living room sofa while he cried.

The same sofa, preserved in the same clear plastic covering, still graced the room. Lenore ran a hand along the cool plastic as she remembered that day so long ago. A frayed blue rug, its floral patterns long faded, covered the hardwood floor. The mismatched chairs and lamps, sturdy ottoman and knickknacks remained the same. The La-Z-Boy recliner was a newer model. The furniture and the room seemed smaller than she remembered. Probably because everything associated with Billy seemed larger than life.

Lenore placed her handbag on the sofa and made her way to the kitchen. The big wooden table had been crafted by Mr. Dixon's own hands. It undoubtedly would last a lifetime or two. A kettle was on the gas stove. Faded yellow curtains hung at the windows and back door.

Near the door Lenore spied a key hook. "Oh, gracious, would you look at that."

She reached a tentative hand out to the painted wood with its five hooks. Carefully, almost as if it would break, she fingered the lettering HOME SWEET HOME. She'd made the piece from Mr. Dixon's scrap wood and had hammered it to the wall so Billy would stop misplacing his keys.

She'd spent just a weekend in this house fifteen years ago, yet she recalled with clarity each and every moment.

Suddenly a week seemed longer than she'd ever be able to bear. Tearing her gaze from the key holder, she looked around the rest of the kitchen. A cookie jar, the same one she remembered, sat on the counter next to canisters for flour, sugar and coffee.

Shaking her head, Lenore walked to the other rooms down a short hallway. From memory she knew one would be Mr. Dixon's bedroom, one would be a guest bedroom and the other one would be a den. She wondered if the upright piano would still be in its place of honor in the corner. Mr. Dixon didn't play, but he always kept the instrument tuned and sheet music in the bench storage area. "Just in case one of my buddies stops over," he'd say.

Lenore glanced into the two bedrooms as she made her way down the hall. A king-sized bed dominated Mr. Dixon's room. The twin beds that had been in the guest bedroom had been replaced by a double bed. She'd probably sleep in there for the next seven days. Or maybe to be safe, she'd sleep outside. She could string a hammock up between the trees. She'd be safer outside than she'd be in the same rooms with Dixon.

Stepping into the den, Lenore smiled. It, too, remained the same. Mr. Dixon liked his recliners. Two of them, separated by a small round table, sat side by side facing a big-screen television. The sofa, this one without the plastic covering, seemed an afterthought. On the walls, covering just about every available inch of space, were pictures of Mr. Dixon and all the stars: Sammy Davis, Jr., Miles Davis, Ella Fitzgerald, Frank Sinatra, Sarah Vaughn. The list and the photos went on and on and on. Lenore smiled as she stepped closer to look at the photographs. Mr. Dixon had great stories about all the entertainers. Music had been his life. And some of the photos obviously had been shot in this very room with some of the greats sitting at DuBois Dixon's piano.

Lenore rested her arms over the back of one of the recliners and gazed at one of the photos on the wall near the television. It apparently had been taken in later years, long after Billy and his dad reconciled. They both mugged for the camera. Lenore fell in love with the photograph.

"I've been here staring at that picture and waiting for you to arrive."

Lenore screamed and jumped back.

A moment later, the figure appeared behind the disembodied voice. Dixon swirled the other recliner around and stood to face her.

"Wh-what are you doing here?"

"I live here," Dixon said. "And for the next week, so do you. Hello, Lenore."

Lenore took three steps back. Dixon advanced two.

"Stay away from me, Billy."

"Why do you keep fighting this?" he asked.

"I . . ."

She paused, suddenly at a loss for an answer. There was nothing to fear from or about Billy Dixon. If anything happened, it would be between two consenting adults. She was old enough and savvy enough to handle a fling. As long as her emotions didn't get involved, everything would be just fine. Besides, he couldn't even steal her heart because he'd had it for years now. Not that she'd ever admit that to him.

That amused half smile she loved so much quirked his mouth.

"What?" she asked.

"Just now, you reminded me of how you looked when we first met."

"And how was that?"

He smiled. "Like an innocent angel come down from heaven to brighten my world."

Lenore's breath stopped. She stared at him.

"Breathe, Lenore," he said.

She took a deep breath. He held his hand out to her. "Trust me?"

Her heart was beating a mile a minute. Agreeing to this week had been a mistake. If she'd harbored the notion that trying to flirt with Gilbert Hobbs put her out of her element, this was floundering in uncharted waters. She didn't stand a chance against Billy Dixon. And when she allowed herself to be true to her heart, she realized she liked it that way.

"You haven't given me a reason to trust you. I'm here because I'm curious, Dixon. I'm here because you put me through unimaginable heartache."

"I'm sorry," he said simply. "I know those words aren't enough to erase the past, but I'm asking for a second chance. I've been through some things, too. I'm going through something right now. But through it all, then and now, I've never, ever forgotten you. If we can't make up for lost time, let's at least remember the good times."

He still held his hand out to her. Lenore looked at it. He offered an olive branch she was willing to take.

She clasped his hand.

Dixon raised her hand to his mouth and kissed it. "Thank you for that," he said softly. His mouth lingered at her hand a moment longer. His tongue licked her delicate skin, and he softly blew his warm breath along the damp skin. Every nerve ending in Lenore's body went on alert. Desire licked through her and left her breathless and weak in the knees.

"Wh-what are you doing?" she said, while trying to control the breathlessness in her voice and failing miserably.

"I'm remembering the good times," he said.

Chapter 12

His head lowered to hers. He gave her enough time to pull away, to change her mind, to establish boundaries. But Lenore missed all the cues. Her eyes fluttered shut, and she met him halfway.

The touch of his lips, a delicious sensation on her kiss-deprived mouth, sent her reeling. Momentarily shocked at her eager response to him, Lenore pushed at his chest.

Dixon deepened the pressure. His tongue rimmed her teeth and fought for entrance. When she allowed him the access he sought, his mouth demanded a response from her.

Caught up in conflicting emotions of need and desire, of passion and past pain, she clung to him, not even aware when her arms snaked up his chest and wrapped around his neck and shoulders.

His mouth was hard and searching. If she'd anticipated tenderness and tentativeness, he quickly disabused her of those things. This kiss meant business. Her mouth burned with fire and with his brand.

She wanted it to go on forever.

But Dixon had other ideas. He mastered her mouth, then sought other ripe territory. He whispered in her ear, ran his hands through the thick hair at her neck, then licked and nibbled and reacquainted himself with the tender erogenous zone behind her ear.

Lenore whimpered and fell into his cushioning embrace. Her body tingled from the contact.

"You're mine, sweet Lenore. All mine."

She blinked. "What?"

The sensual fog lifted. Lenore fought for air, for space, for survival. She pushed at his shoulders.

"Stop it."

Dixon immediately stepped back. But his gaze lingered, assessing, warming her in places she didn't want to be warm.

"Don't look at me like that."

He chuckled. "Like what?"

"Like—like that," she said, waving a hand in his general direction.

"We're two consenting adults," he reminded her.

"That's the problem," she shot back. "Look, I came here to carry out the provisions of Marvin's will so I can do something good for my students and other kids. I didn't agree to this so I could get manhandled."

Without her realizing it, he'd advanced on her. One hand smoothed up her bare arm, slowly, seductively. Lenore's breath caught again. "You call this manhandling?" he said.

"I call it unfair advantage."

He smiled. She was right and he knew it. Lenore had always been a study in contradictions: one minute laughing with him and the next angry about something. It was good to know she hadn't changed in that regard. But with the experience their intervening years had provided, Dixon knew more about women and how to read their moods, the unspoken words, the fire or the laughter in their eyes.

He'd written and produced enough love songs to know

what his lines were supposed to be. But with Lenore, he didn't want to and couldn't run a line. She deserved the truth—or as much truth as he dared to reveal to her this early in their reacquaintance.

"I'm fighting for my life here, Lenore. I think I should be able to use every weapon in the arsenal."

"I don't know what you're talking about," she said, folding her arms across her chest.

"Liar, liar, pants on fire."

He leaned forward and brushed a gentle kiss across her lips. Lenore's eyes drifted close.

She missed his knowing smile. "Let's just call this battle a draw. This is a seven-day campaign," he said. "And I think I'm going to enjoy all the skirmishes."

"You obviously have been reading some military history book. Maybe you have me mixed up with someone else."

He shook his head as he released some of the pressure on her by breaking all bodily contact. "I know exactly who and what you are, Lenore Foxwood."

He didn't elaborate.

"Well, what is that supposed to mean?" she demanded, her nose slightly out of joint at his cavalier demeanor.

But Dixon didn't answer her question. He headed out of the room. Lenore followed him into the hallway.

"After Dad died, I redid the two bedrooms. You can sleep with me or you can hang out in the guest room."

Lenore made a sharp right into the smaller bedroom.

She slammed the door behind her but still heard Dixon's chuckles in the hall.

"I'm sorry I hit you yesterday."

They'd come to an unspoken truce. Dixon had had a restaurant leave food for dinner. Warming the plates in the microwave, they talked.

"No, you're not. You're just being polite. Lenore, if

we're going to survive this week, we need to come to an understanding.''

The microwave beeped. Lenore took the second meal from the appliance and placed it on top of a woven cotton placemat.

"An understanding about what?"

Dixon helped her into her seat, then took his own.

"That I want you. That you want me."

"You can go to hell, Buster Dixon."

Dixon abruptly blinked, then sat back with a stunned expression. "I think I crossed a dangerous threshold. Did Miss Prim and Proper just say a cuss word? That's probably the first one out of your mouth since college, right?"

"You do manage to bring out the worst in me."

"That's why you love me."

Lenore's breath caught. He was right! But she couldn't tell him that. Dealing with Dixon exasperated her; one minute she'd find herself angry, and in the next breath, he made her weak in the knees. She couldn't tell him that, either. Then she got her wits about her.

"Your time has come and gone, Billy Dixon. If you snooze, you lose. And you lost big time."

"I don't think so."

Lenore reached for the glass of raspberry lemonade sent by the restaurant. She sipped from the cool drink, an elegantly arched raised eyebrow her only question.

"You tremble in my arms," he answered.

"I'm recovering from a cold."

"Let me warm you."

Lenore closed her eyes and sighed. When she opened them, she stared him in the face. "Look, Billy, Buster, Dixon—and I'm covering all your names, so you can't pretend one of you didn't understand. We need to get something straight. I am not here out of some misguided loyalty to Marvin. I'm not here because I've spent the last however many years carrying a torch for you. I'm not here to be manhandled, seduced, cajoled or otherwise convinced that there's something still between us. I'm here for one reason and only one reason: to earn a million dollars that I can take back for my students, for deserving kids who need a chance to prove their potential."

For a second, just a second, the half smile playing at his mouth distracted her. Then she caught his game.

"And you can stop trying to play that charming little boy role. First, it's played out; and second, I'm not the little girl you remember, whose head could be turned with a pretty word."

His gaze dipped to her well-defined breasts, the smile became broader. His silent message was clear: He was glad she wasn't a little girl anymore.

Lenore shook her head. "Gilbert Hobbs called me 'a piece of work,' but I can see you deserve that accolade. I don't know what kind of women you're used to dealing with out here in California, Dixon." She rested both elbows on the table and stared him in the eye. "But let me school you on something about me. I ain't them," she said, slowly enunciating every word so he'd be sure to understand.

She stood up from the table, her dinner untouched. "I may not have known Marvin Woodbridge that well, but he sure knew that it would take a lot to get me to agree to this charade. After staying in the same house with you, by the end of this week, I'll have earned every penny and more of that scholarship money for my students."

"Sit down, Lenore," he said as he rose and picked up his plate. "I'll eat in the den."

With not another word to her, he carried his plate and his glass out of the kitchen.

Confident that her speech had gotten through to him, Lenore finished her meal in peace. She found a dishpan under the sink. After rinsing off her plate and utensils, she added dish detergent to the dishpan and ran hot water in it. She left the dishes in the sudsy water, dried her hands and looked out the window.

Her swing was still there!

Grinning, Lenore went outside to examine the old tire swing.

From the kitchen window above the sink, Dixon watched her. She sat in the swing, occasionally pushing it to get a little movement going. Mostly though, she looked as if she were daydreaming.

She'd drawn his attention to the fact that she was no longer a naive little girl. Man, was he glad that wasn't the case. He liked the strong woman she'd become.

She wore her confidence like sex appeal. Lenore had always been a woman of purpose, while he'd been a guy who liked to play. The campaign he'd launched years ago, to get her to see the value of both, had been successful. Unfortunately he'd left before the final exam. And man, oh man, had his student developed through the years.

Lenore had filled out and grown into all the potential he'd recognized in her. He'd zeroed in on that potential the night he'd met her. From her long legs to her delicate hands, she was one hundred proof woman. Dixon's body stirred as he thought about those hands caressing him. Lenore was built for pleasure. Those full hips and big legs would wrap around him so tight, so right. He shifted to accommodate the growing erection in his jeans.

Dixon then moved from the window above the sink to stand in the open doorway where the view was even better.

Her bright smile, still as open and tentatively shy as he remembered, made him smile. Her skin remained smooth and just the cocoa brown he liked so much. Dixon was glad she hadn't cut her hair. Sure, the short cuts and braids some sisters sported were sharp. But he liked to run his fingers through Lenore's hair.

He grinned. She probably didn't even realize that she purred when he did that. He couldn't wait to hear those soft sounds from deep in her throat.

Lenore was a sensual woman, whether she knew it or not. She'd obviously hadn't spent the last fifteen years alone. She could even have a man waiting for her back East. His eyes narrowed with that thought.

"That might be the case, Dr. Foxwood. But you're gonna be mine by the time you leave this house."

Her pretty little speech hadn't fooled him for a moment. She wanted him. And he planned to have her. He had fifteen years of loving stored up for this woman. Man, they were gonna be good together.

"Tell me about your path to the Ph.D.," Dixon said.

They sat in the den. The big-screen television was on, but neither of them paid attention to the sit-com on the air.

Lenore sat in one of the recliners with her leg tucked under her. Dixon, across from her in the other one, looked relaxed . . . and unthreatening. Two tall glasses of the refreshing lemonade and a bowl of pretzels were at the ready on a small table.

Lenore liked it when they talked like this. In college they'd spent so much time on the go, at this party and that one, that the only time they got to sit quietly and talk was when she said she needed to study. Billy kept her engrossed in his world, but he'd respected her thirst for knowledge and her need to hit the books. She liked that then. And she liked his interest in her work now.

She settled in her chair, playing with a small pretzel.

"I went straight through. In the summers I'd work with public school districts, developing curricula or running summer reading programs for kids."

"Where'd you get the big one?"

Lenore smiled. "Ohio State."

Dixon nodded, obviously pleased with her choice.

"I met Simon in grad school."

Dixon sat up. "Simon? Who the hell is he?"

"My husband," she answered. Tell him about J.D., her conscience prodded. No, not yet, she argued back.

She watched his gaze dip to her left hand. "Why aren't you wearing his ring?"

"What's this fascination you have with rings? That's the second time you've mentioned that."

Dixon shook his head. "You used to drive me crazy when you did that."

"Did what?"

"Changed the subject. You do it so smoothly that only someone used to your technique would be able to know they'd been successfully sidetracked."

"Is that so?" she asked. "One of the things I've found with my undergraduates is that they tend to be unfocused in both their studies and their research. They become sidetracked and fascinated by mundane details. Then they lose all sight of their original task."

"Um-hmm, yep," he said, smiling at her, amused.

Lenore nodded. "Theresa—she's one of the students who will benefit from Marvin's largesse—is a perfect example. The girl is bright, talented. She writes poetry that would make you weep. Only problem is, her boyfriend is a gangbanger. How she made it out of her home life situation and to college is a study in perseverance and determination. Theresa's perseverance is a testimony to anyone who thinks one raw deal or bad life choice means the end of the road."

Dixon sat up in his chair. The amused half smile crept in. "That's all quite fascinating, Dr. Foxwood, but . . ."

She spoke over him. "And here's something that should make you smile."

Dixon chuckled. "I'm not going to get sucked into this, but go ahead." Under his breath he added, "You can run, but you can't hide."

"Remember the day you first kissed me?"

Now there was a topic worth getting sidetracked over. He could get back to the issue of the husband later. "I remember that moment very clearly, Lenore. It still ranks as one of the best days of my life.''

He watched her face, her eyes, her body language. The confession didn't even seem to faze her. She was making this as hard for him as she made his body hard.

"My master's thesis was on the use of the magnolia in southern novels.''

"What's a magnolia got to do with me kissing you?''

She frowned. Surely she didn't think he'd ever forgotten that moment.

"We were under a magnolia tree," she said.

"That was a crepe myrtle tree.''

"No way, Dixon. I remember that day like yesterday. The big waxy leaves were definitely of the magnolia family.''

She reached for her glass of lemonade and sipped from it. Dixon's gaze fell to her mouth. Watching him, she nervously licked her lips, then replaced the glass on the table between the two chairs.

Before she let the cool tumbler go, Dixon reached for it. He raised the glass to his mouth, turned it and drank from the same spot her lips had covered. He watched her breathing deepen.

The drink was cold but hot desire shot through him, desire so lightning quick that it was almost painful.

"You always did dance close to the flames," she murmured.

"Dance with me there, Lenore.''

Placing the glass on the table, he watched her fidget in her chair. Her own hands looked less than steady as she clasped and then unclasped her hands.

With an almost shy glance, she peeped at him and then away. Dixon's heart melted again and again. Always for Lenore. He let the sweet melody of an innocent song drift through him.

She was also the reason his jeans fit uncomfortably tight right now. As usual, she'd done a good job of getting him off the subject at hand. But he had her MO down pat.

Yeah, he wanted her, and he knew it would be just a matter of time before he had her—before they had each other. Right now, however, there was an issue that he wasn't about to let come between them, now or later.

Dixon shifted in his seat.

"Tell me about Simon, Lenore. You've had enough bluffing and stalling time, time enough to get your thoughts together and to get me turned on."

She tried to be casual about it, but he caught her quick glance to his lap. When she met his gaze, he smiled. "We have all the time in the world for that. Tell me about Simon."

Lenore blushed. Had she been a lighter-skinned woman, her whole face would have been red. She glanced away from him.

"Simon and I were very . . . very compatible," she answered finally.

Dixon rolled his eyes. "Well, that sounds like a nice boring start."

"It isn't your place to judge me or mold me, Billy Dixon," she snapped back. "You spent an incredible amount of time trying to make me over into a fly girl. But that's not me. It never has been. But you couldn't see that. You've always liked to think of yourself as some sort of master manipulator. Well, the day is gone when you could manipulate me. My husband and I were compatible . . ."

Dixon ignored the anger—she was just pissed off because she was still attracted to him—and focused on the word that gave him hope. She'd said she and her husband *were* compatible. Past tense.

". . . We had the same values, similar goals and similar backgrounds."

"But?"

"What makes you think there's a but?"

Dixon just looked at her.

Lenore shook her head and sighed. "But we disagreed on a few key points in our marriage," she said.

When she didn't elaborate, Dixon sat up on the edge of his chair. Her tense body and strained expression told him whatever was to come next wasn't pretty. He took her hands in his. His thumb caressed her soft flesh.

"So are you going to tell me what those key points are, or are you about to leap into subject-changing mode?"

He watched her fight and lose the smile that threatened. Dixon leaned forward and pressed a quick kiss to her mouth. Lenore's "oh" of surprise tempted him to go back for more, but he controlled himself.

Lenore glanced down at their clasped hands. Dixon gently squeezed, then entwined his fingers with hers.

"One of the big things we disagreed about was the definition of fidelity. My definition meant him being true to me. His interpretation encompassed a much larger framework. When it got to the point where I didn't feel safe sleeping with my own husband unless he was wearing a condom, I knew it was time to throw in the towel. I took our vows very seriously. Simon viewed them as suggestions to follow if the mood so struck. We disagreed on . . ." She paused and struggled to find the words. "Suffice it to say, we disagreed on other important issues as well."

"So what happened to him?"

She tugged her hands free from his.

"I'd rather not talk about this anymore," she said.

The argument died on his lips. Had it not been for the obvious pain in her voice, he'd have pressed the point. Her trembling mouth demanded that he cut her a break. It also begged to be kissed by a man who loved her and knew how to treat her right.

Dixon's mouth covered hers.

Chapter 13

This time she didn't resist. She didn't want to. Out of her chair now, she met him more than halfway. What was the sense of resisting the inevitable? She'd spent years wanting this very thing and sleepless nights tossing in her nightclothes wondering if she'd ever again feel the touch of this man's hands, the whisper of his mouth on hers.

Of course she'd die before she ever told him that.

Lenore told herself that this was for old times' sake. She told herself that she was simply fulfilling the unspecified stipulations of Marvin's will. She told herself all sorts of lies.

When Dixon traced a hot path, she stopped the rationalizing and faced the truth: She loved him, and she wanted him.

His kisses, both challenge and reward, sapped the last vestige of restraint from her.

Gently his hand outlined the circle of her breast. Lenore moaned and arched into his embrace. Dixon took the opportunity to shift her on top of him. The leg rest of the lounge chair popped up. She tumbled into his arms. He tried to right them, but Lenore had discovered the sensitive spot at his ear. She licked and nipped at him.

Dixon trembled and kissed the smile of victory from her lips. His hands traced her face, outlined her shoulders, roamed down to cup and fondle her breasts. Then the slow, maddeningly slow caress moved lower.

Her hands left his body long enough to pull off the light sweater and to unfasten the single button at her collar. Dixon helped her out of the blouse and feasted his eyes on what he'd so often dreamed of.

"I know they're small. I never was endowed like my sisters."

"More than a handful is a waste," he said.

Then he proceeded to show her exactly what he meant by that.

With his hands and his mouth, he pleasured her until she moaned and begged for more.

"Lenore," he said as he stroked her.

"Um-hmm."

"Baby, we're a little old for this chair action. Let me love you in bed, the way it's supposed to be."

She shook her hair so it fell over his hands in a thick mass. "This *is* the way it's supposed to be."

"Honey, if we do it like this, you're gonna have to call a chiropractor to get me out of this chair."

Lenore chuckled and stood up.

"For tonight, Billy, I want you to love me like you would have in college."

Laughing, he struggled out of the recliner. "You want to go outside and get into the backseat of the car?"

She hit him, but he grabbed her around the waist and pulled her to him. His thumbs looped through the belt loops on her skirt. Her chest, bare but for the wispy bra that barely covered her, crushed against his. Dixon buried his head in her neck. She threw her head back and gave in to the hot sensations. In his arms she was sexy, radiant.

In his arms she felt whole. She'd come home. Her pulse, eager and erratic like a summer storm, matched his.

Then their bodies began to slowly sway to and fro as Dixon hummed the sweet melody that ran through his head. Her feet seemed to be drifting along on a cloud. And then with one thrust of his erection to her midsection, he brought her back to earth.

A delicious shudder heated her body.

Taking her hands in his, he led her to the master bedroom. He moved her to the bed. Together they fell to the firm mattress. Dixon swiftly came out of his clothing. His eyes tracked the shimmying motion of her hips as she discarded the rest of her clothing.

He opened the nightstand drawer and drew out a condom. She watched him rip open the package. When he straightened to roll it on the full length of him, she sat up on her knees and leaned forward to get a better view.

His hands began to shake. "What are you doing, Lenore? You're looking at me like I'm a science experiment."

She glanced up at him with wide eyes, then again focused her attention on his erection. Reaching out a tentative hand, she began to stroke him.

Dixon shuddered as if he'd been plugged into an electrical outlet. "Jesus, woman. You're gonna end it before it begins."

Lenore's chuckle came from the woman's place inside her. More than her hand, the sound, throaty and knowing, almost undid him. Dixon took a couple of deep breaths, then joined her in the bed.

She watched him stretch out. When he reached for her, she ducked and scooted down on the bed.

"I want to see."

Dixon was gonna lose his cool any minute now. "Come here, Lenore. The only thing you need to do is feel."

She curled one soft hand around his erection and gently squeezed. Dixon yelped and bucked up.

Before she knew what had happened, Lenore was on her back.

"Teach me how to dance close to the flame," she whispered.

Dixon kissed her eyelids, her nose, her mouth. "Don't you know, sweet Lenore, you are the flame that makes me burn."

Then his mouth began a slow southernmost exploration of her body. He didn't miss an inch. She whimpered in need. Aching for the fulfillment of his lovemaking, she pleaded for him to end the torture pleasure.

"Please, Billy. Now."

He ignored her. He edged himself to the hot place where she wanted him most, then pulled away. Again and again he teased her until he could feel the tiny tremors of her release course through her.

She'd waited for this for so long, part of her wanted to prolong the sweet treasure of Dixon's love. But the other, more impatient, part of her wasn't willing to wait another moment. In Dixon's arms, she found both closure to what was and the beginning of what was to come. She moaned his name, an entreaty, a demand.

She undulated beneath him, her hair fanning the pillow on which they lay. With his large hands, he stilled her hips, then lowered his mouth to hers for a soul-searing kiss.

A moment later, his steady gaze bore into hers. In silent expectation they watched each other. Then something intense flared in his eyes, and he thrust into her.

Lenore cried out his name, over and over and over until his name became the sound of an ancient pagan prayer. He thrust into her until he was spent.

For a long time, the only sound in the room was their heavy breathing. He held her close, slowly stroking her hair and her smooth bare back, while their pulses slowed and returned to normal.

Dixon gently rocked her and began to hum a lazy sweet melody. Lenore drifted to sleep with a song in her heart.

* * *

When she woke several hours later, Lenore stretched.

"Keep making those sounds deep in your throat like that, and I'll put you out for another few hours."

Chuckling, she rolled onto her stomach and turned to face him. "Promises, promises."

Dixon stood in the doorway. An unlit cigarette hung from his mouth. His jeans, unbuttoned at the fly, drew her gaze. But not for long. She feasted on the bare chest. Her fingers ached to again caress the warm brown skin that covered his broad muscles.

"Did I tell you how disgusting a habit smoking is?" she said.

"Did I tell you how sexy you look when you wake up from some good loving?"

He reached for the cigarette and tossed it onto the dresser. Lenore sat up, then remembered she didn't have on a top. Gathering what she could find of the sheet, she tugged it to her breasts.

"What makes you think that was good loving?" The sass in her voice didn't escape him.

He took two steps into the room. Then holding his hands to his head, he mimicked her: "Oh, oh, Dixon. Yes! Buster, please. Now, dammit, now."

She laughed and threw a pillow at him.

"Don't even try it. I don't swear. You obviously have me mistaken for someone else."

That thought made her pause. How many women did he sleep with? He'd taken pains to put on a condom before they made love. Was he being safe, or was he trying to tell her something?

The mattress dipped where he sat on the edge of the bed. He bent his head to capture her lips.

"Stop thinking. That's the problem with you academic types, you want to analyze things to death."

"You don't know what I'm thinking," she challenged.

He slid back on the bed a bit and drew her head into his lap. "Yes, I do. You're having second thoughts. You're wondering if our making love was a wise thing to do. You're comparing yourself to every other woman you think I may have been with. You're wondering how you measure up."

"And when'd you earn a Ph.D. in behavioral psychology?"

"I'm a doctor of desire, Lenore. And you're my only patient."

"That is the corniest line I've heard since 'what's your sign?'"

But in moments, she was on her back again. When he put the condom on this time, she helped. But in the midst of her pleasure, she couldn't stop wondering if the protection was for his good, for her good, or just a sign of the times.

More than an hour later, Lenore was unpacking her single suitcase. Much to Dixon's dismay and grumbling, she'd insisted on sleeping in the guest bedroom. "It's necessary to assert a modicum of decency and propriety."

"For what?" he shot back. "We're the only people here."

In the end, Lenore won. Mumbling about her head being stuck back in the seventeenth century with her dead poets and composers, Dixon stomped off to shave and make a few telephone calls.

Lenore slipped the last pair of panties into the small drawer she'd claimed and then picked up her old journal. She settled in the wing chair by the bay window in her room.

I missed my opportunity to hear the Reverend Jesse Jackson's speech. Billy Dixon held my hand through the entire program. It felt like heaven. I'm so lucky he noticed me. Sometimes I wonder why he even did. I'm smart and I get

An important message from the ARABESQUE Editor

Dear Arabesque Reader,

Because you've chosen to read one of our Arabesque romance novels, we'd like to say "thank you"! And, as a special way to thank you, we've selected four more of the books you love so well to send you for only $1.99.

Please enjoy them with our compliments, and thank you for continuing to enjoy Arabesque...the soul of romance.

Karen Thomas
Senior Editor,
Arabesque Romance Novels

3 QUICK STEPS
TO RECEIVE YOUR "THANK YOU" GIFT
FROM THE EDITOR

Send back this card and you'll receive 4 Arabesque novels!
These books have a combined cover price of $20.00 or more,
but they are yours to keep for a mere $1.99.

There's no catch. You're under no obligation to buy anything.
We charge only $1.99 for the books (plus $1.50 for shipping
and handling). And you don't have to make any minimum
number of purchases—not even one!

We hope that after receiving your books you'll want to
remain an Arabesque subscriber. But the choice is yours to
continue or cancel, anytime at all! So why not take us up on
our invitation to receive 4 Arabesque Romance Novels, with
no risk of any kind. You'll be glad you did!

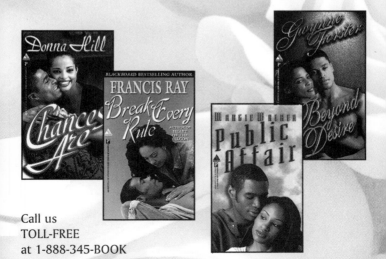

Call us
TOLL-FREE
at 1-888-345-BOOK

Accepting the four introductory books for $1.99 (+ $1.50 for shipping & handling) places you under no obligation to buy anything. You may keep the books and return the shipping statement marked "cancel". If you do not cancel, about a month later we will send 4 additional Arabesque novels, and bill you a preferred subscriber's price of just $4.00 per title (plus a small shipping and handling fee). That's $16.00 for all 4 books for a savings of 25% off the publisher's price. You may cancel at any time, but if you choose to continue, every month we'll send you 4 more books, which you may either purchase at the preferred discount price. . . or return to us and cancel your subscription.

ARABESQUE ROMANCE BOOK CLUB
120 BRIGHTON ROAD
P.O. BOX 5214
CLIFTON, NEW JERSEY 07015-5214

THE ARABESQUE ROMANCE CLUB: HERE'S HOW IT WORKS

AFFIX
STAMP
HERE

*good grades. That means no one's supposed to like me. All
the guys always ask out the sorority sisters. There are so
many other pretty and popular girls on campus, like Kim
for instance. But Billy Dixon picked me!*

I'm the luckiest girl in the world.

*And guess what!? This is the best part. He kissed me
again! I swear there was an earthquake when he did. Now
I know what they mean when they say "the earth moved."
You know, I've never been able to figure out who "they" is.*

*But anyway . . . Billy Dixon kissed me. And he asked
me out on a date, a real date. I can't wait. He said to wear
something funky because we're going to a party.*

*When Kim gets back from her date, I'll ask her what
funky means.*

Lenore laughed out loud at her exuberant naivete. But
one thing had remained the same: The earth still moved
when Billy Dixon kissed her.

After more than fifteen years, they'd again made love.
It was as good as . . . no, it was even better than before. In
college they had always either been rushed or cramped in
one of those dorm room beds. They had sex back in those
days. This time they'd made love.

Lenore thought about their last time together, so many
years ago. Billy walked out on her shortly after that last
time. She leaned her head back and sighed.

"Let it go, Lenore," she told herself. "Everything will
work out the way it should."

She couldn't help comparing Dixon to her ex-husband.
Simon always said she lacked inventiveness in bed. But
he never would explain exactly what he meant by that.
Apparently the young coeds he slept with knew exactly
what he meant . . . as well as how to please him in ways
his wife couldn't.

Lenore had always figured she was the type of woman
who didn't need a lot of sex, that the coldness Simon
accused her of was in truth just a low sex drive. But one

night with Dixon made her question the assumption she'd lived with for so many years. Maybe what she'd needed all those years was a real man to bring out the natural woman in her.

Suddenly embarrassed, she quickly glanced at the door to make sure no one was there.

"You yelled. He said you yelled," she whispered to herself. Over the years, Kim had maintained that there was a wild woman trapped in her just waiting to get out. Lenore had always laughed off her friend's comments. Now she wondered if there was something to it. Then she grinned. She didn't recall screaming, and definitely not swearing or giving orders in bed. Granted, she'd made a few specific suggestions—ones he'd eagerly seen to.

And he'd let her look at him.

Lenore had always assumed Simon was just shy about being naked and having her see him. After Dixon, she knew Simon wasn't shy, he had been embarrassed. Dixon was, well, er, rather large. Before now, she'd had nothing on which to base a comparison.

Her gaze fell to the journal lying open in her lap. She picked up the volume, marked her current page in the narrative, then flipped to the last page.

Sometimes I wonder if my life would have been different had Billy wanted me enough to stay. I know that eventually I'll fall in love with someone. I'll marry him, have his children and be a good wife and mother. But a part of me, well, a part of me will always regret what I didn't have with Billy Dixon.

I saw Marvin, Billy's roommate, and asked him to deliver a message from me to Billy. Maybe that, at least, will make Billy respond. I know Marvin knows where he is. The last four letters I sent him have come back as "address unknown." I know Marv is in contact with him. I could see it in his eyes.

Lenore leaned back and closed her eyes. Her sigh was deep and weary. She wouldn't have guessed—couldn't have guessed—that her story with Dixon would have yet another chapter. But this time she would script the ending.

She'd finally made love with the long time fantasy. Now it was time to say hello to reality. Now that she'd slept with Billy Dixon, Lenore figured she could get on with her life, close the book on the loose ends. She'd finally had some closure with Dixon. She'd get through the end of this week. She'd keep her emotions in check. At the end of the week, she'd set up the Woodbridge Achievement Scholarship fund, she'd take her reminisces, her journal and her sweet memories and head back to Ohio where she belonged. There was no use pretending she could fit into Dixon's world, not if it were truly as Kim had described—constant parties, groupies, tours and one loud concert after another.

With her plan in place, Lenore nodded her satisfaction. Unfortunately Buster Dixon had other ideas.

Chapter 14

Dixon finished his business, then met Sarge. They'd worked out the details of the announcement. Dixon gave three of his key staffers a heads-up and offered a generous severance deal if any one of them wanted out before the shit hit the fan.

All three—Monique, his personal assistant, Ashley, the office manager and Kelvin, his all-around roadie—opted to hang with him.

"We got your back, Buster," Kelvin announced, speaking for the group.

Buster was proud. Knowing that his people supported him made the hard road ahead seem a little easier to face.

Buster and Sarge timed the press conference to miss the early evening news. BET, MTV and the Nashville Network would all probably break into regular programming for special reports. The networks would wait until the late-night news. The newspapers, trades and radio jocks would eat him alive in the morning.

But the late announcement meant he bought himself time, time to tell Lenore.

Lenore had been a wild woman in his arms last night. She'd been all he knew he'd been missing and more. Despite what he'd done in his professional life, he had enough decency left in him to feel guilty about using Lenore. But it felt so good, so right having her in his arms. No doubt about it, though, he'd used her all right. Lenore wasn't the kind of woman to accept deceit and dishonesty. Years ago she had tried to teach him integrity, but Buster had come to the conclusion that you couldn't learn integrity, you just had to have it. Just thinking about the censure he knew he'd find in her eyes hurt him. She'd believed in him when he didn't believe in himself. He'd turned around and used that trust with little regard for the woman.

It was gonna be easier facing reporters and record company execs than it would be to tell Lenore what he'd done. Maybe she'd find it in her to forgive him. But before he could concentrate on that hurdle, he had to clear the first one.

In one of his trademark white suits, Buster climbed into the white limo before Sarge. The ride was short and silent. In a box on the seat between the men were the music awards Dixon had won.

A few minutes later, Buster and Sarge stepped out of an elevator and into the inner sanctum. Sarge had arranged the meeting.

Buster looked over the smiling, eager faces of the people who'd put their trust in him and had backed up that trust with millions of dollars in advertising and promotions.

If one of the acts or groups he managed had come to him with a similar story, he'd have thrown them out on their ears. Yet here he stood, about to throw his career and everything he'd worked for out the window. All for Lenore—and she didn't even know the depth of his deception.

He blew air out of his cheeks. "Oh, God."

"Steady, man. It'll be over soon," Sarge said softly, adding, "It's not too late to change your mind."

He had an out! He could take it and run. The thought tempted Buster in a big way. Sarge was good on his feet, he could come up with some plausible reason for their presence here.

Dixon opened his mouth. Then he snapped it shut. Turning back now would be the coward's way out. He'd held on to this secret for too long now. It was eating at him in ways he couldn't stand. His long dormant conscience was kicking his butt left and right.

Dixon shook his head. Sarge sighed.

After everyone was seated, Sarge began.

Then Buster got up. The music he made with Lenore played through his head. He focused on that, on dancing close to the flame. And then he explained . . . and apologized.

When he reached the door of the pink stucco house, he was again clad in jeans and a white T-shirt. Buster D had been transformed back into Billy Dixon. With Lenore he could be himself. Not a celebrity, not a household name—he could simply be a man, a man without the weight of a monumental decision on his shoulders.

As he pulled open the door, he got assaulted by the fresh smell of herbs, tomato sauce and something cinnamony sweet. Lenore had cooked. Dixon grinned. Lasagna or spaghetti. He couldn't remember the last time he'd had an honest to goodness, home-cooked meal. His diet consisted of a steady supply of take-out and restaurant food—only the best, of course, but there was nothing like real home-cooked food.

He looked at the flowers in his hand. The scene with the industry folks had been ugly. This had the potential to be worse.

He sniffed the air. Oregano, cheese, garlic.

"Maybe true confession can wait until after dinner," he mumbled to himself. He had a few hours before the late news. Sarge warned against pulling a disappearing act, but Dixon had had no intention of going back to the penthouse. It was the first place reporters and fans would flock to. Monique would deal with any problems at the apartment.

Lenore was here, at his real house, his hideaway. The few neighbors who knew his other identity respected his privacy, just as they'd respected his father's. When his father lived, the sight of famous people coming and going from the small house didn't even faze the neighbors. Here, Dixon could keep the business away, away from Lenore.

He kicked the door shut.

"Honey, I'm home!"

Dixon grinned. He'd always wanted to say that.

A moment later Lenore came into the room, a plaid pot holder in one hand. She'd wrapped one of his old man's leather aprons around her clothes to keep them clean.

"Hi."

Dixon smiled. "Hey. I missed you." He pulled the flowers from behind his back and presented them to her.

"Thank you," she murmured. "I cooked. I hope you don't mind."

"If you can burn in the kitchen like you did in my bed last night, I just might have to barricade you in this house."

She hooked a finger through the belt loops on his jeans and tugged him forward.

"Why don't you come do a taste test and see."

Dixon grinned. "There's nothing I'd like better."

He wrapped his right arm around her shoulders, and with his left hand drew her face and mouth to his. The moment his lips touched Lenore's, he relaxed. He hadn't even been aware of the tension in his body. The stress of the day seeped out of him as her arms circled his neck. In her arms he'd truly come home.

Lenore gave herself up to sensation. His firm mouth

demanded a response. Opening her mouth to allow him access, she pulled his head closer. He deepened the kiss. Lost in a swirling vortex of need and desire, Lenore pressed herself even closer to him. Their tongues danced a fierce ballet.

His hand smoothed down her face and neck to her full, aching breast.

She wondered how she ever thought she could blithely walk away from this man. A few short hours ago, she'd nearly convinced herself she could have a physical relationship with him, then go back to being plain Lenore. Now she wasn't so sure. The wild woman in her threatened to emerge. The only reality that mattered was the hot touch of his hand, the trembling in her knees, the fire racing through her body, and the forced truth that there was no place else she wanted to be except in his arms.

When he finally let her go, Dixon pulled her to him for a fierce hug. He closed his eyes. "Thank you, Lenore," he whispered.

She looked up at him. "For what?"

Framing her face in his large hands, he gazed into her brown eyes. "For being you. For the gift of last night. You mean more to me than you'll ever know. You're the melody that's been missing from my life. You're my music, Lenore."

She smiled. "Then write a song for me."

His answering grin melted her heart. "Come here."

Taking her hand, he led her to the den. He sat at the piano and patted the edge of the bench for her to join him.

Lenore slipped the apron over her head and dropped it and the pot holder in one of the recliners. Joining him at the piano, she sat while he, with one hand, played a simple melody on the high keys.

Then he closed his eyes, picked up the music with both hands sliding over the keys. He gently swayed as the song developed and grew. The tune, gentle and hauntingly painful, reminded Lenore of the moonlit nights they spent walking along the lakefront on campus in college.

Soon he began to hum, then words, at first soft, then sure, flowed freely from him as the melody continued. Lenore placed her hand on his thigh and let the music envelop her in a cocoon of gentle emotion. She watched his nimble fingers skim the keys. He played the piano as if it were a lover, teasing, coaxing, always considerate.

It ended as it began, with single notes, the melody fading like butterflies in the breeze. Lenore wiped away tears she hadn't realized she'd shed.

Dixon sat quietly; his eyes clenched shut, his hands still poised over the piano's keys. Lenore wrapped her arms about his waist.

"Thank you. That's the most beautiful thing I've ever heard."

He blinked several times as if coming back from a trance. She watched the motion of his throat as he swallowed deeply.

"It's yours," he simply said.

Lenore smiled. "Does it have a name?"

Dixon turned to her. She couldn't read the emotion in his eyes. Was it love? Regret?

"It's called 'Close to the Flame.'"

Lenore's gentle "oh" was followed by a shy smile as she recognized the title from their love talk last night.

"I've never inspired a song before," she said.

"Yes, you have," he said quietly.

Dixon closed his eyes. She hugged him close.

"Are you hungry? Dinner's about done. I remembered how you liked lasagna, so I made some."

"You go on. I'll come in and set the table in a minute."

"Okay." She kissed him on the cheek. "The song is beautiful, Billy. Thank you."

When he knew she was gone, Dixon bowed his head in resignation. She'd called him Billy just like she used to so many years ago. Maybe giving her the gift of his music now was best. She'd remember how much she liked the song and not be so hard on him when he told her the truth and confessed his sin.

Dixon glanced at the big gold Rolex on his wrist. She'd cooked for him. Now he'd have to spoil dinner.

Taking a deep breath, Dixon got his resolve up. He reached for the small notebook on the piano top and quickly jotted down the words of the song as he sung them to Lenore. When he finished, he played the song again, and then again.

Lenore had been back in his life a few short days, and he'd already composed two songs. If she stayed around long enough, he'd have a new collection of love songs he could record. Then he remembered that he was supposed to be quitting the biz.

Lenore made it pretty clear that she was with him because her students needed Marvin's money. But there had to be more to it than that. She was headed back to Ohio as soon as possible. He had a few short days to make her change her mind about him—and to forgive him.

Dixon stared at his hands and at the ivory keys that had been his stock in trade as long as he could remember. After he told her about the plagiarized songs, she'd probably head home and as far away from him as fast as she could.

He just wasn't sure how he was going to be able to live without her.

After dinner Lenore served some sort of sweet sticky pastry thing that melted in his mouth. Dixon patted his stomach.

"A man could get used to this."

Lenore stood up to remove their plates. She patted her thighs. "So could a woman."

Dixon chuckled and reached for her. He nuzzled her

stomach and cupped her behind. "I like big-legged women, so you just keep right on eating."

Laughing, Lenore sashayed out of his embrace. "You say that now. But if I made those all the time, I'd put on fifty pounds in no time. And it would all be right here," she said pointing to her hips and thighs.

"Ain't nothing wrong with that," he said, assessing her, liking what he was seeing and imagining what she described. He grinned.

Lenore shook her head and started to carry the dirty plates to the kitchen.

"Leave the dishes. I'll get them later," Dixon said. "Come here, Lenore. There's something I need to tell you."

She turned, the edge in his voice alerting her that something was amiss. She put the plates on the end of the table and sat in the chair next to his. "What's wrong, Dixon?"

He took her hands in his. "There's something I need to tell you. I should have told you last night—but, well, I just didn't want to spoil things between us."

Color drained from her face. Lenore stopped breathing. Oh, my God, he's HIV positive, she thought. Celebrities slept around all the time. They used drugs, particularly musicians. Then with a semi-sigh of relief, Lenore remembered they'd used a condom. Was one enough? She hadn't brought any additional contraceptives with her. She really couldn't have anticipated that they'd have sex. That was a lie and she knew it. She could have had some of those female condoms. She'd let physical pleasure overtake better sense. And now, all the things she worried about with her ex-husband came crashing back.

She'd gone through this terrible uncertainty with Simon. Those old fears sprang to the surface now as she faced Dixon. Simon had come to her with the same dire words: "Lenore, sit down, there's something I need to tell you." And then he'd proceeded to tell her about a string of encounters he'd had.

Lenore didn't for a moment doubt that Dixon had other women. Everyone knew about the groupies who followed musicians and athletes.

Thank God, Simon had never transmitted anything to her, but she'd lived in fear of herpes, syphilis and AIDS until finally she had tests done. Not once, but twice. Both times she'd come back from the doctor's with a clean bill of health and boxes of prophylactics. To go through all of that again would be unthinkable.

Belatedly Lenore snatched her hands from his and folded her arms across her middle.

"Wh-what is it you have to tell me?"

Dixon closed his eyes. "I don't know how to tell you this," he began.

"Oh, my God," she whimpered. Her heartbeat quickened. She tried to remember to breathe. At least he had the decency to tell her. She doubted if Simon would have given her that much consideration.

"I had a conference today. That's what I was out doing during the day. I had an announcement to make. It'll be on the news tonight and in all the papers tomorrow. But I wanted . . . I needed you to know before then."

Lenore's frightened gaze darted over him. Did he have full-blown AIDS? "What, Dixon? Just tell me."

He took a deep breath.

"I had a meeting today with the head of the record label I work with. My manager and agent was with me. Lenore, . . ." He paused, staring in her eyes.

Trembling and near tears, Lenore snapped, "What? Just tell me and get it over with!"

"I've returned the six music awards I just recently won. I couldn't in good conscience keep them. I plagiarized the music."

Lenore waited for the rest, the part about him being sick. When he didn't continue, her eyes widened. "What did you say?"

Dixon swallowed and reached for her hands again. She

folded them in her lap. Dixon sighed. "The music, in particular 'Soul Fire,' the piece I won Songwriter of the Year for, isn't entirely my work."

Wide-eyed Lenore stared at him. "That's it?"

He nodded.

Open-mouthed and stunned, she stared at him. Then Lenore's overwhelming relief came out as a bark of laughter. As tears rolled from her eyes, she doubled over laughing. She wiped them away, then tried to stifle herself by holding her hand to her mouth. She sat up and stared at him. She reached for his hands and kissed them.

Perplexed, Dixon watched her.

Still chuckling, she said, "Dixon, you don't know what kind of scare you just gave me."

He glared at her. "I don't see what's so funny about this. I stand to lose everything, *everything,* Lenore."

She wiped at her eyes and smiled at him. "Dixon, I thought you were going to tell me you have AIDS."

Suddenly stonefaced, he stared at her. "You think AIDS is funny? That AIDS is something to laugh about?"

Abruptly she stopped chuckling. She'd never heard him sound so cold. "No, no, Billy. There's nothing funny about that. That's not what I meant at all."

His jaw clenched, his eyes slightly narrowed. He watched her. "What, then, did you mean?" he said coldly.

"Nothing. It's not important."

He folded his arms. "Yes, it is. Forty thousand people die of AIDS every year. That includes men, women, teenagers and babies. Another forty to fifty thousand will get infected with HIV every year. That's nothing to laugh about, and it is important."

Lenore watched him, the tense, almost angry set of his jaw telling her there was more going on than she knew. "What are we really talking about here, Dixon?"

He was silent for a long time. He stared at her, as if plumbing her soul. For what she didn't know.

Then quietly, "Marvin died of AIDS."

Chapter 15

Lenore reached a hand out to his. "Dixon, I am so sorry."

But he rejected her sympathy. Yanking his hand away from hers, he walked out of the room. Minutes later she could hear him playing the piano in the den. He started with pounding angry notes. Lenore cleared the table and went to the kitchen to wash the dishes. From the den, the music shifted to mellow blues. Since his feelings obviously ran deep, she wondered if Dixon, like some other entertainers, held AIDS and HIV research fund-raisers.

The music coming from the den changed. Lenore blinked and looked up when she recognized first the Beethoven, then Bach piano concertos he played.

It was then she realized why she liked his song "Close to the Flame" so much. It combined classical elements with jazz, blues and what Billy used to call "old-school R&B."

Like a moth to a dangerous flame the music drew her. She dropped the dishrag in the sudsy water, dried her hands and followed the melodies.

He knew she was there, standing in the doorway. He could sense her presence. He ignored her though and played on. Whenever he wanted to think, he played classical music. Long ago Lenore had taught him how soothing it could be. He'd never forgotten the lesson.

She stood over his shoulder now. His head bowed and his shoulders slumped as he played. He'd plagiarized music, and his friend died of a disease with no known cure. No wonder he looked so dejected.

"I'm sorry, Dixon. I'm sorry about Marvin, and I'm sorry we quarreled."

His mouth quirked up even as his hands stilled over the keys. Quarreled. No one but Lenore talked like that.

He shrugged. "It's okay. I guess I'm still pretty torn up about it. I wasn't there when Marv needed me most. I promised I would be there for him, and I let him down."

Lenore placed one gentle hand on his shoulder. "I'm sorry, Dixon. I know those words probably don't make you feel better, but I mean them."

When she felt his shoulders heave, her eyes widened. Was he crying? Not sure what to do, what to say, she patted his shoulder, then stepped away to sit on the edge of one of the recliners.

With one hand Dixon played the melody of an old Gershwin tune.

"Tell me about Marvin."

He turned on the piano bench so he faced her. For an instant, a wistfulness stole into his expression. Then his features hardened and his glance flicked over her. "You don't have to pretend interest."

"You're being unaccountably rude to me, Dixon. I've apologized. What else do you want? Marvin Woodbridge is a man I haven't seen in more than fifteen years. Out of the blue he leaves me enough money to live comfortably for some time and the option of another million at my disposal. I think I ought to know a little about the man."

He didn't answer at first. Then he locked his hands together and stared at the floor.

"Marvin doesn't—he didn't—know where he picked it up. When we were in college, AIDS was just starting to get real attention. It was something that happened to gay men in California and New York. If you recall, Marv called himself an international playboy. While you were sitting in an econ class, he was aboard a yacht in the Greek Isles or in a casino in Monte Carlo. He paid some guy to go to class for him. It's not likely that he picked it up then because so much time passed, but the incubation period is so long, who knows. But with Marvin at least, he knew getting AIDS was a direct result of his life-style."

Lenore tucked one leg under her and settled back into the chair.

"Marv had more money than he knew what to do with. Between what he inherited from his family, and his investments, he could do whatever he wanted. But he couldn't buy a healthy body, he couldn't buy a cure for the disease that ate him alive and left him a shell of the man he used to be."

Dixon got up and walked to the wall of photographs. Pausing at one of him, his dad and Marvin, he smiled. "My dad died a wealthy man partly because he was frugal, mostly because he listened to Marvin's investment advice. I did, too. Marv liked for people to think he was just a party guy. He said it disarmed them. In a lot of ways, he was right."

"I never saw him at any of the parties you took me to."

Dixon turned to her and smiled. "Marvin Woodbridge wouldn't be caught dead in a sweatbox party. At that time my idea of good liquor was Thunderbird and wine with twist-off tops. If I was gonna impress a girl, I bought Riunite."

Lenore smiled. "I remember a couple of Riunite picnics. With plastic wineglasses from the grocery store. You were trying to impress me, huh?"

His answer was a grin. Then he turned back to the photos. "Marv's running buddies were people who owned French vineyards that had been in their families for centuries. Princes and European royalty attended the parties Marv went to and the ones he put on."

"How did the two of you ever end up together?"

"We were assigned together as roommates freshman year. Marvin took one look at that tiny dorm room and said, 'I don't think so.' We decided on the spot that we could be friends or we could hassle each other. Friends seemed easier."

"You stayed in touch through the years like my roommate and I did?"

He nodded. "Kim, right? Isn't she like a clothes designer or something?"

"She does some costuming for films and I think music videos. She owns a boutique and does a lot of original work for clients."

Dixon nodded again. He plucked a pack of cigarettes from a bookshelf. Then he glanced at Lenore and sighed. He ran the cigarette under his nose, inhaling the tobacco smell, then tucked the cigarette behind his ear.

He made his way back to the piano bench and sat down.

"Marvin's number-one goal was to get as much pleasure out of life as he could. As for sex, he did it all. Gender and race didn't matter to him. The only thing that mattered was feeling good. I don't think he ever ventured into hardcore drugs, but with Marv you could never tell. I went to the reading of his will with his family there. What a mess. An ex-wife, three girlfriends, a boyfriend and somebody who claimed Marv had adopted him showed up. The girlfriends all thought there was just one other woman. Two of them shared one of the homes Marv had. None of them knew about the ex-wife. The guy was appalled to discover that his lover had three children and slept with women. The supposed adoptee didn't speak English. In typical Marvin fashion though, he'd provided for all of them."

"That's what Mr. Hobbs was referring to."

"Huh?"

"Gilbert Hobbs told me that he needed the services of a mediator and referee at the reading of Marvin's will. He didn't go into any detail though."

"It was a circus . . . in every sense of the word."

Glancing again at some of the photos scattered about the room, Dixon continued. "Sometimes I can't believe both he and my old man are gone. They . . . and you . . . are my links to the past."

"Dixon?"

He looked at her.

"Mr. Hobbs said something else I've been wondering about."

Dixon leaned back and crossed his feet, one heel resting on the toes of the other foot. The insolent pose was back. "What's that?"

Lenore leaned forward, balancing her elbows on her knees. She was in a quandary. It was obvious Dixon knew nothing about his friend's duplicity. Lenore wasn't one to speak ill of the dead, but Marvin Woodbridge wasn't the good friend Dixon thought he was. Dixon needed to know that, but was it her place to inform him? How could she tell him without admitting her own feelings?

Lenore decided to test the water. "Mr. Hobbs said Marvin left me so much money because he felt guilty about coming between us, meaning me and you. He also said that you and Marvin fought over me. What does that mean? Maybe the two of you weren't as close as you thought," she added quietly.

"What I know is Gil Hobbs talks too much."

"Dixon?"

He nodded. "The last part is true. We did fight over you."

"But why? I was as plain as they come. I wore bottle-cap glasses. I was a nerd."

Dixon shook his head. "You just wouldn't understand. It was a guy thing.

"Try me."

His appreciative eye traveled from her feet, lingered at her breasts and finally moved to her face. Lenore squirmed under the scrutiny. She wasn't surprised when heat pooled in her middle. How could he make her want him with just a look? She licked suddenly dry lips. When she heard him sharply inhale, her gaze met his. Lenore stopped breathing for a moment, her total being concentrating on this man.

Dixon cleared his throat.

Finally he spoke. "Marvin and I both had a knack for picking out diamonds in the rough. You were one of the first water—that's what the highest-grade diamonds are called. I saw the potential in you. So did Marvin when I first introduced you to him."

"My potential as a scholar? Neither of you, as I recall, had any particular fondness for books or classrooms. And you just said Marvin didn't even go to class. How he got away with paying someone to attend his classes is an outrage. And—"

Chuckling, Dixon held up a hand. "Hold it, Dr. Professor. You're heading off into a tangent. As for the classes, yes, Marv eventually got caught. His parents hushed the whole thing up, though, with a significant contribution to the college's general fund. There's a performing arts center named for the Woodbridge family on the campus now. The university gave the dude who was going to the classes credit. He was a stockbroker until he got convicted of insider trading or something."

"I feel like the country mouse compared to you guys."

"The country mouse?"

Lenore shook her head and waved her hand. "It's a children's story. Never mind."

"Do you have kids?" he asked.

Wary now, Lenore eyed him. "Now who's changing the subject?"

Dixon grinned. "Guilty. But did you and what's-his-name have children?"

Lenore shook her head. "No. Simon and I did not have children together. That's something I'm grateful for. If we'd had any, he'd still have to be a part of my life. Back to you, me and Marvin. I'm not easily distracted—so stop trying."

He sighed and shifted on the piano bench. "Lenore, maybe you couldn't see it in yourself then, but you were a hot piece of flesh. Under the clothes and the glasses, there was potential in you. The kind of potential that makes a man take notice, the kind of 'hmmm' speculation that gets talked about on the block."

"Talked about on the block! I was the subject of prurient speculation?"

"If 'prurient speculation' means guys wondered what it would be like to do you, yes."

Lenore sat back in a huff. "That's really crude."

"I told you you didn't want to know."

Annoyed now, "And you and Marvin argued about this?"

"Why don't you take this time to do one of your subject-changing segues?"

"All right, fine," she huffed, clearly in a snit. "All right. Then whose music did you steal?"

Dixon winced at both her tone and the word steal. "For Christ's sake, Lenore. I didn't . . . See, it's . . . You were . . ." he started and stammered. Then he backtracked. She was irritated with him now. If he told her the whole truth, she might walk out the door and out of his life forever. He couldn't risk that. Not after finding her again. If she left, he wouldn't get the chance to tell her how much Marvin's death had affected him and his outlook on life. But before he could confess that to her, she had to accept that he still had feelings for her, that he wanted their story to be a real-life love song.

"It doesn't matter," he said. "What matters is that I wasn't straight up about the whole thing. I could easily have attributed the material to the songwriter or said I was 'inspired' by the writer's work. But I didn't do that, and now it's too late to go back and right a wrong."

Lenore blinked. He'd just hit on the whole reason for her being with him now. From his grave, Marvin was trying to right a wrong. Was it too late?

She forced her attention back to the conversation they were having. It was far easier to shift attention and blame to Dixon than confront her own fears about the uncertain future.

"But you didn't. And some poor guy out there trying to pay his light bill or put food on his table to feed his kids is missing out on the royalties you stole from him—probably millions of dollars, right?"

Dixon jumped up and threw his hands in the air. He started pacing the room. "Lenore, stop being so melodramatic. Look, I did wrong. I'm trying to fix it. Cut me some slack already."

"It doesn't sound like you deserve any. How could you steal someone else's work? I thought you were a better person than that."

Dixon's shoulders slumped. He paused in front of the television and stared at the blank slate gray screen. This is what he'd feared. "I . . ." He shook his head and closed his eyes. "I don't have a defense. I'm sorry."

Lenore unfolded her legs from the chair and stood up. "I'm not the person you need to apologize to. You need to be talking to that songwriter . . . and to your attorney. You're likely to get sued, you know."

"It'll probably be worse than that," he mumbled.

"I'm going to go finish the dishes."

He didn't respond. Lenore stared at his back for a few moments. Then shaking her head, she left the room.

Dixon rested his hands on the side of the television and dropped his head between his arms. Maybe he should have kept her talking about Marvin.

Then for the first time in a long time, he prayed.

*   *   *

Lenore finished the dishes and went outside to her tire swing. A slight breeze in the early evening made it cool, just the right temperature for soul searching. She thought about all Dixon had told her that day. It was too much to digest.

The back storm door squeaked . She glanced up. Dixon stood there. She watched him approach her. He moved with a masculine grace that had her recalling the night of passion they'd shared. That night, just last night, seemed like a lifetime ago.

"I have to go out," he said. "I have some business to tend to. I'll leave you keys to the car in case you decide to leave."

Lenore nodded.

"Lenore?"

She met his gaze.

"I lo . . . I . . ." He paused again and ran his hands over his face. "The song I played for you earlier today. That is my own. I composed it for you."

Tears welled in Lenore's eyes, but she wasn't sure why. Was this goodbye? Had he been about to tell her he loved her? Why—after all the time that had passed between them—would he start to say something like that?

"Are you gonna be okay out here?"

She nodded again. "I was just getting some air."

He shoved his hands in his jeans pockets. "The news will be on in a little bit. You should look at it. I also left a tape for you to watch. It might answer some of the questions you have."

"Okay."

"Well, I'll see you around."

Lenore nodded. That sounded like goodbye.

He pulled a crushed pack of cigarettes from his shirt pocket. He tapped one and lit it with a lighter he pulled from his pocket. After a deep drag on the cigarette, he slowly exhaled over his shoulder.

Lenore watched the smoke. When she didn't say anything, he reached out a hand to her. Then changing his mind, he tucked his hand in his pocket, turned and walked away.

It was obvious to Lenore that he didn't expect her to be there when he returned.

Chapter 16

Lenore pressed the remote and watched as a huge color image filled the screen. She channel-surfed until she found one of the networks. A news brief promised details of the Buster Dixon story after the feature film. Lenore muted the sound as the TV movie concluded. She picked up her journal and opened it to a random page near the end. If today constituted the final chapter, she may as well see what that last goodbye had been like.

> *Dear Billy, I keep asking myself why you left. What I did that made you not love me anymore. I ran into your friend, Raheem, but he said he hadn't seen you around. I even went to see your roommate, Marvin. He promised to get in touch with you and to give you this letter. The others have come back to me. All I ever did was love you. Why did you leave me like this?*

Lenore closed her eyes and sighed. She'd forgotten that she used to write drafts of her letters to Billy in her journal.

She wanted each letter to be just right before she copied it onto her good stationery.

The period after Billy left had been a terrible time in her life. Her grades suffered, she'd lost weight. The desolation, the confusion and the loneliness threatened to completely overwhelm her. Funny, she felt much the same right now.

She glanced at the television long enough to make sure the news hadn't started. Then she flipped backward to another page, a page about happier times.

I made Alpha Kappa Mu, the honor society!! We went to a party tonight to celebrate. It was loud, but it was really nice. Kim made this red dress that I was terrified to wear. It's so short! And it's tight with a capital T. There's practically no back to it at all. Kim said I looked to die for in it. Kim loaned me some high-heeled strapped sandals. She did my hair and put some of her makeup on my face. When I looked in the mirror, I couldn't believe it was me!

When Billy picked me up, he took one look at the dress, he grunted and then he backed me up to the wall and kissed me. I felt like I was going to melt. I didn't want that kiss to end—ever!!

I could feel his you-know-what. It felt like a big stick in his pants. And it kept getting bigger! Then my panties got wet. I must have accidentally urinated on myself. I was so embarrassed. I ran back up to the room and changed panties. I wanted to put a pad on, but they're so bulky. Sometimes I walk funny when I'm on my you-know-what. I didn't want it to show through the dress, and I didn't want to walk funny tonight.

Lenore's face flamed at her youthful candor and innocence. Her first encounters with passion and desire had been with Billy Dixon.

She closed the journal and fanned herself with the volume. Then glancing at the television, she picked up the remote control and turned up the volume. A smiling blond anchorman delivered the news.

"Record producer and songwriter William Dixon has admitted today that he, quote inappropriately borrowed unquote, lyrics for his award-winning song 'Soul Fire.' According to a spokesman for Power4You Records, Dixon returned the six awards he won two weeks ago, including Record of the Year and Songwriter of the Year." Images from an awards program flashed on the screen while the newscaster continued a voice-over report. Lenore watched Dixon's trademark grin as he held an award high over his head.

"Dixon, who is also known as Buster D, has produced music for some of today's top acts. His own solo career took off like lightning a decade ago with his first release of jazzy R&B ballads. No one at Dixon's production company, Foxhound Ltd., could be reached for comment."

The anchorman turned to his pretty dark-haired news partner. "This is really a blow for the music industry," he commented as he passed the story off to her.

"Indeed it is," she said. "I understand the record company said a press conference will be held in the morning."

"That's right, Renata."

The woman smiled and nodded, then faced the camera. "We'll have more details for you tomorrow on 'First News.' And in other stories . . ."

Lenore muted the sound.

"Inappropriately borrowed, that's a mouthful, Billy."

Lenore looked from the television to the videotape Dixon left for her. AWARDS PROGRAM was typed on a bright orange label. Lenore took the tape and went to the television. She opened cabinets and drawers until she found the VCR. Slipping the tape inside, she stood before the large screen. Seconds later Dixon's image popped up. She pressed REWIND, stepped back a few paces, then punched the PLAY key.

Backing up until her legs hit the chair, Lenore sat. The

camera panned over the audience while the program's theme music played. She hadn't watched one of these in years. Lenore spotted Dixon. He sat in the middle of a row of tuxedoed men and glamorous women. When the presenter, a movie star Lenore thought she recognized, called Buster D's name, the place went wild.

Lenore smiled at the exuberance of the audience. Buster D was obviously a favorite son in the music business. The camera focused in on Dixon. He was praying! Then some woman started kissing all over him. Lenore frowned.

She was still frowning when Buster took the microphone. The man looked good in his white tux. He'd combined a red bow tie and cummerbund with the white and was wearing some sort of red pin on the tuxedo jacket.

He waved and the applause grew louder. The camera panned over the crowd. The audience was giving him a standing ovation. Buster eventually silenced them with "thank yous."

In one hand he held the award, the other he wrapped around the microphone.

"Thank you. Thank you. You all do my heart proud tonight. First, I'd like to thank God for all the blessings He provides. And I'd like to thank my dad, who would have been proud to see this moment. I wouldn't be standing here tonight if it weren't for Sergeant Watson and my crew, I love you guys: Monique who keeps me straight; Ashley and Kelvin; K-Rock, who makes sure everything is the way it's supposed to be." Then with a hand out to the audience, "Thanks to all of you who buy my records, who like my music. You made this happen."

He paused, visibly swallowed and blinked back tears. The crowd roared, obviously assuming he'd become overcome with emotion and the moment. Chants of "Bus-ter! Bus-ter!" echoed around.

He held up his hand to silence the enthusiastic throng.

"In addition to my dad, there's someone else who isn't here tonight. I wish to God he could have been. Marvin

Woodbridge, a good friend, died of AIDS a month ago. Marv loved music, and he would have loved this night."

Dixon held the award high over his head. "This is for you, Marv." He fingered the pin on his suit. The camera zoomed in on his hand.

Lenore leaned forward. The pin was a red ribbon folded over.

"Until there's a cure," Dixon said. Then with a final thank you, he exited the stage to thunderous applause.

Lenore fell back into the chair and watched as Dixon's back was slapped behind the stage. Women hugged and kissed him. A camera zoomed in on his face just as he wiped a tear away from his eyes. Lenore punched REWIND and then paused at that moment.

For a long time she sat staring at the frozen image of Buster Dixon.

"Oh, Billy. How could you have gotten yourself in such a mess?"

Eventually she rewound the tape, looked at Dixon's segment again, then picked up a portable phone and called Kim.

"Girl, have you heard the news?" Kim said without preamble. "Your man has been running around ripping off music."

Inextricably Lenore felt compelled to defend him. "He'll explain it all at the press conference tomorrow." She hoped that was true.

"Lenore, did you catch the segment on BET? They got some reax from some of Buster's acts. His people are standing behind him right now. But everybody wants some answers. How was your flight back to the East Coast?"

"I didn't go home."

"You didn't? Well, where are you?" Kim asked.

"At Buster's father's house."

"Get outta town! Are you serious? What's up with that?"

Lenore closed her eyes. "I don't know, Kim. I don't know."

"You want me to come get you? We can grab some eats, talk if you want."

"I'd say yes but I'm not sure where I am."

It took a few minutes, but Kim got enough info out of Lenore to determine where she was and where they could meet. Kim gave Lenore directions. As she jotted them down, she asked, "Hey, Kim. Where can I get some of Dixon's music this time of night? I want to hear what the fuss is all about."

"There's lots of all-night record stores around. I'll get you hooked up."

Lenore rang off with her friend. She watched the awards segment again. Then she sat at the piano and fingered the keys. She'd never learned to play. For Dixon, the gift came naturally. Curious, she lifted the piano bench seat.

Neatly stacked sheet music greeted her eye. She sorted through some of it and smiled. Closing the bench, she went to her bedroom to freshen up and go meet Kim.

Lenore stumbled over a throw rug as she came in the front door.

"I didn't think you were coming back."

"Dixon?" She fumbled her way to the light switch. "Why are you sitting here in the dark?"

When the lights came up, Dixon got a good look at her. Her hair, in wild disarray, looked as if someone had been running his hands through it most of the night. His eyes narrowed. She teetered on sexy high-heeled gold sandals that criss-crossed at her ankles. The figure-hugging gold dress had a huge diamond-shaped cutout in the middle that showed off her belly button and stomach. Long, dangling earrings that matched the dress completed her outfit.

She squinted in the bright light cast by an overhead lamp.

Balancing one hand on the back of a chair, she untied the sandals and kicked them off.

Barefoot, she sashayed to where he sat on the plastic-covered sofa, her bare navel eye level with his mouth.

"Make love to me, Dixon."

"You're drunk."

"Am not. Kim and I had a few glasses of chardonnay. It was good. You people out here make good wine."

"It sounds like you had a few bottles."

Lenore started shimmying out of the dress.

Dixon stood and grabbed her by the shoulders. "What are you doing?"

"Taking the initiative. Men like it when women take the initiative."

"Is that what Kim told you?"

Lenore pulled buttons open and Dixon snapped them back up. "What's wrong? Don't you want me anymore?" she pouted.

Dixon shook his head. "Kim's a bad influence on you. What'd you do—bar hop tonight?"

"I don't frequent bars."

"Um-hmm."

She draped her arms around his shoulders and tried to kiss him. Dixon turned his head away, crinkling his nose at the albeit faint but nevertheless distinct scent of alcohol. "You're drunk, Lenore. Let's get you to bed."

Lenore smiled. "Now that's what I wanted to hear."

Dixon swung her up into his arms. She linked her arms around his shoulders, her head tucked against him.

"Dixon?" she murmured.

"What?"

"I like your song about midnight shadows."

She was asleep before he got to the guest bedroom.

Dixon placed her on top of the bedspread. She murmured his name and rolled over onto her stomach. Shapely brown thighs and long legs beckoned him. His body responded accordingly.

She needed to come out of that tight dress. Dixon

reached forward, then drew back a second before his hands encountered warm skin.

"Don't even think about it, man." Some temptations were best left avoided. Even he had sense enough to know that.

He backed out of the room and returned to the front room. He looked out the door but didn't see his car. Kim had either driven Lenore home or she'd taken a cab. In college Lenore never drank anything stronger than a half can of beer. That had been on just one occasion, and she'd passed out cold from it. While they hadn't been in contact for many years, he seriously doubted if she'd changed much. A couple of glasses of a good California chardonnay would probably put her out.

Dixon shut and locked the front door and went to his own room. He stripped naked and thought of the woman in the next room.

Tonight of all nights he needed his coolheaded Lenore, not the inebriated woman sprawled across the bed in his guest room. It was four o'clock in the morning. Where the hell had she been all this time? And why was she dressed like a hooker?

Lenore's head pounded something fierce when she woke up the next morning. Her body felt like she'd slept in a straitjacket. She twisted around to peer at the clock on the bedside table. It was gone. So was the collectible figurine of a ballet dancer she kept next to the alarm.

She tried to put the pieces of the previous evening together. Slowly it came to her. California. Dixon. Music. Kim. Some scandal. Hanging out.

She fully opened her eyes. She was in the guest room at Dixon's father's house. She and Kim had been out. With that much confirmed, she sat up and tried to swing her legs over the side of the mattress. Her head protested, and her body didn't cooperate, so she sat still for a few minutes. What had happened?

She remembered being in a rather mellow mood by the time she got back to the house. She'd wanted to make love, but Dixon was . . . tired? What had he said?

The friends went to Kim's shop for some comfortable clothes, then they stopped at a record shop and loaded up on Dixon's music. A song about midnight made her cry. Then? Then what? Oh, yes, the café. She and Kim found a café where they talked. She'd confessed all the regrets she had: that she hadn't lived, loved or just had fun. That she'd never let herself just cut loose and nevermind the consequences. Men did it all the time. Dixon had done it. Why couldn't she, she'd complained to Kim.

As memory filtered in, more fragmented pieces of the evening came to her. "Oh, and Armand," she said before falling back on the pillows and closing her eyes. Armand was a friend of Kim's. They'd gone to his house? No . . . His vineyard in France? Lenore stopped trying to figure it all out.

She squinted at the place where the clock was supposed to be. Slowly she made her way up.

She got a look at what she was wearing. "Oh, my God!" There was more of her showing than was covered up. The little dress, what there was of it, had all the trappings of one of Kim's original "tease-me" dresses.

Lenore sat back on the edge of the bed and held her head.

"Let me just die right now."

But she didn't. After about ten minutes, she got herself out of the bed and into a cover-up. A quick look in Dixon's room showed he wasn't there. After a stop in the bathroom and a long shower, she eventually she made it to the kitchen. On the table propped against a glass of water and two packets of Alka-Seltzer was a note.

Had to take care of some business. Didn't wanna wake you. Take the seltzer. It'll help your head. I'll send a car around for you in the afternoon.

D.

Lenore hoped the car was a hearse. The only way she could feel this bad and still be living was if she were already dead. She tore open the blue packets and watched the seltzer fizz. After downing the contents of the glass, she rested her head in her arms on the table and waited for the pounding in her head to cease.

A shower, some tea and a few hours later she felt human again. And she'd never been more mortified in her life.

"What in the world happened last night?" she demanded when she got Kim on the phone.

"Lenore, are you all right? I was really worried about you. You were acting like, well, to be honest, you were acting like me. I've never seen you so wound up."

"Kim, just start at the beginning and tell me what happened."

"First, we were just talking. We were at a little café. You started trying some of the house wines. Then you said you wanted to go to a club where they played Dixon's music. You were dancing like you were on 'Soul Train' or something. I didn't know you had some of those moves in you, girl. But then things started weirding out. You'd picked up some guy named Armand and was about to go home with him when I grabbed you and put you in a cab. Dixon's car is still there, I think."

"Oh, God." It was worse than she'd imagined. "I knew I never should have come out to this state. It makes people crazy."

"Well, after last night, you shouldn't be feeling repressed or suppressed anymore," Kim said. "You danced, flirted and drank enough chardonnay to make up for the last fifteen years. Are you okay, Lenore? Where's Dixon?"

"I'm fine. My head has stopped hurting. As for Dixon, I don't know where he is."

"Well, you need to turn on a television. His press conference has been all over the air."

"Oh, goodness! I forgot all about that."

Before she could get to the television, there was a knock at the front door. "Kim, somebody's at the door. Let me get back to you."

She opened the door to a chauffeur, but it wasn't the man she remembered from her arrival on the West Coast.

"The car is available when you're ready, Dr. Foxwood."

She nodded and shut the door, then leaned against it. *Dr. Foxwood*. She was so far away from her academic life right now that she wondered if it had been in another lifetime. She'd been in California just a few short days, and her world had been turned upside down.

Chapter 17

A newspaper on the seat in the limo provided more than she wanted to know about Dixon's case. The reporter's story was fairly straightforward, but a column in the entertainment section was absolutely scathing. Ugly words leaped off the page, words that maligned his character and everything he'd done in recent months.

Frowning, Lenore folded the paper and put it away from her. She picked up the receiver that put her in touch with the driver.

"Yes, ma'am?"

"If there's any of Buster Dixon's music in the car, would you please put it on?"

"Which CD would you like to hear?"

Lenore didn't have a clue. She just needed to hear his work with the advantage of a clear head. "The latest will be fine."

Moments later a soulful ballad surrounded her. Lenore closed her eyes and rested her head on the leather seat back.

You're my soul fire/the fire that burns me
   hotter than any flame/When I'm with you I can't
   believe we found each other/You're my soul fire

The words, familiar in some odd way, seemed to trigger a distant memory. Then she realized she merely recognized the tune from the awards program video. He'd won Songwriter of the Year for this song. Was this one of the plagiarized ones?

The next cut, an instrumental that featured Dixon on the piano, made her want to weep. Something about the melody haunted her. The music touched a chord deep within her—a chord filled with emotion and longing she'd forgotten she'd ever possessed.

But she'd known those feelings before. She'd known them with a boy named Billy Dixon. She glanced at the newspaper—now he was a man known the world over as Buster Dixon.

Lenore blinked back silent and sudden tears as the melody of the piano wrapped her in unexpected longing, needy anticipation.

She lifted the receiver again. "What's the name of this piece?" she asked.

"This one is 'Distant Dreams,' ma'am."

"Thank you," she murmured as she replaced the phone. 'Distant Dreams.' That's exactly what it felt like.

When the tune ended and a jazzy upbeat song picked up, Lenore was relieved and saddened. She'd wanted the distant dreams to go on forever, even though she thought she'd die of the longing and the need in the composition.

Even after the driver announced their destination, Lenore told him to wait. "Midnight Shadows" had come on. Her face flamed at the memory of the night before when she'd thrown herself at Dixon and he'd scolded her as if she were a recalcitrant child.

"You deserved it," she said. But the coolheaded Lenore

wasn't quite ready to accept all the blame for her behavior the night before. "It was the dress . . . and the stress."

She frowned, not for a moment buying into her own weak rationalizing. What she wanted—albeit unconsciously, but nonetheless wanted—was the ability and the chance to live free. She wanted to be the wild, passionate creature Dixon had seen in her so many years ago. Just for a moment, she wanted to recapture some of the happiness she'd known in college. Home was three thousand miles and a world away. Surely she could live a little now. Wasn't that the purpose of spring break?

The song ended. As if on cue, the chauffeur opened her door.

Minutes later all heads turned toward her when Lenore walked into Dixon's office. She'd worn the magenta suit to make an impression. It was the boldest, hippest thing she owned that hadn't come from Kim's couture collection. The outfit, conservative enough to wear at her university, also made her feel powerful.

She walked and looked like she owned the place.

Conversation ground to a halt as she stood in the open door.

Dixon hopped up and approached her. "Lenore. Come in." He held out a hand.

In this environment, he looked like a record producer—slick, suave, ready to do a deal, even though she still wasn't quite sure just what that job entailed. Some sort of jade pin served as the collar on his white band shirt. The people in the room had the bored predatory looks Lenore had seen in some of Kim's magazines.

She adapted herself to the climate—considerably frosty and with much attitude.

She took his outstretched hand and glanced at the faces as Dixon led her to an empty chair.

"This is Lenore. She's with me," he announced. Then he went around the table introducing her to his crew: Monique, who flicked disdainful eyes over Lenore. Lenore raised one cool eyebrow at the woman, then moved her gaze to the next name and face. K-Rock, Mouse, Ashley, MC African or something that sounded like that, Cool Light and RastaMan.

If she had been expected to recognize the names and suitably fawn, Lenore failed the test. Not only did the names sound just as ridiculous as Dixon's stage name, she wondered how they ever kept track of who was really whom. It was like old times. Dixon would introduce her around at a party, she'd smile and pretend like she was having a good time.

The last person introduced was a big man in a tailored suit. Other than Dixon's, his was the only friendly face in the room.

"Sergeant Watson," he said as he stood and reached across the table to shake her hand. "I've heard a lot about you."

"I hope it was good," Lenore answered even as she wondered why she thought she could pull this game off. She didn't belong here, not in this office, not in this world. She tried to think of something clever to say, but nothing came to mind.

She looked to Dixon. He got her seated, then turned his attention back to the meeting in progress.

Crossing her legs, she gratefully sat back in her big chair. She felt Mr. Watson watching her legs. Dixon cleared his throat, scowled at Mr. Watson and then picked up the conversation. They talked of an ad campaign, profits and losses, rescheduled concert dates, studio times for acts. And then the talk shifted to the immediate problem and how to do damage control.

Cutting her eyes at Lenore, Monique brought up the point no one else seemed willing to broach. "Buster, I don't think it's a good idea to have a stranger in while we're discussing this."

Lenore slowly swiveled her chair. "Let me assure you, I'm no stranger. Just because *you* don't know me, don't jump to conclusions." Lenore's eyes widened at her own audacity. She didn't know these people. She could only attribute her rudeness to the headache she still had and maybe some vestige of that wild woman she didn't recognize in herself.

Monique glared at Lenore, then slammed a pen on the desk and turned to Buster. "You need to handle your guest."

In Monique, Lenore recognized a rival, an enemy. She started to fire back a flygirl retort, then decided against it. She didn't know these people and didn't want to know them. It had been years since she was down with the juvenile one-upmanship she'd learned at Dixon's side years ago. Did people even still say they were down with things?

Since she hadn't been given a play book and didn't understand the rules, what was the sense in playing the game and antagonizing his associates? This was Dixon's turf, his people, his world. She was the one who didn't fit in. She belonged in Ohio at her quiet little conservative college where everyone played by the rules. People who colored outside the lines were frowned upon. And right now, Lenore felt like a beige crayon in a box full of ultrabrights.

"Dixon, where might I find the powder room?"

Monique rolled her eyes, then a gleam appeared. "I'll show you," Monique said sweetly.

Ashley and Kelvin exchanged a look between them. One of the others snickered.

Dixon sighed. "All right. Let's take five. We're almost done."

"This way, Miss Foxwood," Monique said.

When Ashley made to follow the two women, Dixon called her back. Rising, Lenore took a deep breath, anticipating the confrontation to come. She'd let her adversary throw the first punch.

It wasn't long coming. The ladies' room door had barely shut behind them when Monique rounded on her.

"Why are you here?"

Lenore stood in front of the large mirror and shook her hair out. Then she reached a not steady hand into her small bag and pulled out a compact.

"I'm here to powder my nose," she said to Monique's reflection in the mirror.

"Let me get you straight on something, Miss Lenore."

Lenore's eyebrows rose at the use of her name as slur. She dabbed the powder puff over her nose.

"There can be only one queen bee around here. And she's already on the throne."

Lenore pulled a small vial from her bag. "Good thing I travel with insect repellant." With that she sprayed a dab on her wrist and behind her ear. Then, without a backward glance, she left Monique standing in the ladies' room.

Shortly after the group reconvened, a secretary called Monique out of the meeting to take an important call. Lenore figured she'd heard more than she wanted to know about Dixon's work world.

She leaned toward Dixon. "I'll wait for you in the car."

When she rose, so did Sergeant Watson.

"I'll see you downstairs," he offered.

"Sarge. Don't get any ideas," Dixon warned.

Sarge simply smiled and guided Lenore with a large hand at the small of her back.

Then they were alone in the elevator. "Why are you here?" he asked, unable to mask the belligerence in his voice.

"Excuse me?"

"This whole mess is your fault."

"My fault? First of all I don't know you. And second, I don't know what you're talking about."

"I'm talking about my number-one client's sudden burst of morality. You show up on the scene, and all of sudden he's had a great epiphany and is ready to turn his life and my life upside down. This mess you created is costing me a shitload of money."

Hands on hips and eyebrows raised, Lenore fired back. "I don't know who you *think* you're talking to Sergeant Watson. But I'd suggest you watch your tongue and your tone when you address me."

Sarge pressed the STOP button on the elevator. Lenore glanced at the closed doors and then at the big man. A shiver of apprehension coursed through her.

She swallowed, hard, but managed to keep the tremor out of her voice. "What do you want?"

Lenore reached for the elevator buttons, but the big man blocked her access.

"If you're trying to intimidate me, it's not working."

She watched Sarge assess her from the top of her head, and the wispy tendrils of dark hair she'd arranged around her nape, to the plain but high-heeled black pumps shielding her size eight feet.

Lenore put one hand on her hip and bit down on the fear that had goose bumps popping out all over her arms. Thankful that the long sleeves of the suit's swing jacket shielded her, she stared Sarge in the eye.

"What will it take to make you go away?"

She blinked. "I beg your pardon?"

"Buster Dixon's sudden burst of conscience is very— and I mean *very*—out of character. The only thing that's changed in his life that I know of is your arrival. You showed up and now he's acting crazy. I know your part in this. And let me tell you something that may not have crossed your mind—this little morality and integrity trip you have him on is gonna cost some big bucks when it's over. I want to know how much you're going to demand to just get the hell out of here and forget you ever met him."

Lenore pulled on all the reserve courage she had. She was in costume and playing a role. She could keep up the act for just a while longer, just until the curtain call.

Rallying all the diva she had in her, she gave him a cold stare and an even chillier smile. "You must think I'm out of my mind."

Sarge swore. Lenore just barely managed to keep from flinching in the face of his anger and animosity.

He pointed a beefy finger in her face. "This fiasco you've prompted is likely to cost millions of dollars. If you think you're going to bleed Buster dry, you can forget it, lady. It ain't gonna work. I've busted my ass and Dixon's too many years to watch some squeeze from his past waltz in here and take it all away. Name your price."

The elevator jerked. Sarge lost his balance. Lenore ducked to the left as he stumbled. She punched the elevator button and the car lurched down a floor.

"I wouldn't worry too much about those millions. If I were you, I'd be concerned about an assault charge."

When the elevator doors swooshed open, Lenore stepped out of the car and moved past an annoyed man waiting for the elevator. She didn't fall apart until she was safely tucked in the limousine.

"Take me home, please," she told the driver.

"I'm sorry, ma'am. I have instructions from Mr. D to wait for his arrival."

Lenore snatched the door open. "Fine. I'll walk."

"That won't be necessary," Dixon said as he slid into the car. "Get on the coast and go north. I'll tell you when to stop."

The chauffeur nodded. Moments later the luxury vehicle glided into traffic.

"I don't like being manhandled and harassed by your flunkies, Dixon. I don't care how famous you think you are."

Chapter 18

Weary from answering an hour's worth of caustic and accusing questions from the press, and then a decidedly tense and frosty meeting with his crew, Dixon sighed. Monique had been a particular pain. Maybe it was time to kick her butt to the curb. She got big money to keep the waves outta his life, and here she was making more grief than anybody else. The absolute last thing he needed was Lenore on his case and copping an attitude. Sarge had been bad enough.

Nobody had given him props for doing the right thing. This decision to go straight up had been to give himself a little inner peace, to atone for what he'd done. All he'd managed to do, however, was create turmoil. Everything he said people either took the wrong way or got what he said all out of context.

His crew, his people, the very ones he thought he could count on—the very ones who'd assured him they had his back—had his back all right. They'd ripped him to shreds with the daggers they had waiting after the last camera shut off and the microphones were all packed away. All he wanted to do was crawl in Lenore's lap and let her love the pain away.

But instead of Lenore, he got this carpy woman nagging at him. She sat there like some ice princess, accusing him of injustice. All he'd ever done was love her. And look what that got him.

"I am famous. Just because you didn't know about it, doesn't make it not true," he finally answered her.

"I hate it when you get like this."

Dixon sighed. "Join the club. I hate me, too."

Dixon sighed again, then closed his eyes and rested his head on the seat back. He didn't even bother to look at her. A fact Lenore noted and was stung by.

"What are you talking about?" he finally asked.

On one level he knew that a cooler head would allow him to remember he'd done everything for Lenore—*everything*. Lenore was the reason he was where he was today. She'd believed in him, and he fed on that belief. She wouldn't see it that way though. And truth be told, he was still ticked off about her leaving him last night. Sure he didn't mind if she went out, did some tourist things, got to see the city, maybe a studio backlot. But she damn sure wasn't supposed to be having fun without him—especially not the kind of fun that brought you home at four o'clock in the morning looking liked you'd just been sexed.

Lenore studied the still life of Dixon's insolent, indolent pose. He'd perfected it to an art form. If he cared, truly cared, about how his friends treated her, he'd show a little sincere interest in her plight. Painfully obvious, however, remained the fact that his first loyalty went to someone else—probably that Monique woman with the daggers in her eyes.

Lenore well remembered the lessons Dixon taught her so many years ago: "Attitude is everything," he'd say. "Act like you own the place," he'd whisper before they walked into a crowded house party. "Demand respect. Expect nothing less."

She stiffened her back and looked straight ahead.

Dixon rubbed the spot between his eyes and willed the pounding in his head to cease. "Lenore, I'm not in the mood for any games. What's going down?"

She turned to stare at the stranger sitting next to her. It was past time to go back to the real world, her secure life of students, exams and the flat lands of Ohio. And until she got there, she could take care of herself in Dixon's world. Sure she had to step carefully sometimes and play the political games of academe, but at least she knew the rules and was a better than average player. Here, in Dixon's world, she floundered.

Jealousy, however, remained universal. She could handle someone like Monique. And she'd come up with a solution on her own to handle Sergeant Watson. He thought he could intimidate her with his size. At her former university, Lenore had known that kind, too. She'd just apply the same foot down, "don't even try it," attitude she used then. She might not have all the fly attitude like Dixon's cronies, but Lenore wasn't a complete pushover.

"Nothing I can't handle," she answered.

Something in her voice, maybe the steel, maybe the pain, made Dixon sit up. What had she said first? Something about being manhandled and harassed? He reached for her, but Lenore snatched her arm away.

"I don't think that's a good idea, Dixon. As a matter of fact, I've decided to forfeit the money from Marvin. I'll use what he left me personally to set up a scholarship program for my kids. And *we* can end this farce right now."

Farce? Is that what she thought of the loving they'd shared? How little she knew about him. Lenore's loving constituted the only reality in his world. He'd even come up with another song, this one about honesty and second chances. She couldn't give up on him now, not when his redemption was within view.

"There's no sense in us continuing this. I feel like a

complete idiot," she said. "I'm sorry about last night. I didn't mean to embarrass you."

Lenore plucked at imaginary lint on her bright suit. Now embarrassed to look him in the eye, she gazed out the window on her left side. California coast zipped by too fast for her to enjoy the view.

She indicated the bright suit she wore. "I, I was trying to make myself over into the kind of woman who would appeal to you."

That got his attention. "What do you mean, make yourself over for me?"

But she ignored his question. "I feel like such a fool," she said. "And today I didn't mean to barge in and interrupt your meeting. I was just . . . I don't know. I think it's past time I head home. This has all been a mistake."

Dixon edged closer to her and took her hands in his. "Lenore, you're the best thing that's ever happened to me. Without you, I wouldn't be where I am today. Nothing you have ever done has been a mistake. Not where I'm concerned."

She turned to him. With one finger he wiped away the tears glistening at her eyes. His smile warmed her. And then his gentle kiss loved all the hurt away.

Well, she reasoned, maybe she was being overly dramatic, taking things too fast. She'd gotten a little tipsy, she'd interrupted a meeting. Surely worse crimes had been committed in the world. That bully in the elevator was another story.

"What's your military buddy's problem? I didn't appreciate him cornering me in that elevator."

"Who . . . Sarge? He's never been in the military. What elevator?"

"He threatened me."

Dixon sat up. Peering at her face, her hands, her body, he demanded, "What happened? What did he do to you?"

Lenore related the incident to him.

Dixon swore. Lenore did flinch this time. His harsh words tinged more than her ears blue.

"Nobody, and I mean nobody, puts a hand on you. That SOB is fired!"

Dixon reached for the telephone. Lenore put a restraining hand on his thigh.

"Don't do anything rash. I told you I can handle it. He was just looking out for your best interests."

"The only interest Sarge Watson is concerned with is the kind that increases his bank balance." Dixon's hand gently cupped her face. He studied her as if expecting to see a wound or bruise show up on her face. "What did he do to you?"

Lenore clasped his hand in hers. "It's not important. We just failed to see eye-to-eye on something. Everything's fine," she lied.

With a raised eyebrow, and the anger still etched at his mouth, Lenore knew he didn't believe her. Solicitously she patted his hand. "We're cool. Honest."

Slowly Dixon put down the phone. "If he so much as looks at you wrong, I want to know about it."

Lenore, unwilling to promise, looked down at their hands. This wasn't going to work. She should have known better. She didn't belong in this world, in Buster Dixon's world. She belonged at home, with J.D., where things weren't perfect, but at least she was in her element.

"Billy . . . I mean Dixon, it's been great seeing you again after all this time. Thank you for your kindness."

He frowned. "That sounds like an hasta la vista to me."

She smiled. "No. It's not a farewell, yet. But it will be. There's really no sense in me staying here. You're in the midst of this record thing. I'm in the way, and I'm sure there's more you'd like to concentrate on without the distraction of my presence."

"Please stay."

He nestled her head and shoulders in the crook of his arm. "You just don't know how much seeing you again means to me. When I dropped out of college I never thought I'd see you again. And then when you walked back into my life—when I saw you in that lawyer's office—I knew you were there for a reason."

"Well, money isn't everything," she said.

"Not that reason." He leaned forward to position her to accept his kiss. "You're here to give me a second chance to love you right."

Lenore smiled as he eased her back onto the long, plush length of the seat. She wrapped her arms around his neck. His welcoming weight settled over her.

"I'm still going home. But I wouldn't trade this moment for anything."

When Dixon lowered his head, his mouth grazed hers. "Maybe I can convince you to stay."

He did.

As Lenore placed the white-rimmed floral pattern plates on the table for their dinner two nights later, she wondered how he'd so swiftly changed her mind.

"Well, it wasn't exactly swift," she said with a soft smile. In the last two days and nights, Dixon had been friend, lover, tour guide, teacher and historian. In a few days he crammed a master's degree program worth of information at her: percentages, how CDs were made, the cost of studio work versus location work. They dashed through the city on a whirlwind tourist's tour, with Dixon pointing out the homes of the stars—his neighbors.

At his side she got to see a music video being produced. Dixon had laughed at her when she didn't recognize the triple platinum R&B crooner who flirted with her, then signed an autograph for her. She and Dixon, decked to the nines in white-on-white outfits—him in a suit and her in a short little fringed chemise—left the studio for a party at a club. Stepping from the white limousine, they looked the parts they played: wealthy, high profile, in love while living and loving the good life.

But through it all, Lenore felt like Cinderella. Even as Dixon showed her his town, his world, she knew that midnight would soon come. She'd return to reality.

She and Dixon had crammed fifteen lost years into five short days. They'd gotten to know each other better. With Dixon she could be free: free to laugh, to live and to make mad, passionate, sweaty love. All those wasted years. The time she'd spent with her ex now seemed like a prison sentence. Simon never liked to perspire. He thought perspiration savage and unseemly. Lenore grinned. Getting sweaty with Dixon had been the most fun she'd had in years.

Lenore eyed the daffodils she'd cut from the flower bed in the backyard. The arrangement filled the dining room with the fresh scent of spring. She fingered one of the golden yellow petals and smiled. Spring was a good time to be in love.

Two more nights and Cinderella would have to take the carriage back to the rental office. Without a doubt, this had been the best spring break ever. But the fantasy had to come to an end sooner or later. Sooner was catching up with her. The stifling reality of the papers she hadn't graded and the course work she would return to weighed heavy on Lenore. That thought made her pause, a small frown marred her features.

Her academic life wasn't stifling. In the past she'd always gotten a measure of comfort and satisfaction in teaching, in molding young minds and encouraging her students to explore new avenues of thought. Except for this week, she couldn't remember the last time she had had or had taken the opportunity to do the same for herself.

Dixon, she concluded, just had a way of altering her perception of reality. He was like Tinker Bell and Peter Pan, all play and no work.

"Stop it right now, Lenore," she advised herself. "This

is but one fleeting interlude. When you get on that plane, it will be business as usual. No wild parties, no hanging out meeting the stars, no lovemaking, no . . .

She stopped. This train of thought was going nowhere quickly.

She fiddled with a daffodil, rearranging the arrangement she'd created. "Enjoy the time you have left with him and let it go."

With that, Lenore slipped flatware into two porcelain rose napkin holders, then went to check on dinner. For her last full evening with him, Dixon had promised a night on the town, starting at one of L.A.'s best restaurants. That was the plan for tomorrow. Tonight she'd prepared a special meal for them: comfort food—all the things Dixon said he never got to eat because no one he knew, including himself, could cook. He had, however, impressed her with his coffee-making skills.

"Man cannot live on French roast and Colombian beans," he'd told her laughing.

So tonight, after checking in with J.D. to let him know she'd be home soon, Lenore cooked like a mother—or a wife: pot roast, potatoes and apple pie.

Lenore added seasoning to the vegetable medley and turned down the heat under the pot. Dixon had a lot on his mind this week. By mutual agreement, they hadn't turned on a television since the night when one of the entertainment magazine programs skewered Dixon's music, his producing and his character—all in a five-minute expose segment.

Out of respect for Dixon, she refrained from buying newspapers to see what was being said and exactly how far-reaching this scandal was. But Kim had kept her fully briefed on the situation.

Kim also insisted that Lenore take a proactive role in her relationship with Dixon. Kim supplied Lenore with a cute little number guaranteed to take Dixon's mind off his troubles. The bodysuit, in an exact shade of Lenore's dark skin tone, looked as if all that covered her body were tiny patches of shimmering gemstones in strategic places.

Lenore, not quite sure she had the guts to wear the get-up, knew for a fact Dixon would love it—right before he ripped it off her body.

Kim had also dropped off a couple of outfits made for partying: a black mini that looked like a man's tailored dinner jacket and another gold dress, this one a gown with a split that would show off her leg clear to her thigh. Lenore had taken one look at the dresses, said, "No way," then listened to Kim's laughter as she hung them in the closet.

"Trust me, Lenore," she'd said. "Not only will you have Buster Dixon's undivided attention, you'll stop traffic. You have the body to pull these off, girl. Not everyone I design for is so blessed. Go for it. Strut your stuff."

Lenore glanced at the clock on the kitchen wall. She had just enough time for a pampering bath before Dixon got home. The dresses, however, were out of the question. She seriously doubted that a mere dress could transform her into a femme fatale.

Dixon smacked his lips and licked his fingers. Lenore grinned.

"I take it that means you liked dinner."

He patted his stomach. "Woman, I'm gonna have to watch myself around you. I can't pull up to your table too often. If you keep feeding me like this, I'll get fat."

Lenore glanced at him with a shy smile. "I know a few exercises to keep you in shape."

His eyes narrowed as sexual awareness replaced thoughts of food. "Come here."

Lenore complied, then settled on his lap when he patted the place for her. He smiled when she wiggled her bottom getting comfortable. "You're trying me. Why don't you kiss me? I'm tired of doing all the work."

She just smiled.

Dixon couldn't help but smile back. This woman he didn't deserve had been a rock for him this week. Her sheltering arms held him at night and loved the stress and strain away. Luckily she hadn't shown a whole lot of interest in what had been going down and so didn't know that his whole world was falling apart.

But when he held her, when the sweet music she inspired flowed through him, Dixon felt invincible. She kissed his chin and he grinned.

"Umm, that's not what I had in mind," he said.

She kissed him on the cheek.

"Hmm, I see a need for a few remedial lessons."

She parted her lips to tell him something, but Dixon's mouth closed over hers. He spread a series of slow shivery kisses along the rim of her mouth, then settled in for passion over instruction. His lips, warm and sweet on hers, coaxed and pleaded. When she succumbed to the forceful domination of his lips, she opened her mouth to him.

A moan in the room had Dixon wondering if it had come from him or from her. Then he lost all thought except the feel of his woman in his arms.

She had a burning desire, an aching need, for something more potent than a kiss, more intimate than sitting on Dixon's lap. She could feel his lengthening arousal and lowered a hand to stroke him through his pants.

"I had plans for us tonight, but I think I'm being convinced that home is the place to be."

Home. That's where she always felt in Dixon's arms. Tonight she'd be his fantasy woman, tonight she'd pretend that all her tomorrows included this man.

"What did you have in mind?" she said, while her finger danced a light ballet along the sensitive area behind his ear. When he tremored, Lenore smiled.

"Witch," he accused.

"Let me put a spell on you."

"Too late. I'm already under your power."

He spoke the truth and proved it to her. But after several moments of heavy making out, Dixon sighed.

"Baby, what's up with you and these chairs?"

Lenore shrugged and licked the rim of his ear. Dixon shuddered and closed his eyes.

"I don't know," she said. "You bring out the wild woman in me."

His response, more grunt than greeting, made her smile. With one last kiss, she rose. "So what plans did you have for tonight?"

Dixon, lost in a fog of arousal and need, stared blankly at her. "Plans?"

At his befuddled look, Lenore chuckled, the sound coming from deep inside. Dixon buried his head in her neck. She smiled.

"You said you had plans for us tonight. Plans to go out," she prompted.

"Oh, those plans." His palm slid up and down her thigh. "I'm thinking about producing a new group—if they don't run for the hills and treat me like a piranha like some folk have been doing. The group E.P. Nasty is doing a show tonight. I thought we'd check it out and then go do L.A., the nightlife, not the tourist stuff."

"What kind of music group calls itself E.P. Nasty?"

"It stands for Electric Power. Nasty just happens to be an acronym for all the group members' names. They do rap. Nathan, Anthony, Sean—"

Lenore interrupted. "Rap?"

Dixon chuckled at her expression. "It's music, Lenore. Not toxic waste."

She struggled out of his embrace. "That depends on your definition. In my book the two are synonymous."

Lenore started clearing the table. Dixon took the cue and helped, following her into the kitchen with dishes. "Um-hmm, yep. And you're a rap connoisseur."

"I've listened to enough to know that the whole purpose of it is to demean women and disrespect authority."

"That's not true."

Lenore dumped the leftover gravy into the trash. Then she rattled off statistics that startled him: arrests of rap artists, convictions, gang-related violence directly attributable to the music, shooting incidents at concerts.

"What are you—the rap police?"

"I've had enough arguments with . . ." She paused, then started again. "I'm on a campus and community committee at home that has been working to ban music that demeans or belittles people. That particularly goes for the gangsta variety of rap."

Dixon threw the dish towel down and rolled his eyes. "Oh, for God's sake, don't tell me you're one of those holier-than-thou right-wing witch hunt types."

"If you feel like the subject of a witch hunt, maybe that's your conscience telling you that that music is doing more damage than good."

"You people have been giving me, and the industry, unnecessary and undeserved grief for too long now. First you wanted warning labels on albums. All that did was give the kids you called yourself protecting an easy ID on what to buy. If you'd wanted to do some good, you should have put warning labels on that precious classical music of yours. Give Bach a warning label and watch sales skyrocket."

Lenore, arms folded across her chest, stared him down. "If you call yourself convincing me that rap is a legitimate musical art form, your argument is sorely lacking."

"I don't need to *convince* you of anything. Rap is here to stay. Fifty years from now, people like you will be throwing your hands up in the air screaming about whatever new music is out there in the next century. Rap is the jazz of the juke joints in the twenties and the rock 'n roll of the fifties."

He took in her militant pose, then shook his head. "You know what burns me up?"

"I'm sure you're going to enlighten me," she said.

He ignored her sarcastic tone. "Most of the people like you have never even listened to a rap artist."

"Artist? How can you call that garbage art?"

The dishes forgotten, the battle lines drawn, Lenore and Dixon faced each other down on opposite sides of the kitchen table.

Chapter 19

"You know what irritates me the most about people like you? The only reason you don't like rap is because it's different. It's outside your little norm. Because they aren't like you, you feel threatened by the people who perform the music and by the people who enjoy listening to it."

"That's right—I feel threatened," Lenore fired back. With her fingers she ticked off all the reasons. "First of all, any illiterate man who stands on a stage or screams from a record that women are nothing but 'bitches and ho's' does not respect me or any other female, including the ones who struggled, fought and died to give him the opportunity to stand on that stage.

"Second, volume level. Everybody in the world does not want to hear megadecibels of profanity pouring from the vehicle stopped next to them at a red light or at the gas pump."

Warmed to her argument, Lenore counted off the next argument. "And third, the music perpetuates violence and exacerbates the stereotype that black youth are thugs."

In her face Dixon shot back, "That music—that you very

obviously don't understand—is providing a much needed creative outlook, not to mention an economic boost, to young people."

"Oh, yeah, right," she said. "So they can go out and buy two hundred dollar athletic shoes and designer shirts for their ten kids they have by ten different girls. I suppose you'd use the same line of reasoning for crack and heroin dealers. 'They provide an economic boost to the community' huh?"

"There you go, twisting my words. Just tell me one thing, Lenore. Have you ever even been to a rap concert? Could you name any two rap artists at the top of the charts right now?"

"I know that several of those so-called artists of yours have been arrested and convicted on all sorts of charges—everything from drug possession to murder. Some have even died as a direct result of their life-styles."

Dixon nodded. "Um-hmm, yep. Just like I thought. The answer is no."

Lenore picked up their dinner dishes and ran cold water over them. After rinsing each plate, she slipped them into the dishpan and starting washing.

"I don't have to experience everything firsthand to know I don't like it. And for your information—not that it's any business of yours—I am familiar enough with the *music* that I know I don't like it."

"Um-hmm. Afraid. You're still afraid to try anything that doesn't conform to your neat little bourgeois world. I thought you'd expanded your horizons. I thought you'd stopped being a cultural snob."

Lenore sucked in her breath. The barb hurt. It reminded her of all the times when she'd missed the joke while hanging out with Dixon's friends years ago. Often she'd come to the conclusion that *she* was the punch line. Well, no more.

She counted to ten and then slowly turned to face him.

"Now I know why Marvin Woodbridge wanted us to live

together for a week. It was his revenge. I don't know what I've ever done to you or to Marvin, but I don't have to stand here listening to you call me names. If calling me a cultural snob makes you feel like a big man, go ahead and call me all the names you need to to make you feel strong."

Without looking at him, she glanced around the kitchen to make sure everything was put away. Then she dried her hands.

"Where are you going?"

"I told you the other day. This has been a mistake. I'm tired of arguing with you. I'm tired of forgiving you just so you can turn around and fling things in my face. I'm tired of the stupid premise of this entire week. You can't make amends. Sometimes it's just too late to try to fix the past. You want to know where I'm going: Lenore Foxwood is going home where she belongs."

When she marched out of the room and toward her bedroom, Dixon realized she was serious. He stood there for a moment, trying to figure out when the conversation had taken a turn for the worst. One minute he'd been sitting there copping feels and getting busy. The next minute she was screaming at him about rap.

Dixon grinned. An angry Lenore was a glorious sight. He'd gotten even more turned on by that, by the passion that ran so deep in her. He well remembered how wild she could be in his arms.

Dixon looked at the dishes, then figured he'd better give her a minute to cool off. With nothing else to do, he washed up the dishes, rinsed them and then went to Lenore.

In the guest bedroom, she meticulously folded clothing, creating small piles around her suitcase. Dixon smiled. She probably used pink tissue paper between the layers. His idea of packing for a trip was grabbing a toothbrush and some underwear. Monique and Ashley took care of everything else.

Lenore worked in silence. She didn't even acknowledge

his presence. Not even when he reached a hand out to still hers. She simply paused. When he released her hand, she continued folding.

"Lenore, I hurt your feelings. I'm sorry."

When still she ignored him, Dixon took both her hands in his. Her gaze met his.

"I'm sorry," he repeated. "I didn't mean to pick a fight with you. I've been under a lot of stress this week. This is the place where I come for refuge. You're like the only stability I have. I haven't been telling you about a lot of the mess going down simply because when I'm with you I don't want to think about that stuff."

He placed a finger on her chin and lifted her mouth to his. He stopped just short of kissing her. "The only thing that's gotten me through is knowing you were here, knowing that when all the mess I've gotten myself in played out each day, I'd have you here for me."

He let her hand go long enough to push aside her suitcase. Then he sat her on the edge of the bed and perched next to her.

"You called me a cultural snob," she sniffed.

"You are. You always have been."

Lenore smiled. He was right and she knew it. J.D. had all but called her the same thing. Hearing it from Dixon was just so . . . Lenore let the thought go. There was no time for regrets.

"I've taken some heat from the conservatives about this deal with the new group I'm going to produce," Dixon said by way of explanation. "Some people feel their music conflicts with everything I've ever done. I've been trying to explain to these people with no vision that to stay fresh a recording artist has to occasionally venture away from the known. It's the same thing with what I do. When I did a deal with some country music artists, I got flak from people. 'Buster Dixon is abandoning his roots, selling out to crossover,' they all said. But it's not about selling out or crossing over or anything like that. Music is music," he said. "You taught me that."

Lenore looked at him and swallowed the lump in her throat. He'd done it again. He'd made her angry in one breath and then turned around and showed a depth of emotion and sensitivity that made her love him even more. Surely she could trust her heart to a man like Buster Dixon.

She looked in his eyes. What she saw there—desire, contrition, a silent plea—let her know she'd forgive him and keep on loving him. She also realized she needed to tell him the truth.

"Dixon, there's something you need to know."

He took her hands. "Lenore, I already know everything I need to know. I know we can't go back and change the past. I know you still have some reservations about me. I want to show you that I'm a different man now. I've been doing a lot of soul searching lately. What I've found is an emptiness in my soul. You fill that spot."

He was making this so difficult. "Oh, Dixon," she sighed. "You don't understand. I have—"

"No more regrets, Lenore. Let's start over. We can begin with your opinion of rap. Come with me to this show tonight. Listen to the music and then decide if you like it. Give rap a second chance while you give me a second chance."

Unable to bring herself to look at him, Lenore nodded her acquiescence.

A few hours later, Lenore wondered at the fact that she'd let Dixon talk her into this. The long white limousine pulled into the arena entrance. She had second thoughts about agreeing to go to a rap concert. But she wasn't about to let him get away with the charge of being a cultural snob. She would listen and then come to her own conclusion, a conclusion she had no doubt would bolster her already poor opinion of the music.

Lenore could hear the mob outside. Dixon looked at

her, grinned and squeezed her hand. He planted a quick kiss on her lips.

"You look fabulous," he said.

Lenore glanced down at her lap, her right thigh exposed from the deep split in the gold sequined evening gown. "I don't know about this dress. Kim—"

"Kim knows how to show off your best assets. And those assets . . ."

"Watch it, now."

He grinned.

Lenore cast a worried glance out the window. "There are so many people. I thought you said we were coming in a quiet way."

Dixon followed her gaze out the darkly tinted windows. "This is the quiet VIP entrance. Had we gone around front, it would have been a real zoo. This is nothing, just the fans who figured out which entrance the groups would use." The car came to a stop. "Ready?"

She nodded and he squeezed her hand again.

"It'll be fun," he assured her. "And I'll prove to you that rap is just like any other musical art form."

A moment later the door opened, and Lenore was assaulted by the noise and the camera flashes going off in her face. She lifted one long, shapely leg out of the car and was offered assistance by the chauffeur. Dixon was beside her seconds later.

The crowd went wild when they recognized him. "Buster! Bus-ter!"

Dixon wrapped a protective arm about Lenore's waist as fans thrust paper at him for autographs and microphones were pushed into his face. He released Lenore long enough to smile for a few pictures and sign some autographs for adoring fans, even while reporters shouted questions at him. Then he took her hand again.

"Buster Dixon, tell us about the charges."

"Are you still going to work with E.P. Nasty?"

"Who's the pretty lady, Buster?"

"I love you, Buster!" a woman yelled out as lacy panties sailed through the air toward Dixon. Lenore's eyes widened. Dixon smiled and waved in the general direction from which the gift had come. A photographer caught the panties and stuffed them in a pocket. Dixon grinned.

And then to the reporter who'd asked about his lady, "That's for me to know, and you to find out."

Clasping Lenore's hand in his, he led her to the doors guarded by security officers. The reporters followed. Fans and professional photographers alike continued to snap pictures.

"Come on, Buster, give us a clue," the writer persisted.

Dixon wagged a finger at the entertainment reporter and pulled Lenore closer to him, a hand wrapped about her slim waist. He kissed her cheek, and then with Lenore, ducked into the arena.

Backstage it was just like old times. Lenore smiled when he introduced her around. Everyone knew Buster Dixon. To some degree she felt like she did when they were in college: like pretty window dressing, all form and no substance. And just like in those days, Dixon never let her out of his sight. Any man who got too close or showed too much interest got a cold look. Since no one obviously wanted to be on Buster D's bad side, the men backed down.

Dixon managed to come off as both overly possessive and attentive. But Lenore knew he was just doing business. There was always a deal to be done, a "thing" to be worked out. A female on his arm simply remained part of the package, one of the fringe benefits of doing business.

Someone pressed a glass of champagne into her hands. Remembering her chardonnay night, Lenore placed the glass on the nearest tray.

As they eventually made their way to their seats in the front row of the arena, Lenore watched as Dixon worked the crowd. Then in a relatively quiet moment, "You can't possibly know all of these people."

He grinned. "Not even close. A lot of the folks backstage where Whitney wannabe's and brothers who think they're the next Boyz II Men."

"And this nasty group of yours?"

He smiled. "Well, they may be."

"Do they sound like Run Dempsey and Cool O?"

Dixon looked at her and laughed out loud. People nearby smiled at his exuberance. He hugged her close, then helped her into her seat. "That's Run DMC and Coolio."

Lenore rolled her eyes. "Whatever."

Before he could say anything else, a shirtless announcer with gold teeth and black combat boots took the stage. For the next hour, Lenore's eardrums protested, and the English teacher in her cringed every time the language was butchered. Her ears burned at the profanity that spewed forth from two of the acts.

E.P. Nasty, the group Dixon had come to see, performed. To Lenore, they sounded like all the others, minus the profane language. Lenore couldn't understand a single word. But the audience ate it up. They hollered back, chanted, whooped it up and jumped in the aisles.

After the next act, the announcer came back on stage. He'd at least covered his chest with a leather vest this time.

"Yo, yo, you. Listen up. I got some bad news."

Grumbling and grousing started up in the arena.

"If ya'll hold it down, I'll tell you whazzup."

Lenore got the gist of the news. The headlining rap act would not be performing, something about strip searches at the airport and confiscated equipment.

The murmuring of the crowd turned ugly, and people who had been dancing in the aisles minutes before surged forward.

Dixon leaned over to her. "Let's bust a move."

Lenore wasn't sure what that meant, but it sounded like "let's get out of here" to her. She nodded and took his hand.

As she started to rise from her seat, sequins on her gown caught on the chair. She turned to free the snag as people around her started to chant a demand for refunds.

"What's wrong?" Dixon asked.

"My dress." She glanced at the angry faces of the people behind and around them and tugged on her dress.

Someone rushing the stage pushed in front of them and shoved a hand in Lenore's face. "Get outta my way. I want my money back."

"Yeah, we want a refund."

"Watch it, buddy," Lenore fired at the man. She took a fistful of the dress and yanked. The fabric ripped, but then Dixon was yelling for her and frantically looking about for his bodyguards. When Lenore looked around, Dixon was nowhere in sight.

He whirled around in time to see Lenore stumble. She saw him and reached for him, but he wasn't fast enough. She went down and he lost her.

Fighting mad at being pushed to the floor, Lenore came up swinging. Her fist connected with skin.

"Hey, what the f—"

In seconds a fight erupted all around them. The person Lenore hit thought he'd been hit from someone behind him. He swung a right hook out and connected with an unintended victim who fought back.

Then a gunshot rang out in the arena.

The place went completely wild.

The announcer dived to the floor of the stage for cover. Screams and shouts filled the air. Concertgoers scrambled over the seats, trying to head for safety.

The arena's emergency siren system started up with an automated repetitive voice telling people; "Walk—do not run—to the nearest exit," while the announcer could be heard above it all, screaming in a microphone for somebody to call the police.

Dixon whirled about, trying to find Lenore, to spot the

gold dress she wore. Someone grabbed his wrist, and he breathed a sigh of relief in the pandemonium.

"Lenore."

The stampede for the doors completely jammed the area all around Dixon and Lenore. With all his might, Dixon held on to her as he fought to get them to the exits.

And then she was yanked from his arms.

Chapter 20

In numb shock Lenore watched as the officer pressed her fingers into the ink and rolled the imprint of her fingerprints onto the page. Then eyes wide and disbelieving, she stared and blinked as the bright light of the flash went off.

"Turn to your right, ma'am."

Stumbling, Lenore turned to her left.

"Your other right," the voice snickered.

Lenore looked up at the voice, then blinked and turned, this time following the directions.

"There's been some mistake," she mumbled.

"No talking, please. Follow me."

Lenore hop-limped after the police officer. At some point she'd lost her right shoe. Maybe it had been at the arena, maybe when she'd been pushed, along with the surging crowd, into the waiting arms of police officers and the paddy wagon. Pausing now, she reached down, unstrapped the ties of the remaining gold sandal, and then carrying the shoe in one limp hand, resumed walking behind the man.

She gulped back the hysteria that threatened to consume her. So much for Dixon's calm assurances about rap.

Surely this madness was but a dream. Surely any minute now her alarm clock would go off, and she'd awaken in her very own pink floral coordinated bedroom in Ohio. At worst she'd awaken in Dixon's bed, her body nestled against his hard one.

But the cacophony of sound around her told another story. Three menacing teenagers shoved and cussed at each other as two uniformed officers held them apart. A man to her left in the room, his voice rising above the others, yelled profanities at a harried-looking clerk.

"I just want my money back," another voice boomed. "I paid thirty-two fifty each for those tickets, and I ain't leaving this damned place till somebody gives me my money!"

Lenore passed by an Hispanic woman who herself cried as she comforted a crying baby. Lenore could pick up snatches of the fractured Spanish as she walked by.

". . . last two hundred dollars . . . arrest him . . . how will I feed my baby?"

Lenore closed her eyes to the sights, but the sounds still assaulted her. Ringing telephones, shouts, broken English, misery. All around her people seemed to be yelling. They demanded attorneys, threatened to sue, screamed about police brutality.

"I don't know nothing 'bout no stolen CD players. I was just walking down the street minding my own bizness."

"What do you mean there's nothing that can be done? I bought that car last week. I haven't even made the first payment on it."

"That bitch can't just slice me and get away with it!"

Lenore shuddered.

Her eyes snapped open when she walked into the back of the police officer.

"Watch it," he warned.

The officer led her to a cage filled with about fifteen

women. Her guide opened the door and stepped aside for her to enter.

Lenore, in her stocking feet and holding a gold shoe, stood stock still, rooted to the spot.

"Get a move on, lady. We don't have all night."

Feet cemented to the floor, Lenore didn't move.

She stared at the faces before her. Hostile. Hateful. Curious.

A shove at her back sent Lenore sprawling into the holding pen. She landed on one knee but caught her balance before her face kissed the dirty floor. The barred door clanked shut with a finality that made Lenore cry out.

"Ooh, chile, look at that dress. Where you boost that, beauty queen?"

"Did you lose your tiara, Miss America?"

"What 'appened to yer other shoe, luv? That a new thing the gents like?"

Laughter crackled around the cell. Lenore glanced up, then closed her eyes. It couldn't be. This just couldn't be happening to her.

"Ya'll leave her alone. Look like she scared, and you all ain't helping none."

Surprisingly soft hands helped her rise from the floor. Unaware that silent tears streamed down her face, Lenore stared at her rescuer.

"Thank you," she murmured. Then she took in the woman who addressed her. Orange short shorts with a green fringed bra were all that covered the woman. Cheap gold earrings dangled from her ears, and matching orange and green thick-heeled platform shoes adorned the woman's large feet.

Steady on her own feet now, Lenore clutched her shoe to her chest and surveyed the rest of the room.

"What you in for, honey?" the orange and green lady asked.

"I . . ." Lenore faltered. Any minute now this nightmare

would end. Surely she wasn't in jail, calmly talking to someone who looked a whole lot like a prostitute.

Lenore looked around the cage. A smiling face here, an encouraging one there, an openly hostile one there. She stepped backward a pace. No, she wasn't standing in jail talking to a prostitute. She was standing in jail with a cell full of them!

Lenore swayed on her feet.

"Make way."

Moments later Lenore was sitting on the edge of a hard wood bench, her head between her knees.

"Breathe deep," a voice said. "You don't need to be passing out in here. You could be bleeding to death, and they wouldn't get a doctor."

Lenore looked up into the kind eyes of the woman in orange and green. The woman pressed a tiny paper cup into Lenore's hand.

"Drink the water, honey. It's about the only thing fresh and cool you're gonna find in this place."

Lenore dubiously eyed the cone-shaped cup, but she sipped from the rim, found the liquid to be clear, cool water and downed the remaining contents.

"Welcome to paradise," the orange and green woman said. "My name's Rachel."

"Don' know why you being so nice to Miss America, Rach. She ain't one of our kind. Look at her. Bet she a uptown girl. One of them by-appointment-only ones that have stock portfolios and 'booking agents.' Lemme see them earrings she wearing."

Another woman reached for Lenore's hair. "Who does your head? Is that a weave?"

Lenore shrank back on the bench. Fear and panic glazed her eyes. "Please don't hurt me. I've done nothing wrong."

Laughter rippled through some of the crowd.

"Didn't I tell ya'll to leave her alone?" Rachel said.

"You gots the right of it," a woman in a lavender jumpsuit said. "When they take you, just keep saying that, and you'll be fine."

"But I haven't—"

Rachel shook her head. "Don't worry about it, honey. I'm sure your man'll come get you soon. He know you got snatched? We here waiting for Elroy. That sorry SOB probably off looking at a basketball game while we in here losing bizness. What you call yourself?"

"Lenore. My name's Lenore."

Rachel nodded. She then turned and introduced Lenore to some of the other women in the holding cell: Kim, Sunni, Daphne, Anatasia, Tyee, Gloria. Clio, Calliope, Thalia, Terpsichore.

Lenore blinked. "Muses?"

Rachel let loose with a deep infectious laugh. "Go on with your bad self, sistagirl! Not a lot of people figure that out. Elroy was reading some book and decided some of us should be goddesses. The Zeus girls even have an act."

"Oh, God," Lenore moaned. She closed her eyes and counted to ten, hoping that when she opened her eyes again, she'd be home in Ohio.

She slowly peeked out of one eye. Rachel and the daughters of Zeus were still there. Before she could ask another question, a commotion outside the cage caught everyone's attention.

Cussing and scrappling in the hall came more officers and more women.

Cops rustled another ten females into the cage. This group was loud, rude and pissed off. Lenore thought she recognized one of them from the concert.

"This shit don't make no kinda sense!"

"All we was doing was listening to a show, and some fool gon' go and shoot off a gun."

"Get me out of here. I am not a criminal!"

Lenore's own sentiments echoed that outraged woman's. She scooted down on the bench to let others take a seat.

Someone in a corner began playing cards with another prisoner. Rachel lit up a cigarette. "What happened to you?"

Lenore looked up at the prostitute and decided she wanted to be an equal standing with the woman. Lenore stood, her spot on the bench quickly replaced.

"I was at a concert with a friend. My dress caught on the seat. There was some announcement. And then shots were fired. The next thing I know, I'm here."

Rachel exhaled smoke over her shoulder, straight into the face of a wretched-looking woman. "Don't even think about it, Betty," she said without turning around.

Lenore watched the woman named Betty sneer and then turn away.

"Eleven of us be Elroy's girls. We were working a party that got busted. Betty, she's a regular in here. A drunk," Rachel added by explanation. "Don't know these other divas. You must be with the group they just hustled in."

"No. I'm just . . . I'm by myself."

Rachel nodded knowingly.

"Really," Lenore said. "I'm not a . . ." she floundered.

"Hooker, honey. It's okay to say it. That's how I make a living. Been at it a while. Know how to take care of myself. This here thing is a pain though," she said, waving her hand around the jail cell. Lenore watched cigarette ashes fall to the floor. "This is a time waster. I could be working."

Lenore had nothing to add to the conversation.

"Where'd you get that dress? That outfit is hitting."

Lenore glanced down at the gold dress. No wonder the girls picked on her. She probably did look like a beauty pageant contestant. The expense of the gold gown, even while ripped and torn in two places, couldn't be masked.

"A friend designed it for me." A thought struck Lenore. "Did you already know about the muses from Greek mythology. Before Elroy's book, I mean."

Rachel laughed. "Ain't always been a whore."

Lenore cringed at the word. But Rachel continued.

"There was a time, long time ago, when I had dreams. Came out to California to make a name for myself. Wanted to be in pictures. Even had a little college before I got out here."

When Rachel didn't volunteer any additional information, Lenore probed. "What happened?"

Rachel shook her head. "Life happened, honey."

For a while the two women were quiet. Then Rachel sauntered off to break up a scuffle between one of the concertgoers and one of the hookers. Lenore slumped against the wall.

Rachel checked on her off and on, and the two women talked again. It seemed like hours passed before there was another commotion in the hallway. Two uniformed officers, two men in suits and Dixon converged on the cage.

"Get her out of there this minute!" Dixon roared.

"Calm down, Buster. We're on it," one of the suits said.

"Buster Dixon! Look ya'll. It's Buster Dixon."

The women crowded the front of the cage, waving, blowing kisses, asking for autographs.

Dixon ignored them all. He scanned the faces, looking for the only one that mattered.

And then he saw her.

Relief surged through him.

"Hurry up and open that damn thing," he barked at the cop.

"Mr. Dixon, please do not harass my officers."

Dixon ignored the police captain and dashed into the cage when the door sprang open. The women, still calling out to him, opened a path from Dixon to Lenore.

She stood against the back wall of the holding cell. She hadn't moved an inch. She didn't even acknowledge his presence.

"Lenore?"

She ignored him.

Lenore looked beyond Dixon. "Are you my attorney?" she asked the man in the blue double-breasted suit.

"Yes, Dr. Foxwood. I'm sorry for the delay in getting to you—"

Lenore cut him off. "Rachel, how much is your bail?"

Dixon reached for her. "Lenore."

She stepped aside. "This is all your fault," she hissed at him, not bothering to lower her voice. "Whatever trifling explanations you have, you can save them for a time when I don't feel like killing you."

"Wooo," a couple of the women in the cage said, even as others backed up a few steps.

"How much is your bail, Rachel?" Lenore asked again.

Rachel the prostitute looked from Lenore to Dixon to the lawyer, then at the cops and back to Lenore.

"The same as usual I reckon," she finally answered.

Lenore walked down the path created by the women. She stepped out of the cell. "Get her out, too," she told the attorney.

He glanced at Dixon.

"Lenore!"

"Dr. Foxwood, I don't think . . ." began the other suit, the police captain.

Lenore stepped back into the cell and bumped into Dixon. He steadied her, but she jerked out of his embrace. "Either Rachel gets out, too, or I stay."

"For God's sake, Lenore. I have enough problems as it is without you adding some—"

Lenore's glacial glare defied Dixon to say anything derogatory about the woman with the lace green bra and fringe.

Dixon threw up his hands in defeat. "Jackson?"

"Done," the attorney said, pulling out a flip phone and making a call.

"If you'll come this way, please, ma'am," one of the uniforms told Lenore.

Lenore turned back to the women in the holding cell.

Her gaze met Rachel's. "Pen and paper," Lenore demanded over her shoulder.

A cop quickly supplied the requested items. Lenore jotted her name and telephone number on the paper and handed it to Rachel.

"If you ever decide that you want to pursue those early dreams or maybe chase some new ones, call me. Okay?"

Rachel nodded.

With nothing left to say, Lenore, in her stocking feet and holding one gold shoe, was escorted away. She walked with the dignity of a goddess, her head held high, her back straight.

The moment they emerged from the police station, a flash went off. Dixon lunged for the photographer. Police and Dixon's own bodyguards held him back, handled the photographer and hustled Dixon and Lenore into the waiting car.

A few minutes later, safely ensconced in Dixon's limousine, all the rage, the anger, the fear and the hurt erupted.

Lenore threw her gold shoe at Dixon's head.

Chapter 21

"Owww! Dammit, what'd you do that for?"

The high heel of the shoe glanced off Dixon's temple. He tossed the weapon out of Lenore's reach, then turned to her.

Her nostrils flared with fury. That was the only warning he got before Lenore was all over him, kicking, scratching and pounding at his chest.

He took every blow, deflecting the ones that may have done real damage. The lack of fight in him seemed to infuriate her all the more.

"How could you leave me like that? You let them drag me away like I was a criminal. Jail! They put me in jail!" She clawed at him and punched him until her tears and her anger became one seething mass.

When she ripped at his collar, Dixon lost his own temper. The gnawing fear that had ripped at his insides for the last three hours exploded. One minute he'd had her safe in his arms, and the next she was gone, swept away in a crowd panicked by the gunfire in the arena.

"If you hadn't gone at the guy like Mike Tyson, I'd have been able to hold on to you.

"How dare you blame me!" she raged.

Angry at himself for exposing her to danger, and doubly PO'd with her for disrespecting him at the jailhouse, Dixon fought back, his verbal weapons stronger than her fists.

"You were standing there, looking like you belonged with the rest of those streetwalkers. Did your girlfriend Rachel give you some tips on how to treat a man who takes care of you? Is this how she taught you to express your gratitude?"

Lenore's sputter of outrage coalesced with rage. She made to slap him, but Dixon caught her wrist.

"Let go of me," she said, while wresting her arm from his grip. He let go, then without another word she turned to the door and tried to yank it open it and escape. Dixon lunged for her, trapping her beneath his large body.

"Is anything wrong, Mr. D?" The voice of the chauffeur came at him.

"Keep driving and mind your own damn business."

Lenore struggled under him. Dixon breathed in the scent of her—her still seething anger, the lingering fear in him that she'd been injured in the fight, his own pulsing guilt over exposing her to danger in the first place. The only thing that registered in his mind was that she was safe in his arms again.

His body hardened, his mouth closed over hers.

Lenore fought and kicked until he let up.

"Don't ever touch me again. I hate you."

Dixon wiped his mouth. "Well, I'm finally starting to believe it."

"Let me out."

"We're in the middle of the freeway."

"I'll walk."

Weary now, "Lenore, be reasonable."

"Reasonable!" she screeched. "Reasonable? Let me tell you about reasonable. You drag me to some concert run by hoodlums. You subject me to hours of blasting, unintelligible so-called 'music.' You stand by and do nothing, *nothing!*, while I'm yanked and pulled and fingerprinted and arrested like some common criminal.''

Her voice rose with every charge against him and ended in a shrill screech that made Dixon wince.

''So just shoot me and get it over with,'' he said sarcastically.

''Where's the gun?''

Dixon eyed her. Unfortunately she didn't look like she was joking. If she had a weapon right now, she probably would shoot him.

The interior of the limo seethed with suppressed fury on both of their parts the rest of the long ride home.

Lenore hopped out of the car before it came to a complete stop in front of the house. Barefoot she stomped to the door and then had to wait for Dixon to arrive with the key. Once inside she went straight to her room.

Without a care for wrinkles or expensive fabric, she jammed the rest of her clothing and toiletries into her bags. Yanking open the bottom bureau drawer, she scooped up the few things there and dumped them into a bag. She grabbed her leather briefcase and brushed by Dixon, who stood in the doorway quietly watching her.

In the kitchen Lenore called for a cab.

''That's not necessary. The car can take you.''

She glared at him. ''I'd rather walk from here to Ohio.''

Unmindful and uncaring of the fact that he followed her, Lenore went back to the bedroom, wiggled out of the form-fitting golden gown and slipped on a pair of jeans, a white top with a lacy collar and a brown sweater. A pair of flat loafers went on her feet.

The expensive designer original gown lay puddled in a golden shimmering heap on the floor. Dixon eyed the gown and then turned to follow Lenore.

''Why won't you talk to me? I know you're mad. I'm

mad, too. The guards never should have let you out of their sight. I fired them both."

Lenore glared at him. "Leave me alone."

He'd prefer that she rage at him. He couldn't stand the silent treatment. Frustrated and angry at both himself and Lenore, Dixon cussed a blue streak.

She looked at him as if he were a specimen in a petri dish. "Does profanity make you feel like a man? Is that why the groups you produce use so much of it?"

With that comment Lenore stepped on Dixon's last nerve.

Had she been Sarge or a man, he'd have busted her mouth open. If he'd been the type to hit a woman, she'd have gotten slapped.

Instead he grabbed a pack of cigarettes and stormed out of the house.

At the airport Lenore booked herself on the first flight home. Then she called her sister.

"Erica, I'm coming home early. My flight will land . . ." She glanced at the ticket in her hand and gave her sister the information. "Is J.D. there?"

"Yeah, just a sec. You okay, Lenore? You sound horrible."

"I'm fine. Let me speak to J.D."

A moment later his deep voice came on the line. "Hey, Mom. Aunt Erica said you're coming home early. Did you get to see any stars?"

At the sound of her son's voice, Dixon's voice, Lenore started crying.

"Mom, what's wrong? What happened?"

Lenore couldn't believe how much he sounded like his father. How was she ever going to explain this mess to J.D.? He deserved to know his father. He needed a man's direction and guidance in his life. Simon had resented his presence and made no attempts to be a father to J.D.

The arguments she and J.D. had about his music, his hair, his propensity to want to party instead of study were all nothing when stacked against what she had to tell her son. She had to tell him about his father. If he found out some other way, she'd never forgive herself.

Lenore was already trying to come to grips with Marvin Woodbridge's vindictiveness. She'd told Marvin she was pregnant and needed to talk to Billy Dixon. But Marvin had smiled in her face and stabbed her in the back. He'd known up until the day he died that Dixon had a son. But he'd never said a word to him. Now Lenore was left to pick up the pieces.

"Hey, Mom?"

"I'm here, Jason," she answered. "Listen, when I get home, we need to talk, okay?"

J.D. sighed. "Mom, why are you still hassling me about—"

"J.D., let's not argue now. I'll be home soon. We can talk then. I love you, baby."

He mumbled something incomprehensible, and Lenore smiled. She wiped her eyes. "Put your aunt back on the line."

A little while later, Lenore was in her seat on the plane. She cried the first hour of the trip. By the second hour and the flight attendant's concern, she'd gotten herself together enough to drink a cup of tea.

From her carry-on bag, she pulled out the papers she should have been grading during the week instead of hanging around playing house with Buster Dixon. When she dug in the bag for a red inkpen to mark the papers, her hand brushed the slim volume of her journal.

Pulling the book out of the bag, she stared at it. William DuBois Dixon had busted every romantic notion she'd ever had. She wondered how and why she'd wasted so much of her life thinking about him, loving him.

"Well, you're definitely not in love now."

Lenore pushed the journal aside on the tray table and reached for her students' papers. She read through the second one when she conceded defeat. Her attention wasn't on seventeenth-century poets but on Billy Dixon.

Capping the red pen, she opened the journal to a back page. There she found yet another draft of a letter to the boy she'd fallen in love with. She didn't know why she'd loved him. As college students they had little in common. As adults they shared a passion that couldn't be quenched and a fifteen-year-old son with musical gifts like his father.

Lenore sighed but she read the letter. And her eyes widened in surprise and then mounting fury as she read the too familiar words. Once before she thought something sounded familiar. Now she knew why. She flipped forward several pages, looking for her draft letters to Billy Dixon. Almost an hour later, she sat seething, sore and stiff from not moving a single muscle the entire time. She sat there stunned at her own naive stupidity and angry beyond belief at how Dixon had used her.

It had all been a lie. One big lie. Even now he was probably laughing his head off at her gullibility.

Lenore slumped in her seat. Tears blinded her vision just like love had once blinded her to Dixon's deceit.

Dixon sat in the empty penthouse apartment. His world had completely collapsed in on him. He had no career, no hope, no Lenore. Nothing to live for.

His fingers curled around the neck of the expensive burgundy. Disgusted, he put the bottle on the table. He didn't even know how to get down and dirty sloppy drunk anymore. He wasn't down with the homeboys. He was persona non grata in the industry. Even Sarge had stopped returning his calls.

Buster Dixon had come to the end of the road.

It had been a week since The Night. A week since his heart had been ripped from his body, since he'd stormed out of his daddy's house and away from Lenore. He hadn't been the least bit surprised to find her gone when he'd returned with a willing groupie, a woman who knew her place and wouldn't try to scratch his eyes out. *Even if you deserve it,* the voice of reason taunted.

Disgusted with himself, and surrounded by sweet memories of Lenore, Dixon gave the woman a large sum of money, some CDs, an autographed eight-by-ten glossy of himself and sent her on her way.

He'd then walked from his father's house and didn't look back. When he got home, Monique had been there to soothe him. That, however, didn't last long, and he sent her on her way, too. He didn't want Monique. He wanted—and couldn't have—Lenore.

Now he stared at the music scattered about on the floor near the white grand piano. Music had been pouring from him nonstop, but it was too little, too late. He should have just told her. With the look in her eyes and the softness of her resting against him, he should have told her. Before the concert. Before he'd made a mess of things. But now it was too late to make things right between them. He'd literally pounded "Storm of Passion" out of the keys. The song, like Dixon, reflected anger, hurt and passion. The composition was thunder and lightning in a lashing night storm.

But the anger was gone now. All that remained was a hollow loneliness he couldn't drown in a bottle of liquor, a loneliness that wouldn't be soothed in some other woman's arms.

He pushed himself up from the sofa, now stained with spilled liquor and cigarette ash. Dixon stumbled to the piano bench, kicking his way through the tumble of sheet music.

Pressing PLAY on the small recorder atop the piano, he positioned his hands over the keys.

First softly, then with growing power, he played. He played of regret and sorrow; of love, time, healing, tenderness. His fingers embraced the keys the way his heart embraced Lenore.

The music rang through him, for him, for what was and what would never be. The music was beginning, middle and end, alpha and omega.

Passion and tears poured from him, and still he played. On and on. Over and over. Until finally, spent, the sweet melody gently faded in the still apartment.

Dixon stared unseeing at the black and white keys of the piano. Then, folding his arms over the keyboard, he wept.

A long time later, he remembered the tape in the recorder. It had long since played out. Dixon extended a hand to press the REWIND button. But there was no need. The song was etched on his memory and in his heart as surely as his DNA, as surely as the love he'd found and lost with Lenore.

He reached for his mechanical pencil and paper. On blank pages he wrote the notes, he added the parts for violins, harp and percussion. In the now quiet penthouse, he listened to the music in his head and scored the greatest piece he'd ever composed. And when he was done, he stared at page upon page of sheet music. On the first page at the top center, he wrote the title of the composition: "Rhapsody." Then he labeled the tape, "Rhapsody for Lenore."

Chapter 22

Lenore's life resumed its normal dull pace. She taught classes, talked with and counseled her students, graded papers and cried herself to sleep every night. She'd convinced herself that J.D. didn't need to know about Buster Dixon, even though his very name reminded her of her son's father: Jason Dixon Foxwood. She'd chosen the name for her newborn son while she was still in love with his absent father.

Tears welled up in her eyes. Fifteen years later she was *still* in love with him, a man who callously hurt her and who'd robbed her of the one thing she'd still held dear: sweet memories.

The voice of challenge, reason and perspective that her colleagues and students had come to enjoy and expect was no more. J.D.'s voice alone was enough to make her cry.

She willed her heart to stop breaking, but in the time she'd been home, the ache had become as much a part of her as the circles under her eyes. She tried to forget him, she tried to concentrate on the betrayal she'd discovered in the pages of her journal. She tried to focus on his lies, on jail, but her stubborn heart gave her no peace.

Just yesterday she'd gotten a notice in her mailbox about a registered letter. Her heart soared at the possibility. He'd written! But when she retrieved the envelope from the post office, her hopes were yet again dashed. The envelope contained a letter from attorney Gilbert Hobbs and a cashier's check for two hundred fifty thousand dollars.

Standing in the post office, she'd read the letter: "With regret I must inform you that in not completing the stipulations of my client's last will and testament, you forfeit all claim and right to the one million dollars . . . It gives me great pleasure, however, to present you with the enclosed check in the sum of a quarter million dollars to be used at your discretion. Humbly yours . . ."

Not caring and with nothing to do with the money, Lenore, at the astonishment of the teller at the bank's drive-through, deposited the entire amount into her savings account. The money sat in her account like a cold weight on her heart.

Weeks had now passed since the night she'd been arrested in California. The charges, according to a letter from Dixon's attorney accompanied by a written apology from the chief of police, had all been dropped and her name cleared.

And still not a word from Dixon.

While she'd not heard *from* him, she definitely heard *about* him. With a morbid fascination she could neither control or fathom, Lenore soaked up all she could about Dixon. She sat glued before her television, watching him on entertainment programs and the BET network, even on Leno. He answered questions, made assurances about his fate, signed the E.P. Nasty group to his record label. And always, always, he appeared in the company of a beautiful woman.

Lenore's heart ached when she recognized Monique in some of those television interviews. But there was nothing she could or would do about it. Buster Dixon had shown just how much he cared about her when he let her get assaulted, when he shortchanged her feelings, when he betrayed her trust.

In the midst of it all, Kim sent a long letter with a shipment of funky dresses and outfits. The gift was supposed to lift her spirits and cheer her up. But all the clothes served to do was remind Lenore of how far apart her world was from Buster Dixon's. She stuffed the labor of her college roommate's work to the back of her closet. She had no reason to get dressed up. She had no one to dress up for and no reason to wear the flash and dash, tease-me creations that were Kim's signature.

Lenore had, however, engaged in a pity party to beat them all. Triple chocolate ice cream and every CD or cassette ever recorded by William "Buster" Dixon had been her conflicting solace.

She ate ice cream until she was sick, then watched the rest melt in a puddle in a large bowl. She listened to Dixon's tender love songs until she cried, then every night, she hugged a pillow until she fell into a fitful sleep.

And now, now she sat at the desk in her office, ostensibly preparing lecture notes for her next day's class. Lenore jumped when the telephone rang. She blinked back the tears that these days hovered at her eyes just about every waking moment.

She sniffled, wiped her eyes with a tissue and reached for the receiver. "English Department. This is Dr. Foxwood."

"Dr. Foxwood, this is Miss Engles. Dean Altimack would like to see you in his office."

Lenore flipped her appointment book to the next day's page. "I have an open time tomorrow afternoon. Will that be soon enough?"

"The dean would like to see you immediately, Dr. Foxwood. As in now."

"Oh," she said, surprised. "All right. I'll be there in a few minutes."

She replaced the receiver, dried her eyes and pulled out a small makeup kit from her purse. Lenore touched up her lipstick, smoothed her hair back, the thick waves securely bound in a neat bun at the back of her head.

Her sensible one-and-one-half-inch-heeled black pumps were a perfect accompaniment to the navy skirt and the black with navy trim sweater she wore. A neat little bow at the neck of her navy blouse offered a smidgen of feminine relief to the austere clothing.

Lenore felt comfortable.

From a file cabinet, she pulled the folder of notes on the faculty committee on academic regalia. Since she chaired the group, maybe the dean wanted an update on the choices the committee selected for students' new graduation caps and gowns.

With a purpose in her step that had been missing the last few weeks, Lenore made her way to Dean Altimack's office. She was immediately shown into his book-lined office.

"Have a seat, Dr. Foxwood."

Lenore sat. The portly dean paced the area between his desk and a bottled water cooler.

"How long have you been on the faculty here, Dr. Foxwood?"

Lenore frowned. He knew the answer to that question; he'd hired her. "Two and one half years, Dr. Altimack."

"And in that time, Dr. Foxwood, would you say that you have come to a full understanding of the way we govern ourselves here at the college?"

"Yes, but I—"

"And would you say, Dr. Foxwood, that you personally ascribe to the policies set forth by the university for faculty, staff and students?"

Confused now, she said, "Yes, I do. Of course."

The dean stopped pacing. He looked over the rim of his half-glasses and peered at Lenore. She tried not to squirm.

"What is it, sir?"

A sound, a cross between a huff and a sigh, escaped him. "You, it seems, are a contradiction in terms, professor. You do aspire to full professorship, am I correct?"

"Yes," she said, not at all sure where this was leading. "I'm on tenure track."

He moved his wide girth behind his desk. "If you believe in and abide by the policies set forth by this institution, and you aspire to tenure, would you please, Dr. Foxwood, explain these to me."

Lenore sat up as he pulled items from a large white envelope. The dean spread the newspaper and magazine articles out over the desktop.

STILL WATERS OBVIOUSLY RUN DEEP screamed one headline. In a photo on the left, she was highlighted as "Buster's Bitchin' Babe." She was in a sexy little white number, he in a white-on-white suit. They looked the perfectly coordinated Hollywood glamour couple. Lenore cringed at the sight.

The photograph on the right, called "Nerdsville or Bust," was obviously from the day she escaped from L.A. Her red-rimmed eyes, coupled with the dowdy brown sweater, faded blue jeans and loafers made her look like a completely different person. The article asked readers to determine if the photographs were of the same woman.

If only those two articles had been the worst of it.

She dared a glance up at the dean. His glacial stare proved he was not amused. Lenore sighed and lifted up one article to see the one beneath it.

She wished she hadn't.

DESIGNER'S GAL PAL STRUTS HER STUFF

Someone had taken a photograph of her and Kim at the cafe! The picture looked as if they were in an intimate embrace. Since Lenore's chardonnay-fogged memory couldn't exactly recall the details of that night, the only thing she could figure was that was the moment when Kim was trying to get her in a cab home.

She didn't bother to read the story. What would be the point when a picture in this sort of publication was worth a thousand words—and probably a thousand dollars?

Two other photos in the tabloid paper featured the knockout dress Lenore had worn that night. The gold enhanced her warm brown skin tone. The diamond-shaped hole at her navel teased and enticed, particularly since the photographer had captured her on the dance floor with a man lapping at her navel.

Lenore's shoulders slumped. So that's what Kim meant when she'd said, "I didn't know you had it in you."

With trembling fingers, Lenore moved to the next of the visual case stacked against her.

BUSTER MUM ON NEW LADY LOVE

Lenore audibly groaned. This entertainment magazine was sold at every supermarket and drugstore in the country. She well remembered the night of the rap concert. Flash-bulbs had gone off all around as they'd stepped from the white limousine. Dixon had joked with the reporters about finding out who she was. Unfortunately some had taken him up on the offer. Her background, including the name of the very conservative college where she taught, was there for all the world to see.

Lenore cocked her head and critically eyed the photo. Kim hadn't lied about one thing: She had the legs to do that gold gown justice. Leg practically clear up to her waist was displayed in the albeit flattering photo as she stepped out of the car.

And if those weren't bad enough, there was a picture of her being escorted from jail—her hair a wild tangle, the gold gown ripped and torn, exposing more skin than even Kim had counted on. The police officers looked grim, one even had his hand on his revolver as if she posed a threat! The picture looked like she was being arrested rather than released from jail. The headline said it all though: BUSTER'S BEAUTY BEHIND BARS: PRODUCER BAILS HIS SEXY ESCORT OUT OF JAIL.

Lenore didn't want to even think about the disaster that night had been. Then a more horrific thought occurred to her. She snatched at the papers, looking for the dates they'd been printed. All this week! If her stodgy old dean had this trash already, J.D. was bound to see the stories. She had to get home. She had to tell him. But first . . .

She swallowed hard, lifted her chin and boldly met the dean's piercing gaze.

"I can explain."

In the end though, her explanations weren't sufficient in the eyes of the faculty review board. She was in flagrant violation of the moral turpitude clause of her contract with the college. And they had the damning evidence in living color. In the space of three days, she'd gone from being a respected member of the faculty and a Ph.D. scholar on seventeenth-century literature to the call girl lesbian girlfriend of a fashion designer who also shared her affections with one of the nation's top R&B record producers.

Being kind, the dean had given her a week to clear out of her office. She did it in two days.

The situation with J.D. was going to take longer. The same day she'd gotten fired, he'd come home from school with two of the tabloid newspapers.

With nothing left to lose, she told him everything.

When she finished, J.D. sat with a stunned expression on his face. Lenore watched the conflicting emotions flicker across her son's countenance as she poured out her heart to him: first, his profound embarrassment over his mother shown half naked in a trashy tabloid, then proud that his mom knew Buster Dixon, then shamed that she was being called a slut. Anger followed over her being fired for something that wasn't her fault. Then came the hardest part: telling him that Buster Dixon was his father.

J.D.'s mouth opened, and he stared at her. "I don't believe you," he accused.

Lenore handed him the letter from Marvin Woodbridge.

After reading it, J.D. let the sheets fall to the floor. Without a word, he went to his room. He hadn't come out or talked to her since. But she heard his music: sometimes the keyboard, sometimes his saxophone. The music pierced her soul.

Too weary for tears, Lenore sat outside her son's door and listened as he, like his father, retreated into music in times of stress. Eventually J.D. would want to talk. Right now she understood he needed time to absorb it all.

Lenore could have railed about the injustice of it all. A disastrous five days in the company of Buster Dixon had left her reputation in shreds, her dignity impugned, her academic future in jeopardy and her relationship with her teenage son tottering on a dangerous precipice.

When J.D.'s last notes faded away, Lenore realized she had few options. She called her sister and arranged for J.D. to stay with her. Then too angry to think of the consequences, Lenore did the one thing that made sense in a world gone mad: She packed a bag and got on a plane to confront Buster Dixon.

Chapter 23

Lenore checked in with Kim and dropped her bags at her girlfriend's house.

"Since I'm your 'gal pal,' the least you can do is put me up."

Kim chuckled. "I wondered if you'd seen that trash."

Lenore's smile faded as she related to her friend all that had transpired.

"Oh, my God. What are you going to do?"

"Well, first I have some bones to pick with that so-called record producer and singer Buster Dixon. He's cost me my job and my reputation. And for what? So he could benefit, that's what."

Lenore went to a small bag. She pulled out the evidence against Dixon and played her case before Kim.

A few minutes later, outrage burned in Kim's eyes. "That lowlife scumbag. Of all the nerve."

Lenore put a restraining hand on Kim's shoulder as her friend got herself worked up. "Don't waste your energy on that. I've already been there. Right now I need your help."

"I've got your back, sisterfriend. Name it."

Lenore smiled, a pretty smile but one that spelled trouble of the worst kind for Buster Dixon. She sauntered to Kim's triple-size closet and opened the French doors.

"I need some attitude. It's time for Buster Dixon to meet his match. It's time for that woman who looks like me in those tabloid pictures to fully come out of the closet," she said, stepping into the vast space of Kim's closet.

The beginning of a wicked smile tipped the corners of Kim's mouth. "Well, it's about time. I always knew a wild woman was locked up inside you. And I've been dying to teach you how to bring a man to his knees."

Figuring it unlikely that he'd still be hiding out at his father's small house, Lenore went to the one place she might locate Buster Dixon.

Heads turned when Lenore strutted into the office building. Like a Hollywood diva of old, she ignored every one of them. Kim's houndstooth suit made her feel powerful. The black and white checked design, with a wrap that hung off her shoulder just so, couldn't be worn by just anybody. It highlighted her legs, her hips and the attitude she'd perfected under Kim's tutelage.

Kim had hooked her up with some earrings to match the outfit, a wide-brimmed black hat that any preacher's wife would have killed for and a pair of expensive sunglasses.

"Keep the shades on even inside," Kim had instructed. "Unless you have a point to make."

The security guard at the front desk stumbled to his feet in her presence, his mouth hanging open, even as he assessed her and accurately concluded she was way out of his league.

"I'm here to see Buster Dixon."

The guard, finally and apparently over his momentary

speechlessness, remembered his job. "I'm sorry, ma'am. Unless you have an appointment . . ."

Lenore had a point to make.

With one steady hand, she reached up and pulled the gold-rimmed sunglasses an inch below her eyes. She stared the guard down with attitude that wouldn't take no as an acceptable answer.

"Uh, yes, ma'am. Right away."

When the elevator doors swooshed open, Sarge Watson stood before her, barring her entrance to the floor.

"Well, well, well. Look who's back. Didn't do enough damage the first time, huh?"

For a moment Lenore faltered. Then she straightened her back and walked forward. Watson could either get out of the way or get run over.

At the last possible moment, he stepped aside. Walking at her side, he steered her to an office. Not, Lenore noted, the same room she'd entered before.

Sarge did some hand motion thing that sent a secretary scurrying. Lenore swept into the office and without waiting for an invitation, took a seat in front of a large desk devoid of any paper. As a matter of fact, the only items on the desk were a telephone and something that looked like a rock.

Sarge Watson came to the edge of the desk, propped one powerful thigh on the rim and smirked at her. The chartreuse suit he wore would have looked ridiculous on another man. He pulled it off with attitude just like she was doing.

"Who is your bankroll?" he asked.

Lenore crossed her legs and stared at him through the dark lenses of the sunglasses.

When his gaze finally lifted from her legs, she smiled a cold calculating smile. "Now that I have your attention, where's Buster?"

"That's for me to know and you to find out."

Lenore lifted a hand and pulled off the glasses. "Don't be childish. You need me."

The big man snorted. Then went around the side of his desk and settled into his chair.

"Let's just cut the crap, all right?" she said. "I'm the one who can make things happen. If I so choose," she added. She paused long enough to get his attention. "Make it worth my while."

Sarge stared her down, but Lenore didn't flinch or blink.

What seemed like hours later, but in actuality was just a couple of minutes, he exhaled a long breath. Opening a drawer, he pulled out a piece of paper. From his inside jacket pocket, he pulled a thick black fountain pen. In long, angry strokes he wrote an address and telephone number on the paper and pushed it to the middle of his desk.

Lenore, growing weary of the power struggle, knew she wasn't going to be able to hold up this facade much longer. She looked at the paper, looked at Sarge and raised an eyebrow.

He leaned back in his chair and steepled his fingers.

She leaned back in her chair and put the dark glasses back on.

Long minutes passed as the silent tug-of-war waged.

Finally Sarge sighed.

"You two are probably like oil and water," he said. He reached for the paper, leaned forward and handed it to her. "It doesn't matter anymore anyway. It's all over tomorrow."

"Thank you," she said. Lenore glanced at the address, then tucked the slip into her small handbag. She rose, and Sarge did likewise. "I'll be in touch."

With that she swept from the office.

He'd given her the address but didn't tell her how to get into the apartment. The doorman, like the security guard, bowed to her superior attitude. Or that's what Lenore wanted to believe. More likely, that insufferable Sarge Watson had called ahead and let the security force at Dixon's building know she was coming.

Holding a small black leather bag, Lenore stood in front of Dixon's door, not quite sure what to do now. She could play the ice princess role for only so long. And Dixon was unlikely to be fooled by the performance.

She tried the door and let out a small "oh!" when she found it unlocked.

Lenore pushed the door open and stepped into demolished luxury. Everywhere her gaze landed, there was trash, mostly balled-up paper. She stepped into the room, then bent down and picked up one of the papers. Smoothing it out, she recognized sheet music. The meticulous handwriting with its whole and half notes in pencil she didn't recognize.

"What are you doing here?"

Lenore started at the voice. Dixon!

She looked up and there he was, standing in an arched doorway, glaring at her. A pair of dark baggy pants were hanging off his hips, a dingy white shirt with two buttons covered the rest of him. He looked like a hoodlum. And he looked like heaven. Lenore soaked in the sight of him, then she took a deep breath and recalled her anger. She wasn't going to let him off the hook so easily this time. This time there was too much at stake.

She dropped the paper back into the debris. "I came to have it out with you. You owe me explanations and apologies."

Dixon took a swig from the beer bottle he held. "Stand in line. Take a number."

"You're drunk."

He shook his head. "Unfortunately I'm not. Want a drink?"

"No."

He sauntered forward. "Still Miss Prissy Little Lenore."

He walked across the room until he stood before her. He flicked a hand on the wrap draped over her shoulder. "This something your 'gal pal' made for you? Like that hot little number you wore so some guy could lick your stomach."

Lenore smiled. He sounded jealous. She ignored his taunts. "Why'd you lie to me?"

"I never lied to you."

"Don't play with me, Dixon. I loved you with all my being. All you did was use me. You've been using me for the last fifteen years."

He turned away from her. "I don't know what you're talking about."

"Now look at who's trying to change the subject. Let's see if this jogs your memory."

She opened the small bag she held, went to the piano and placed a CD in the combination cassette/CD player. She pulled her old journal from the bag and opened it to a marked page.

"Dear Billy," she began to read. *"Each day I think of you. Each night I dream of you. The love we shared burns my heart. My love for you is eternal."*

She pressed start and Dixon's rich baritone voice filled the room. "Each day I think of you, each night I dream of you, baby. My love for you burns like an eternal flame. Each day I think of you."

Lenore took the CD out, pulled the tape in the player out and popped in a cassette. Then she turned to another marked page in her journal.

"Dear Billy, I lay awake at night asking myself why you left me, what I did wrong, why my love for you wasn't enough to make you stay. When I wake each morning I hope and pray that this will be the day I hear from you, that this will be the day you call. Or maybe that I'll go to the mailbox and there, waiting for me, will be a letter from you. Where did our love go, Billy? Why did you leave me?"

Angrily Lenore punched the START button on the boombox. A haunting, lovesick melody washed over the room, the intro to the sound a heartbreak. And then his voice.

"When I lay awake at night I ask myself why you left me. What I did wrong. I wonder why my love for you wasn't enough to make you stay, to make you stay. I spend each day hoping and praying that this will be the day I hear from you, hear from you. When I go to my mailbox, will there be a letter waiting for me, from you, baby, only from you. Where did our love go, where did it go? I spend each day hoping and praying this will be the day I hear from you."

Lenore turned the volume down as the refrain of Dixon's soulful crooning continued.

"I have other examples. As a matter of fact," she said, "I have a whole heck of a lot of examples. Would you like to hear your award-winning 'Soul Fire'? I do believe I have the lyrics right here on, let's see," she said, turning pages in her journal, "here we go, June 25, 1982."

When he just stood there, offering no defense, no explanation, she descended on him. She swallowed hard, trying to hold back the tears and the hurt that threatened to overflow.

She'd loved this man with all her heart and soul for more years than she could remember. She'd loved him so long and so deeply that she still had trouble comprehending this betrayal. In letters to him, she'd poured out her heart, her most secret longings and dreams for them. He'd turned around and pilfered her love for his music. A record store found every one of his recordings for her. And there, tucked on just about every album, was at least one song that had come straight from her heart, straight from the early letters she'd written to him. Love songs and love letters, sad songs and sad letters. To add insult to injury, every one of those songs had been a hit.

She'd wasted her life loving this man. And for what— so he could rape her love and her emotions and then profit from her pain.

"I just want to know one thing, Dixon. Why?"

"I told you," he said. "You're my music."

Lenore's brittle laughter filled the room. "Well, that's one thing you didn't lie about. When you told me I was your music, it didn't cross my mind that you meant literally. Most people take inspiration from their lives and transfer it to their art. You just pillage. How many other women did you use like this?"

The cassette moved to the next song. Dixon put his beer bottle down and went to the machine to turn it off.

"What? You don't want to hear the songs I wrote? You don't want to dance to or groove to the words from my heart that you stomped all over?"

"Lenore, I'm sorry."

"Sorry doesn't cut it, Buster. I want to know why."

He sat down on the sofa. "Because I'm not good enough. I've never been good enough."

Chapter 24

Whatever explanation Lenore had been waiting to hear, that wasn't it. "What do you mean?" she asked as she settled on the piano bench. She crossed her legs and waited.

The man before her was a total stranger. The Dixon she'd known in college had been full of fun, creativity and energy. The man before her now wore dejection and defeat like a shroud. He looked like he hadn't slept in the weeks since she'd last seen him. Then she amended that thought; he looked as if he'd slept in those pants and that shirt every night.

But she knew that hadn't been the case. With her own eyes, she'd seen him on television, looking fit, jovial and well loved by the parade of women on his arm. He looked anything but fit and healthy now.

He reached for a crushed pack of cigarettes on the coffee table. Cigarette butts and ashes in overflowing trays littered the room.

Lenore didn't say anything when he lit the cigarette, took a deep drag then stared at the floor. Though she willed him to look at her, to explain in his eyes and his soul the nasty things he'd done, his gaze never met hers.

He remained silent for so long, Lenore thought he'd fallen asleep. Then he leaned his head back and stared at the ceiling.

"I never meant to hurt you," he said. "The first time I did it I was missing you so bad. All I had was your memory and your letters."

He lowered his head and looked at her. "Do you know I didn't have a single photograph of you? Not one. These days, everywhere I go people take pictures of me whether I want them to or not. But the one photograph I wanted didn't exist on any photographer's film."

Sitting up, he tapped ashes from the burning cigarette in the general direction of an ashtray on the table. He missed by inches and didn't seem to care.

"Your letters and the sweet memory of you kept me alive and motivated through the hard times. The world and the music business can eat alive the vulnerable, the uninitiated. I didn't want to be a loser. So I scraped and clawed my way to the top."

He got up and walked to one of the large windows in the penthouse. Lenore noticed he was barefoot. And she noticed how beautifully sculpted his feet were. She tried to look at him objectively, to see what the rest of the world saw. It didn't work, though. She couldn't see beyond the man she'd fallen in love with so many years ago.

"It's awfully lonely at the top," he said, staring out the window.

Her eyes, hungry for even this stilted stranger Dixon, took in the rest of him. His strong back couldn't be disguised by the rumpled clothing. His hair, trimmed short, still had the small waves she liked so much. He smoked the cigarette like a man who'd long ago stopped getting enjoyment from tobacco.

"One night I was sitting in my little apartment, trying to come up with some music. I was dry, had been for a while. Sometimes it's there. Sometimes it isn't. In those days, back in the beginning, it mostly wasn't. I was writing jingles for commercials, trying to pay the rent. And I turned to your letters for comfort. I guess some part of me figured if there was someone out there who loved me that much, maybe I wasn't a loser.''

Lenore still didn't understand and wanted to know why he thought of himself as a loser. Maybe it was wrapped up in his relationship with his father. Maybe she'd never understand that part of him. But she kept silent, oddly enjoying the stream of consciousness that flowed from him in awkward fits and starts.

Dixon coughed, took a final drag on the cigarette and held the butt until it burned out near his fingers.

"The words from one of your letters kept going through my head. You'd told me you believed in me. If I believed in myself, things would happen for me."

He turned and faced her. "That became my first hit, 'If You Believe.' I was on to a good thing. The inspiration was there. I was hot. I wrote music, the lyrics flowed from me and then I met Sarge Watson. He promised the world, the mountaintop. Together we were an invincible team. And then I hit a dry spot."

He looked her in the eye and then away. He shrugged. "It had worked once before, I figured. It could work again."

She watched him walk away. "Dixon . . . ?"

He didn't answer but went across the room. From a shelf built into a wall he pulled an intricately carved wooden box. Carrying the box to the coffee table, he sat, opened it and pulled out a packet of letters tied with a faded pink ribbon.

Lenore's mouth dropped open in a small "oh." She remembered the day he'd snatched one of her hair ribbons and claimed it as his own. Could that be the same ribbon?

"Every one you ever wrote to me," he said as he placed the letters on the table. Reaching into the box again, he pulled from it another packet of letters. "Every one I wrote back to you but never mailed. You may find a song or two tucked in those as well."

He tossed that packet to her. Lenore caught it and looked down at her name and college dormitory address scrawled on the first letter. A rubber band that had long since lost its elasticity held the letters together. Lenore ran her fingers over each one. There were eight, maybe ten of them.

Her gaze met his. He shrugged. "May as well keep them. They were yours anyway. I just didn't have the nerve to send them. Then after so much time passed"—he shrugged again—"what was the point?"

When she looked up through a haze of tears she didn't realize she'd shed, he stood before her.

"I never meant to hurt you, Lenore," he said quietly.

He stared at her as if burning her image into his brain. Then without a word, he left.

Lenore sat on the piano bench for a long time. When she eventually realized he wasn't coming back, she blinked and looked around the empty room. Luxury was everywhere, evident in the plush furniture, the deep carpet, the strategically coordinated knickknacks. Luxury abounded but so, too, did loneliness.

Lenore glanced about the rest of the room. Then with nothing else to say or do, she took the cassette and CD out of the player, scooped up her journal and the rest of the discs. She dumped them in her bag and let herself out of the apartment.

Back at Kim's place, she called Sarge Watson and arranged a meeting. In his office she dumped her bag of CDs and cassettes, then read for him and played for him the damaging evidence against Dixon.

When she was finished, she looked at him. Sarge sat at his desk, fingering the paperweight with his motto on it.

"Well?" she demanded.

His gaze met hers. "I knew about it. I just didn't realize it was so bad, so blatant."

"What do you mean, you knew about this? You knew and you didn't say anything? You didn't try to stop him?"

Sarge put the paperweight on the desk. "Calm down, Dr. Foxwood. Buster just told me not too long ago. Right before he decided to come clean. I demanded to know why he was doing this, and he told me."

"And?"

He nodded to her. "And now the ball is clearly in your court."

Lenore sat back and contemplated that fact.

"I'll need to think things over," she finally said. "Where can I reach you?"

Sarge opened a desk drawer and pulled out a business card. On the back he wrote something. "My home and cellular numbers. Call me when you decide."

This time there was no power struggle. Sarge got up, walked around his desk and handed the card to Lenore.

She rose. "I'll take my journal. You can keep the rest."

He nodded, saw her out, then made his way back to his desk. He stared at the CD cases as if they were contagions. Then his eye caught the cassette tape mixed with the CDs. She hadn't played that one for him. Sarge reached for the cassette and looked at the label. Immediately he recognized Buster's precise handwriting.

"Rhapsody for Lenore," he read aloud, then peered at the date Buster had written on the label. Sarge opened his desk to glance back at a calendar. Sure enough, that had been the week Buster had been totally impossible to deal with. The tape was dated a week after his precious Lenore walked out on him following that concert stampede. Sarge couldn't blame her though. He'd be majorly hacked off if he'd spent three hours cooling his heels in jail.

Curious, Sarge got up and popped the tape into a component of his state-of-the-art sound system. Moments later

Buster's voice, the voice that had made both of them multi-millionaires, filled the office. The piano was like nothing he'd ever heard before. As the minutes ticked by, and the melody consumed him, Sarge was surprised to find himself a little choked up. He looked around his office to make sure no one was there. Then he quickly ran a big hand over his eyes.

"I wonder if she wrote this one, too," he said.

Then he heard the crying.

Sarge blinked, cleared his throat and stared at the sound system.

No. Lenore didn't write this one. He'd bet his wife's new Lamborghini on that. Only a man hurting and in love could come up with something this powerful.

"Rhapsody for Lenore." Sarge nodded. He rewound the tape and popped it out of the machine.

He kissed the tape. "Thank you, Buster. Thank you, Lenore. You two have given me the answer to my problems."

Sarge went to his phone, made two telephone calls. Then with the tape between two fingers, he kicked his feet up on his desk and smiled broadly.

The next morning Lenore made a call. Sarge Watson was surprisingly cooperative. Lenore got from him all the information she needed. Then with deliberate care, she dressed.

Kim had done her hair and makeup. All that remained to don was the leopard print couture suit Kim had designed and the wild woman attitude Lenore desperately needed to pull off this charade. She would pull on all the reserve she had in her. Too much was riding on her performance today to get cold feet now. Lenore took a deep breath. Compared to yesterday, this would be a breeze.

She slipped on the suit jacket, its big shawl collar the focal point. She buttoned the single button on the jacket and stared at her reflection in Kim's big three-way mirror. Lenore didn't recognize the woman who stared back at her.

She reached for the pillbox hat, positioned it on her head and pulled down the thin veil that shielded her eyes.

Another deep breath and her attitude settled around her. Lenore went to meet the waiting limousine sent by Sarge Watson.

The ride seemed interminable. Lenore bit down on the nervousness that had butterflies on a rampage in her stomach. Eventually the car came to a stop. When the door opened, Sarge Watson slipped in. They were quiet as the vehicle pulled away from his office building.

Finally Sarge turned to her. "I'm sorry I hassled you, Dr. Foxwood."

Lenore nodded.

Sarge cleared his throat and stretched his legs out. "Thank you for doing this," he said. "I realize you don't have to."

Lenore looked at him, her eyes covered by the netting of the veil. "It was my idea. My choice."

Sarge nodded. "You must love him a lot."

"He's the only man I ever loved," she answered quietly.

The confession hung between them the rest of the silent trip.

Like royalty subjected to some menial but necessary duty of office, Lenore swept into the large conference room. The combined power of the people in the room hit her the moment she stepped in, as did the enormity of what she was about to do.

She straightened her back and stood before the assembled men and women. In the car Sarge prepped her on who she'd meet and what to expect. The president of the record label stood at the head of the large marble-topped conference table. The label's PR director, in a gray sculpted suit that could have been designed by Kim, stood to his right. The company's marketing director and three vice presidents, two female and one male, rounded out the group. A secretary sat to the left and back of the president, Jevic Pantenworth. To a person, up to and including the secretary, they looked irritated and imposing.

Lenore sized up Jevic Pantenworth, the president and CEO of Power4You Records. He looked more like a bank president than the head of one of the country's most successful entertainment companies. Music constituted just a small portion of the multimedia conglomerate he operated.

Lenore and Sarge Watson positioned themselves at the two empty chairs. Lenore sat directly across from Pantenworth, not waiting for anyone else to take the lead. She glanced around the room, daring someone to challenge her.

With a throat cleared here and a raised eyebrow there, the others took their places.

"Mr. Watson," Pantenworth began. An iceberg would have offered more warmth than the chill in his voice. "You and Mr. Dixon have made yourselves perfectly clear on several points. What is the meaning of this meeting? We have nothing further to discuss. My lawyers will do all the talking."

With a glance in Sarge's direction, Lenore silenced the man. As Lenore stood and leaned both hands on the tabletop, Sarge sat back to watch the show.

"*I* demand to know the meaning of *this* tiresome little drama," she proclaimed. Obvious was the fact that she spoke to Pantenworth and no one else.

After a considerably pregnant pause, in which the man took complete measure of Lenore, he stood, then met her gaze head on.

"And who might you be?"

Lenore chuckled. Fully into the role and loving the power she felt, Lenore wished she smoked and that she had one of the long, glamorous cigarette holders like 1940s era screen stars.

She straightened and regarded him. "I'm the factor, the person, everyone seems to have forgotten, Mr. Pantenworth."

He nodded. "You have me at a disadvantage."

Lenore smiled, then sauntered around the table to where the record company executive stood. Necks craned and gazes followed the deliberate sway of her hips. Positive that she had each and every person's undivided attention, Lenore faced Pantenworth.

A tall, imposing man, his strong Nordic features and blond hair gave him the look of a conquering, or maybe a pillaging, Viking of old. Even in the high heels, she had to look up at him. But she met his gaze and then held out her hand . . . to be kissed, not shaken.

"You, Viking, can call me Foxxi. That's with two x's."

The bent of a smile tipped the corners of his mouth. Lenore relaxed. This would be easy. Just play to his prurient interests and keep him off kilter, she reminded herself.

He raised her hand to his mouth and lingered there. When his tongue edged out and caressed the back of her hand during the greeting, Lenore managed—just barely— to control her sharp intake of breath. She all but snatched her hand away. A flickering of knowing danced in his eyes. And then the moment was over. He released her. Lenore placed a steadying hand on the back of his chair.

"And what," he said with a glance toward those around the table, "should my associates call you?"

Without taking her eyes off the one who wielded the power, Lenore answered. "Ma'am will do."

Jevic Pantenworth smiled. And then he laughed. "Have you ever been to Scandinavia, Foxxi?"

"I can't say that I have. My travels haven't taken me to those countries."

"Hmm, pity. You'd be spectacularly received," he said. A quick flick of his hand sent one of the vice presidents scurrying to the seat Lenore had vacated. Pantenworth then held for Lenore the newly unoccupied seat next to his own. She settled into it like a queen taking her throne.

"Shall we begin again, Foxxi."

She glanced at him, the tone in his voice telling her he hadn't been fooled or distracted. But Lenore had another weapon in her arsenal, a weapon that Kim assured had a one hundred percent effectiveness rating. Slowly and deliberately she crossed her legs, then slid one leg over the other in a blatant show of sensuality.

Pantenworth sighed. But Lenore heard the wistfulness in that sigh and knew he was thinking pleasure.

"Surely you are familiar with Foxhound Ltd. and with Foxhound Productions," she said. She smiled when his attention finally left her legs.

He nodded, then glanced at Sarge. Sarge's expression revealed nothing. Pantenworth's gaze again met Lenore's.

"I don't appreciate being called away from my duties," she said, pausing just long enough in her enunciation of the word to leave a world of speculation as to just what those duties might be. "And I find this drama tiresome."

"What drama might that be?"

Lenore waved a hand as if she indeed held a long, thin cigarette holder between two fingers. "This plagiarism, stolen songs, lawsuits pending, returned awards drama. This whole thing is inconvenient."

"Inconvenient. Now there's an interesting term," Pantenworth said. He studied her for a few moments. "You're the young woman from the trades. Buster's mystery woman." His statement was posed as a question.

"An unfortunate lapse by personal valets," she answered. "They are no longer in my employ."

Pantenworth's eyebrows rose. "Your employ?"

Lenore laughed, the sound a deep feminine tease. "How long have you worked with Buster Dixon and Foxhound Productions, Mr. Pantenworth?"

"Please, call me Jevic."

Lenore nodded. "Jevic."

Pantenworth leaned back in his chair and folded his arms behind his head. He and Lenore could have been alone in the room for all the attention and notice either took of the other people.

"My relationship with Buster goes back about ten years or so."

"Um-hmm," she purred. Repositioning her legs, she smiled a small, knowing smile when Jevic again became momentarily distracted.

He cleared his throat and smiled at her. "My company's association with Foxhound goes back to its inception, approximately five years ago."

"You are familiar with the notion of silent partners?"

"Of course."

Lenore raised an eyebrow at him before leveling him with a dazzling smile. "There you have it then."

Pantenworth looked confused. "Have what?"

"Mr. Pantenworth, Jevic, I am Foxxi. I put the fox in Foxhound. I'm a fox. Buster is a hound. When he wanted to begin the venture now known as Foxhound, he needed certain backing, shall we say. In exchange for total anonymity, I supplied what he needed. In addition to"—she smiled a seductive smile—"other things, I gave him the exclusive right to use the music I'd created over the years along with his own work. For my own reasons, I lived vicariously through him. And certain unfulfilled needs have been met on both our parts."

Lenore leaned back, hoping he'd fallen for the lies mixed with sexual innuendo.

"And all of that means?" He let the question hang.

Lenore leaned forward, raised the veil on her hat and stared him in the eye. "I thought you were faster than that, Jevic," she chided. "Meaning, for reasons of his own, Buster decided he could no longer remain silent. He felt he could no longer in good conscience claim as his own my lyrics. I'll be honest with you, Jevic, we've argued about this."

She held up a hand. "And before you ask, no. He doesn't know I'm here. He'll find out I've come to you just as I so rudely discovered by means of a television report that he had launched this foolish and meaningless campaign."

"But why . . ." one of the people around the table began.

Lenore's cutting glance, the type reserved for peons, quelled the man's question. But a braver soul dared.

"Why, Miss Foxxi, are you coming forward now?" the woman asked.

Looking at no one but Jevic, Lenore deigned to answer the question in a rambling way. "We have an understanding, so to speak," she said in explaining not quite the whole truth about her relationship with Dixon. "I write lyrics. He writes music. We get profits."

Pantenworth studied her, weighing the validity of her words. And then he delivered his verdict.

"I don't believe you."

Chapter 25

Lenore's eyes widened.

The palpable tension in the room increased tenfold.

"Are you calling me a liar?"

Pantenworth looked from Lenore to Sarge Watson. "I'm saying I wouldn't put anything past the master spin doctor who so very uncharacteristically, I may add, is just quietly sitting there."

"That's because I know who the boss is," Sarge said. "And trust me, J.P., I've been trying to talk some sense into both of them for weeks now."

Lenore didn't bat an eye at the lie. She reached into her handbag and pulled out a compact flip telephone. "If you don't believe me, ask Buster. I'm sure you know the number."

She offered the phone to him.

Pantenworth eyed the woman and the telephone with equal parts suspicion. The room remained quiet as the moments ticked by, and still he stared at her as if divining the truth from her soul.

Someone cleared a throat in the awkward silence.

Lenore continued to hold her breath. Someone else swiveled a chair to and fro.

"That won't be necessary," Jevic finally said.

A collective sigh eased over the room, and then everyone
started talking at once: questions about media handling,
suggestions for the next steps to take, demands for more
information about Foxxi's songwriting skills.

Lenore slipped the telephone back into her purse and
prayed that her shaking hands didn't give her away. Had
Jevic Pantenworth called her bluff, she didn't know what
she'd have done—because there was no Plan B.

After that the rest was easy: a blur of press conferences,
limo rides, and even an offer to star in a film. Lenore
politely declined the star status; Foxxi replied, "Have your
people call my people." But the joke was on the ones who
thought she had star potential. Lenore didn't have any
"people," and Foxxi didn't exist.

Lenore primly sat on the pink wing chair in her open
living room. Clips about her and about the dramatic turn-
around in the Buster Dixon story lay in her lap. The spin,
according to all the stories, was that Buster had done it all
for love.

To J.D. she told the truth.

"Why are you protecting him?"

Lenore looked at her son, the son who looked so much
like a younger version of his father it broke her heart.
"Because I love him, J.D. I know that's difficult for you
to understand. I'm not sure I understand it myself. Love
doesn't always make a lot of sense."

"Is that why you gave me his name for my middle name?"

Lenore nodded. Then started to cry.

J.D. held her until she stopped.

"I don't want you to be angry with me," she said. "Or
with Buster Dixon," she added.

"I'm not. I'm just, well, it's kind of hard to deal with, you know."

Lenore hugged her son. "I know, baby. I know."

"I guess I shouldn't ask you if you can get me an autograph from him."

Lenore laughed. "That's right." But the entire situation was doubly hard to deal with when the real joke, Lenore knew, was on her. Not once, not even one time during the whole debacle did she see Dixon. She'd swallowed her pride and called him. He didn't return her calls. She went to his office but was turned away by a smug-looking Monique and an apologetic Kelvin.

She tried calling one more time and got Monique, who announced, "He doesn't need you anymore. We don't need you. But, hey, thanks for all your help getting us out of that PR jam."

Sarge Watson had been no help. He'd blithely explained away Dixon's absences: an appointment with a lawyer, a meeting, a prior commitment, mixing singles, negotiations with acts, editing music videos. In all the excuses, Lenore finally figured out what a record producer did with his time. And she eventually got the message: Dixon wanted nothing to do with her.

Sarge, or one of Dixon's office personnel, had quick and believable answers ready for media who questioned why Foxxi and Buster were never seen together.

Lenore knew the real deal though. She'd saved his hide, and now that Dixon got what he ultimately wanted, there was no need for him to pretend affection or interest in her. He had no need for that pretense. Without his asking, prompting, or even knowing, she'd stepped in, lied her way through the scariest moments of her life and rescued him. Her own reputation was shot to hell. His, however, was again sterling in the industry, with the media and with fans. The stories all said he'd done it for love. Now that his world had been righted and made secure again, he'd forgotten about her.

Unmindful of the newspaper articles in her lap, Lenore got up and padded barefoot to her refrigerator. The freezer didn't yield any ice cream. She'd have to get some. She grabbed her keys and her purse. Maybe a drive would do her well. "J.D.," she hollered toward his room. "I'm headed to the store. Do you want anything?"

At his negative answer, she locked the front door and went to her car where she strapped on her seat belt and sat in the driveway, staring at her garage door. At first she thought it was raining. Then she realized she was crying.

All she'd ever done was love Billy Dixon. Twice now she'd let him walk all over her heart.

"When are you going to learn, Lenore? When?" she asked as she angrily wiped the tears away. She turned the ignition key and then turned on the radio. Not up for the classical or all-talk stations she usually listened to, she pressed the SEEK button and paused as the first strong station came in. A song ended and then the announcer's voice.

"And now folks, what you've been asking for. This tune literally came out of nowhere and has ripped up the charts. Some of you have been asking me about the special effect used on the track, and why it sounds so homemade."

Lenore wiped her eyes and put the car in reverse to slowly began to back out of her drive.

"I don't have an answer to that, folks. Maybe that's the way the man wanted it to sound. Whatever the case, here it is, the number-one song on the pop, R&B, and even the country charts, 'Rhapsody for Lenore' by Buster Dixon."

Lenore slammed on the brake and jerked forward from the impact. Fumbling for the knob on her dash, she turned the radio volume up. With a foot on the brake pedal and the car running, Lenore sat in her driveway and listened to the soft intro and then the sweet piano. The gloriously rich composition brought more tears to her eyes. She hugged the steering wheel and closed her eyes. The music caressed her, shielded her, healed her, made love to her. And then, at the end, she heard him weep.

Stunned, Lenore blinked back her own tears, then stared at the radio. As the last notes faded away, the announcer came back.

"That's right, folks. That's real crying you hear at the end there. Remember that totally fabulous babe by the name of Foxxi? The one who wrote the lyrics to a lot of Buster's music? Well, word is her real name is Lenore. She lives right here in the great state of Ohio, and Buster D is in love with the woman. But she's not having him. Broke his little heart. I tell you, if she doesn't want him, maybe I'm more to her liking. Foxxi, if you're out there and listening, I can love you right. Call me at . . ."

Lenore smiled and turned the volume down.

"You're wrong, Mr. DJ. He doesn't love me. He never has. And he's the one who broke *my* heart."

Lenore sniffled, wiped her eyes, then released the brake pedal to back out of her driveway. A quick glance in the rearview mirror made her do a double take and then slam on the brakes again.

A black limousine pulled in front of her drive, blocking her access to the street. Dixon stepped from the car, a bouquet of red roses in his hand.

Lenore put the car in park, pushed down the emergency brake, and got out. Silent, she watched him approach. She soaked in the sight of him: tall, dark and as handsome as ever. The crisp white linen shirt displayed a sapphire pin at the banded collar. Hungrily she watched the play of the strong muscles in his legs as he moved. She remembered the feel of her own thighs wrapped about those legs. Stop it! she scolded. What was the sense in torturing herself with those thoughts?

When he stood three feet from her, he held out the flowers. "Thank you. And I'm sorry."

Lenore accepted the flowers but didn't take her eyes off

his. Nor did she feign ignorance. "Thank you. Apology accepted."

Dixon looked around. "Lenore, can we talk?"

When she made no move toward the door that led to her loft, Dixon led her to his waiting limousine. He handed her into the sleek vehicle, and a liveried chauffeur closed the door behind him.

Eyes wide, Lenore drank in the richness of his brown skin, the long tapered fingers that had loved her, the same fingers that made a piano bring forth sweet melodies.

"I have something for you," he said.

Lenore watched and waited as he reached for a briefcase on the floor. He pulled out a white envelope and handed it to her.

"What's this?"

"Open it."

She glanced at him, then ran a finger under the flap and pulled from the envelope a check made out to her. She gasped at the amount and all the zeros.

She threw the envelope back at him. "I can't take this! How dare you! I'm not like Rachel. I don't earn a living on my back."

"Lenore—"

"And at this point, there's no need trying to bribe me or give me hush money. You got everything you wanted from me. I have nothing left to give. This well is dry, so you can just leave."

He picked up the envelope from the floor and held it out to her.

"That's not hush money or anything else like that, Lenore. Those are the royalties you earned through the years on all the music I took from you. All of it. That money is yours fair and square. You earned it as a songwriter."

"I can't take it," she said, shoving it back at him.

He smiled, but he left the envelope on the seat between them. "Then use it to set up the scholarship fund you wanted for your students. Hell, you could probably buy the college.''

Lenore glanced at the check. ''I don't have any more students,'' she said. ''Buster's bitching babe wasn't welcome as a member of the esteemed faculty.''

He winced. ''I'm sorry, Lenore. I'm really sorry about all the mess I created, the trouble I caused you, everything. Jail. Your job. Those awful stories.''

Lenore folded her arms. ''Why are you here?''

For a moment he looked as if he didn't quite know the answer to that simple question. ''I . . . I'm here because I care about you.''

''You're here out of a sense of guilt,'' she said. ''I heard that little song on the radio just now. Is that the spin you and Sarge put on this fiasco? Is that song the price of my feelings? After I come in and save the day, the romantic Buster Dixon puts out a pretty love song guaranteed to go platinum.''

''That song isn't a gimmick, Lenore. As a matter of fact, it isn't even supposed to be a song. That was personal, private. It was just something I did. Somehow a bootleg copy of a tape I'd done at home got out.''

''I'm supposed to believe that?''

Dixon lost his temper. ''Look, dammit. I didn't come all the way out here to argue with you. I came out here . . . I came out here . . .'' he floundered.

''Yes?'' she said, impatiently tapping her foot.

''I came out here to tell you that I love you.''

Lenore's mouth dropped open, first in surprise, then to protest his claim. But Dixon's mouth covered hers to settle the dispute. He pulled her to him so she sat half across his lap. One hand cupped her chin, while the other held her secure in his embrace.

The calm she tried to portray shattered with the hunger of his kisses. He was slow, thoughtful and meticulously thorough. Shivers of desire raced through Lenore. His tongue traced the soft fullness of her lips. She responded in kind and heard him moan.

He came up for air long enough to stare into her eyes, smile and then again lower his mouth to hers. The caress of his lips on her mouth and along her body set her aflame.

Slowly he maneuvered her until he lay on top of her across the seat.

Dixon grinned. "We're in the backseat of a car."

"And?"

"Want to pretend like we're college kids again?"

Lenore smiled up at him. "No, I prefer the adult ending of this story."

"So what's the ending?" he asked.

"You tell me."

Dixon lowered his head and whispered something in her ear. Lenore giggled.

"Now that's creative. Maybe Foxxi and Buster can write a song about that."

When they emerged from the limousine, J.D. was standing on the sidewalk.

"Mom, I saw you get in . . ." His voice trailed off when he recognized the man with an arm around his mother's waist.

Dixon's head snapped up when the teenager addressed Lenore as "Mom." Dixon let go of Lenore and took a menacing step toward the boy. J.D. backed up a step, and Lenore rushed to get between them.

Dixon stared at the boy and then at Lenore. He knew, without being told, that the strapping kid in front of him was his son. In the boy's face, he saw his own features: thick brows, broad nose. The kid had Lenore's eyes but his mouth.

The boy wrapped a protective arm around Lenore's shoulders.

Without taking his eyes off the teen, Dixon addressed Lenore. "Why didn't you tell me? You lied to me. I asked you if you had children, and you lied to me."

Lenore turned toward J.D. and smoothed a hand along his brow. "Go in the house, J.D. Dixon and I have some things to discuss."

"No," the teen responded.

"Don't disrespect your mother," Dixon said.

J.D. raised an eyebrow as if to ask, And-who-are-you-to-tell-me-what-to-do?

"J.D., please. This is something Dixon and I have to work out."

The teenager looked from his mother to the father he'd never known. "I'll wait by the car." He walked the few feet away and gave them privacy to talk. Lenore and Dixon watched the boy fold his arms and lean against the driver's side door.

"He's protective of you," Dixon observed.

"I'm his mother," she said as she turned her attention back to Dixon.

"That's right. And I'm his father—a fact you've kept from me for fifteen years. That's how old he is, isn't it?"

Lenore nodded.

"Why did you lie to me?"

Lenore folded her arms and stared him down. "I didn't. You asked if my ex-husband and I had children. We didn't. So I didn't lie to you."

"Why didn't you ever tell me? You had no right to keep my son from me," he accused.

"You should have asked your good buddy, Marvin Wood-bridge, about that," Lenore fired back. But she regretted the words as soon as they were out. Marvin was dead and wasn't there to defend himself or his actions. She turned away from him.

Dixon grabbed her arm. "What does Marvin have to do with this?" From the corner of his eye, he saw the boy take a step forward. He dropped his hand even while his gaze lingered on his son's.

"You got what you wanted from me all those years ago. And then you ran away. I never saw you again. I wrote you letters you didn't respond to. I spent sleepless nights crying and holding my pillow and wondering why you left. Eventually the letters I wrote started coming back to me. And then I realized I was pregnant. I told Marvin. He promised to tell you and to deliver a letter to you."

"Marv wouldn't withhold that kind of information from me."

"Guess again, Buster. He did. Why do you think he was trying to make things right from the grave?"

"What are you talking about?"

Lenore folded her arms and stared up at him, willing him to see and hear the truth. "The money, the stipulation that we live together for a week. Marvin wanted to undo the wrong he'd done."

"Oh, please."

"You don't believe me. Okay, fine." She turned to her son, who had inched his way closer to where his parents stood. "J.D., go get that letter I had you read. It's in the top drawer of my desk."

Moments later the teen came back with the letter. Lenore handed it to Dixon. "Gilbert Hobbs said Marvin left this for me to read after he'd died. Read it and come to your own conclusions." Lenore turned to walk away. "Tell your driver to move that car. I'm going to the store."

She left her son and her lover standing on the sidewalk, looking after her. Lenore then backed her car out of the drive and waited for the limo driver to move the long black vehicle.

When she actually drove off, Dixon turned to the teen. He found himself at a loss for words.

J.D. solved the problem. He reached a tentative hand out. "I'm J.D. Foxwood."

Dixon swallowed hard, then shook the boy's hand. "Pleased to meet you, J.D. I'm Buster Dixon."

"Yeah, I know."

Dixon couldn't detect if there was any hostility in that

admission. He was still grappling with the fact that he had a son.

"What does J.D. stand for?"

"Jason Dixon," the teen said.

Breath whooshed out of Dixon as if he'd been punched. He swallowed the lump in his throat. Then with shaking hands, he read the letter Lenore had handed him. When he finished, he cussed a blue streak. J.D. grinned at him.

"That son of a bitch. How dare he not tell me about you."

J.D.'s grin faded to an uncertain smile. "You mean you would have come back to my mother had you known?"

Dixon looked in his son's eyes. "I've never stopped loving your mother, J.D. I'll love her until the end of my time on this earth."

"She cries a lot now."

Dixon grinned. "Does she?" He wrapped an arm around his son's shoulder, and they walked toward the entrance to the building.

"Tell me more about that," Dixon prodded.

The first thing Lenore heard when she came in the door was the music. She made her way up the stairs to the loft where J.D.'s bedroom was. The door was open, and she peeked inside. Dixon was on keyboard, and J.D. was making his sax sing. Lenore leaned against the doorjamb and looked at the two men she loved. Watching them together, she knew that everything was going to work out just right.

Epilogue

The church overflowed with flowers and candles. The sweet smell of vanilla and roses filled the sanctuary. Men in tuxedos and women in shimmering gowns sat packed into the church pews.

At the altar, Buster Dixon stood next to his son, J.D., and his friend, Sarge Watson. Raheem stood beside record company president Jevic Pantenworth. A minister in black robes and kente cloth smiled at the assembly. Dixon's black tails, highlighted by the candlelight, added an extra touch of elegance to the assembled men.

To Dixon's left, along a path strewn with pink and white rose petals, and at a white baby grand piano, sat a keyboard genius. His long braids swayed as he played the piano and sang one of his greatest hits, "Isn't She Lovely," into the microphone.

When the song ended, Dixon turned to his bride. There was just one thing he wanted to do about that long, white wedding dress Lenore wore: He wanted to peel it right off her body.

He glanced over his bride's shoulder and winked at Kim,

the maid of honor. The other bridesmaids smiled. Then Dixon heard the words he'd been dying to hear.

"You may now kiss the bride."

Dixon raised one hand, not bothering to hide the trembling in his fingers. He caressed the side of her face, the fullness of her lips. Then his head lowered. Just a small taste, a chaste peck, his mind kept reminding him. But his body and the woman in his arms demanded more, much more.

Dixon's mouth slanted over Lenore's. It was supposed to be light, flirtatious, just the sort of kiss to end a beautiful wedding ceremony. But, oh well.

When Lenore's hand snaked up his chest, and he heard her moan, Dixon grinned, his fantasy now complete. Lenore was his wife, and the sweet music they'd share forever rang out in song through his heart.

Dear Reader:

If a love song on the radio has ever made you laugh, cry, sigh, or remember when, you'll know the potent wonder of a love song.

People frequently ask where story ideas come from. Buster and Lenore's came straight from the radio. As I listened to a song a few years ago, I wondered if the words had been taken from a long-ago written letter. That wasn't the case, but the thought alone was all I needed to launch me into Buster and Lenore's love story.

If you'd like more information about my books, please send a long self-addressed, stamped envelope to:

Felicia Mason
P.O. Box 1438, Dept. R
Yorktown, VA 23692

Thank you for reading RHAPSODY. I hope music holds a special place in your heart.

May love, joy, and music be yours,
Felicia Mason

ABOUT THE AUTHOR

Virginian Felicia Mason is an award-winning novelist and has worked as a newspaper reporter, columnist, copy editor, editorial writer and as a college journalism professor. She is active in several writers' groups and is a member of Romance Writers of America.

SIZZLING ROMANCE FROM
FELICIA MASON

For the Love of You 0-7860-0071-6 $4.99US/$6.50CAN
Years of hard work had finally provided a secure life for Kendra
Edwards but when she meets high-powered attorney Malcolm
Hightower, he arouses desires that she swore she would never let
herself feel again . . .

Body and Soul   0-7860-0160-7 $4.99US/$6.50CAN
Toinette Blue's world is her children and her successful career as
the director of a woman's counseling group . . . until devastatingly
handsome, much younger attorney Robinson Mayview rekindles
the flames of a passion that both excites and frightens her . . .

Seduction   0-7860-0297-2 $4.99US/$6.50CAN
C.J. Mayview goes to North Carolina for peace of mind and to
start anew. But secrets unravel when U.S. Marshal Wes Donovan
makes it his business to discover all there is to know about the
beautiful journalist . . .

Foolish Heart   0-7860-0593-9 $4.99US/$6.50CAN
Intent on saving his business, Coleman Heart III turns to beautiful
consultant Sonja Pride. But Sonja has a debt to pay the Heart
family, and she is determined to seek revenge until she finds out
that Coleman is a caring, honorable man to whom she just might
be able to give her heart.

USE COUPON ON NEXT PAGE TO ORDER THESE BOOKS

Own These Books
By *Felicia Mason*

__**For the Love of You** $4.99US/$6.50CAN
0-7860-0071-6

__**Body and Soul** $4.99US/$6.50CAN
0-7860-0160-7

__**Seduction** $4.99US/$6.50CAN
0-7860-0297-2

__**Foolish Heart** $4.99US/$6.50CAN
0-7860-0593-9

Call toll free **1-888-345-BOOK** to order by phone or use this coupon to order by mail.

Name _____

Address _____

City _____ State _____ Zip_____

Please send me the books I have checked above.

I am enclosing	$_____
Plus postage and handling*	$_____
Sales tax (in NY, TN, and DC)	$_____
Total amount enclosed	$_____

*Add $2.50 for the first book and $.50 for each additional book.

Send check or money order (no cash or CODs) to: **Arabesque Books, Dept. C.O., 850 Third Avenue, 16th Floor, New York, NY 10022**

Prices and numbers subject to change without notice.

All orders subject to availability.

Check out our website at **www.arabesquebooks.com**